COUNTY
KILDARE

B.E. KENNEDY

Kennedy Books
25 Wagoners Trail
Guelph, ON N1G3M9

First Kennedy Books trade paperback edition October 2025

For information about special discounts, author visits or bulk orders please contact baileykennedybooks@gmail.com.

Manufactured in Canada
Library of Congress Data is available
ISBN 978-1-0690493-2-2

For my mom,

who has given everything to be the mother she
never had.

The strongest evidence of love is sacrifice.

-   Carolyn Fry

Table of Contents

Part I

1

Maeve

Guelph, Ontario, Canada
Summer 2011

Maeve used her forearm to squeegee away the fog from the glass shower door, which was obscuring her view into the bedroom. She squinted, straining to see the digital clock that sat on her bedside table. She was trying to determine just how late for work she would be. It was 7:21 a.m., later than she'd hoped. Maeve groaned, stepped out of the shower and wrapped an oversized towel around herself. She padded out to the bedroom, leaving a trail of water droplets on the hardwood floor from her loose wet curls. Maeve tied her wet hair up in a towel that teetered atop her head as she stood in her closest contemplating her outfit, as if she weren't going to wear the same utilitarian work uniform that she did every day. She almost exclusively wore a seasonally appropriate button-down top and a pair of well-worn denim to work, casual for most office jobs but perfectly acceptable for a journalist working at *The Guelph Tribune*. While the look might read *sloppy* on most, Maeve's broad shoulders and long legs somehow made the oversized shirt, and loose jeans look effortlessly put together. She unwound her wet hair from the towel and let her copper curls tumble down her back, setting off her sharp features.

Dressed for the day, Maeve walked down the creaky Victorian staircase, each step groaning out its own complaint under her weight. The cacophony of sounds this old house produced had become so familiar they were like company to her. On days when Ethan wasn't home, she could count on them to greet her in the morning.

Maeve wound her way into the kitchen, poured herself a cup of coffee and wandered over to inspect a pile of mail that had appeared on the kitchen table overnight. Maeve picked up the stack and leafed through the flyers and coupon books, ready to discard it all until she came across an envelope addressed to her with an unfamiliar return address. Curious, she turned the envelope over in her hands a few times before slipping a finger under the fold, finding a loose spot to tear open. She pulled the folded paper out ungracefully, ripping at all seams of the envelope. The letterhead read "Government of Ontario," and Maeve brushed it off as another likely attempt to get her to register as an organ donor when her license came up for renewal. She tossed it back on the table as Ethan rounded the corner into the kitchen, also eager to caffeinate. He leaned in to kiss her on the cheek before pouring himself his own mugful of coffee and settling into a seat at the table.

"What's that?" he asked, nodding his head toward the stack of papers discarded on the table in front of Maeve. He took a sip from his mug and reached across the table to try to grab the mail and inspect it.

Maeve picked it back up before he could reach it and unfolded the papers. She was quiet as she leaned against the table with her hip, holding the mail with one hand and her coffee with the other. Her face narrowed in concentration as she read, and a sick anxiety rose in her stomach.

"What is it?" Ethan asked again. He assessed Maeve, his eyes searching for clues while she stood seemingly frozen in place.

When she didn't answer, Ethan stood up and walked around the table to where she was still standing and took the letter from her shaking hands to read it.

> Dear Ms. Maeve Grisham,
>
> An Ontario law recently passed allowing all children surrendered by their birth mothers between the years 1940 and 1980 access to their adoption records in full. As a child who was a ward of the province you are entitled to send in an application request for more information. The application and corresponding return envelope are included in this package.
>
> If you have further questions, please call 1-555-676-8827 or visit our informational website at adoption.on.gov for more details.

"I'm going to be late for work," Maeve said abruptly. She took the paper from Ethan's hands, folded it neatly and placed it back into the torn envelope.

"Maeve," Ethan said, grabbing her hand as she

tried to stand up, "we should talk about this."

"Not now. I have to go to work," Maeve said, trying to gently shake him off. Her eyes scanned for a clear path to the door. Her fight-or-flight instinct was surface level, even after eleven years of being with Ethan, Maeve still was ready to run at any moment if things went sideways.

"Maeve," Ethan said as he stood. He was getting in her way again, putting a hand on her shoulder, this time in an effort to comfort her. He didn't realize how badly that made her want to scream.

"Let go of me," Maeve said, recoiling from his touch. She hadn't meant to sound spiteful, but she seemed to have lost control of her emotions.

Ethan put his hands up in surrender and hurt shot through his face.

"Sorry," she said quickly, embarrassed by her outburst. She walked toward the front door and slung her bag over her shoulder. "I really need to go," she said, now standing in the doorway looking back at him.

Ethan walked down the front hallway and met her on the front mat. "Okay," he said. "Don't forget about dinner at my parents tonight," he added, closing the door behind her.

"Yep," Maeve said as she ran down the front steps.

Maeve walked to work, the feel of the pavement beneath her feet a sturdy reminder of the present. She walked at a brisk pace, breaking a sweat, intent on pouring her energy anywhere other than that letter. Maeve was mere months away from her wedding to Ethan and was quite possibly the most disorganized bride in modern existence. She knew she didn't have any energy to spare chasing down ghosts.

"Good morning," Maeve said as she walked through the doors to her office. She gave a curt nod to the receptionist.

"Morning, Maeve," she called as Maeve walked with her head down to her desk.

Inside the office building, the air was warm and stale. Maeve could feel sweat beginning to collect at her temples. She wiped at it with her fingertips, trying to save her hair which was teetering on the verge of going from manageable curls to an unruly mane of frizz. In an attempt to avoid any unnecessary small talk with her fellow journalists today, Maeve wore an obnoxiously oversized pair of headphones and powered up her laptop. Maeve wasn't good at small talk. In fact, there was nothing she cared for less than chatting about inane facts and obvious observations of the weather. While she almost never had anything playing in her ears, the prop worked ninety-nine percent of the time to keep people from stopping by her desk to chat.

Maeve's fingers hovered above the keyboard, tempted to look into the adoption legislation change. She opened her search engine and typed in the words, taking a deep breath before hitting Enter. She had spent the last thirteen years building up an armor to her past, a thick protective barrier needed to keep her from feeling the pain of rejection and abandonment that ruled her childhood. She wasn't sure if she was ready to undo it all.

In her haste to leave the house this morning Maeve left the letter on the kitchen counter, restuffed in its torn envelope. All she wanted to do was scrutinize each word of that four-sentence note. It was vague yet succinct. She knew each word would have been chosen carefully by the writer to convey a very particular message. There were no apologies or certainties, just the news of a legislation change and a next step. Maeve closed her eyes and tried to see the words on the page again in her mind, but they were slipping away. When she'd read it, she saw threads of hope and possibilities, but she knew it was her mind playing a trick on her and reading through the lines. She needed to review the words against the facts, not the fantasy of possibilities she was weaving together in her mind.

While the letter seemingly came out of the blue, Maeve knew as an investigative journalist that these types of government changes were often the result of a long and arduous fight. She had tried to look for her birth mother once before, many years ago, without success. At the time she was young and had been met with closed doors and sealed records, and she'd lost her momentum after a few weeks. She was disappointed, but without any leads, she let it go, accepting the fact that she would never know who she was or where she came from.

Maeve rubbed her hands over her face, pressing her fingertips into her eyes to try to relieve some of the pressure that was building up behind them. It felt as if every muscle in her body was having a physical reaction to this, tensing up for a fight. She exited her search engine and opened her email instead. She scanned her inbox as she tried to focus. Rather than doing anything substantial, she just forwarded off emails to junior employees and starred some important ones to go back to later. She stood up and stretched, then headed for a bathroom break and bartered with herself. If she wasn't going to be productive anyways, she would allow herself one hour of research before she got to work. She would never be able to focus with all the unknowns hanging in the balance around her.

Happy with her plan, she sat back down with a fresh glass of water and opened her search engine back up. She scanned the links that popped up, each one as vague as the short letter she received this morning. She kept being rerouted to the landing page for the website that prompted her to apply for more information. Maeve scanned the site repeatedly but couldn't bring herself to fill it out. If she did, she would find out information about her birth mother she never before had, but where would that lead her? What if her mother was dead or a drug addict or in jail or didn't want to meet her? Maeve had spent so long narrating a story to herself about who she was and where she came from that she feared a search for the truth would most certainly bring all of those carefully built walls crashing down.

Maeve turned her attention to the legislation behind the change, focusing on the hard, tangible facts. First, she needed to understand why there was a sudden change and, second, what she was to make of it. Maeve typed in **Ontario adoption records unsealed** and hit Enter. Within seconds, a growing list of links appeared on her screen. Maeve methodically sifted through the results. While the basic search engines would get her some information, she was hitting a wall and needed a more robust database. Today required utilization of academic search engines to do more thorough research. She scanned articles and scholarly journals, collecting as much information as possible. There was a wealth of data hidden behind the wall of public information, and as she kept finding more, she queued the articles in tabs across her monitor for future reading.

Ten years earlier, Maeve tried to find her mother on her own after she had freed herself from the foster system through emancipation. She spent months sending letters and doing research at the library, but at the time, search engines weren't as powerful, and record digitization was just starting to become popular. Because of this, Maeve had put her efforts on hold as she came to terms with the only answers she had. But now it was all here, everything she had searched for ten years ago. Maeve stared at her screen, overcome by a sudden wave of emotion, all of the words blurring together through the glaze of her wet eyes. When she was able to regain her composure, she wiped her tears, took a deep breath and focused on the screen in front of her.

The headlines read Mothers Forced to Give Up Their Children, The Sixties Scoop, and Unwed Mothers Forced into Government Homes to Give Birth. Maeve felt a familiar prickling of heat creep up the back of her neck as she read on.

> While the initial concern to address the rising challenges of unwed mothers such as poverty, stigma and infant care education, the policies and practices varied greatly over the years, allowing other factors to manipulate the system. Between the 1940s and the 1980s, there were several socioeconomic trends that impacted adoption rates. The rise of the post–World War II nuclear family impacted the desire for many childless married couples to seek out adoption. This coincided with a period of increased births to unwed mothers due to changing sexual mores and limited access to birth control. The general public still saw unwed mothers as unfit to raise a child, and that's when the maternity houses started to play

a sinister role in the adoption system.

Maeve bit down on her knuckle as she read. The story she had constructed to soothe herself over the years was a heavily rationalized tale in which her mother was the heroine, giving Maeve up in hopes of a better life than the one she could offer her. In her naivete, she had never once considered that she could have been taken away against her mother's will. Maeve felt like the ground was slipping out from beneath her feet. Unsteadily, she walked toward the bathroom, where she collapsed beside the toilet, her head filled with a dizzying wave of vertigo.

"Maeve?" a voice called from the other side of the stall door. "Are you all right?"

Maeve braced herself on the toilet, but the nauseating moment passed with relief. She stood shakily to open the stall door. On the other side of it, she found Natalie, her boss, standing there. Maeve nodded and walked toward the sink, splashed water on her face and patted it dry with a paper towel. Once she was sure she was steady on her feet, she leaned against the sink and turned to face Natalie.

"I'm good. Too much coffee on an empty stomach," Maeve said, offering a forced smile. The last thing she wanted to do right now was talk about it.

Natalie frowned. "What's going on?" she asked, not fooled by Maeve's unconvincing brush-off.

Maeve sighed.

Natalie was her boss but also a friend. They had started together at the paper, and Natalie brought her along as she moved up the ranks. She knew Maeve too well to just let this go.

Maeve turned the tap back on, stuck her head under the faucet and took a gulp of water. Beside her, Natalie reached into her bag and pulled out a lozenge, which she handed to Maeve.

"Thank you." Maeve popped the lozenge into her mouth, and her body instantly responded. Her tongue tingled, and the vapor from the eucalyptus caused the air traveling into her throat to feel cool and fresh. "Much better," she said with a real smile this time.

"Come on, let's go to my office," Natalie suggested.

Maeve nodded and followed her out of the bathroom and across the newsroom into Natalie's private office, where they could escape the eyes and ears of the other journalists.

As Natalie closed the door behind her, Maeve took her regular seat at the sprawling mahogany desk that took up almost the entire width of the room while Natalie squeezed into her place behind it. Their office downtown was in an old building, a similar era to her home, and while charming, the rooms were small, and the air-conditioning was limited to a window unit in the main room. With the door closed now and no airflow, the office was getting stuffy, so Natalie turned on the ceiling fan overhead. Maeve watched as the papers strewn around Natalie's desk started to flutter, and she rushed to gather them and slip the pile beneath a paperweight on the corner of her desk. She picked at her nails, anxiously debating what to tell her. She could, of course, lie and say she just had the flu, or she was nervous about the wedding, but Natalie had a bullshit detector that went far beyond Maeve's ability to pad the truth. Natalie sat on the other side of the desk expectantly, her fingers steepled under her chin as she gave Maeve that look, the one that could see right through people and extract the truth from them. It was how she became editor of the paper before she was even thirty.

Maeve weighed her options. She could politely ask for privacy on the matter and go back to her desk to dive down a rabbit hole of research, or she could be up front with Natalie and get a little support. She looked at Natalie's earnest face, full of concern over her well-being and decided it was time Natalie knew everything.

Maeve's story began when she was born; there was no other way to tell it. Everything that had happened in her life cascaded from the moment she was given up by her birth mother. Maeve was given up as an infant but never adopted; therefore, she grew up as a child of the foster system. For the first twelve years of her life, she was raised by a kind older woman named Orla Doyle. While Orla was the maternal figure in her life, she insisted that Maeve call her by her name, never to mistake her for a real mother. There was always an arm's length between the two of them, which Maeve could now see as a protective measure of sorts. As far as Maeve could recall, Orla didn't have any living family. She hadn't ever married or had any children of her own; she just had Maeve, and Maeve had her.

Orla's philosophy for child-rearing was simple: give children the opportunity early and often to be resourceful and independent. She was adamant that if you gave children practical life skills, they would figure out the rest on their own. While as an adult, Maeve agreed that there was merit to that philosophy, it always felt like Orla took things too far. Then, when Maeve was twelve, Orla, who was seventy-two at the time, began to have episodes of delirium that later were diagnosed as Alzheimer's. Even after her diagnosis and working with a specialist on a treatment management plan, her ability to care for Maeve properly was not fit for the foster system, so they took Maeve away from the only home she'd known. As an adult, Maeve could understand what she'd thought to be cold and too harsh as a child was necessary to keep them together as long as they were able to. Orla needed to be cared for herself, and she wanted to make sure Maeve would be okay on her own.

After she left Orla's, for the next two years, Maeve was thrust into a new reality, moving from foster home to foster home. Her new life was a stark contrast from the steady predictability she'd been accustomed to. She learned quickly that adoptive families are looking to take in babies and young children, but no one wanted a teenage girl. This proved difficult for a foster care system that was now dealing with a thirteen-year-old girl, so Maeve was handed over several times, unable to get settled in one place. Each home brought its own set of challenges. Either Maeve didn't get along with the other kids, or the house was too full, and she had to be moved.

When Maeve was fourteen years old and started high school, she met her now fiancé, Ethan Clarke. Ethan was smart, handsome and athletic, with auburn hair and bright green eyes, and he made Maeve feel special. Until she met Ethan, Maeve had always felt like an outcast. She was different from her peers, who all had loving families and stable homes, and wasn't accepted by them. But, instead of casting her out, Ethan pulled her into his inner circle, and they quickly became a pair.

The first time Ethan brought Maeve into his family home, Maeve saw that he had exactly what she wanted, and she decided to be a part of it. His mother, Rose, spent her days baking homemade cookies and meals from scratch. She braided his sister's hair and was on the PTA at their school. Rose was kind and caring and took Maeve in like a daughter of her own.

Now Maeve and Ethan were about to get married and start their own little beautiful family, and she had finally been ready to let her past go—until this morning. This morning the gate into her past was opened, leaving Maeve to decide if she wanted to venture down an unknown path to find out where she came from.

From across the desk, Natalie stared back at Maeve with wet eyes and a hand pressed gently against her mouth. "Maeve, I had no idea," she said. "Why didn't you ever tell me any of this?"

"I don't like to make a habit of telling people my sob story," Maeve said, brushing her off. The pity she could see in other people's eyes when she told them about her past always made her want to crawl inside herself.

"Maeve," Natalie said softly, reaching over to place a hand on her arm, "it's quite the opposite of a sob story."

"I don't need you to feel bad for me," Maeve said, pulling her arm away. She immediately regretted her words when she saw a look of hurt flash across Natalie's face. "Sorry," Maeve added quickly, rubbing a hand over her face.

Natalie held up her hands in an effort to call a truce "How can I help?"

"I need some time to look into this," Maeve said. "Even in the twenty minutes of research I've done, I can see there is a big story here, maybe even a series."

Natalie scratched her head as she contemplated

this. "What about the rest of your work?"

"I'll do both," Maeve said eagerly.

"And the wedding?" Natalie asked, pressing her. She looked expectantly at Maeve, urging her to make the right decision.

Maeve chewed anxiously at the inside of her cheek. "I'll get it all done," she said, her tone not quite as confident as the words coming out of her mouth.

"Okay," Natalie agreed, "but as soon as you miss a deadline or drop the ball on your paying work, you do this on your own time. Got it?"

"Got it." Maeve nodded and stood up. "Thank you," she said, and walked back to her desk feeling an anxious excitement rise in her chest.

This wasn't the first bit of research Maeve had dug up that had caused her to have a visceral reaction to her work. A few years back, Maeve wrote a piece on child abuse, and between the horror stories of the children she read about and her own experience in bad foster homes, it had shaken something loose in her. At the time, Ethan had begged her not to do the piece. He noticed early on the shift that was happening and asked her to get another assignment. But Maeve couldn't let it go. She had felt like it was her duty to educate the masses for all of these children who, like her, had suffered. What she hadn't told him was that it was cathartic, and the process helped heal little bits of her that were long broken.

What she hadn't realized at the time was that healing involved ripping open the scar tissue that she'd built up around old wounds, opening a bigger hole than she realized was there to begin with. All those years of carefully crafting coping mechanisms and building a bridge from her old life to her new one left her fractured and mended with glue. She had been holding steady, but she wasn't quite the Maeve she used to be the six months she spent writing that piece had shattered her and she had to rebuild herself from scratch. The Maeve she was now was engaged to be married, she had a home she was building for their future and a career that was just starting to take off. And while she was itching to dive in, Maeve wasn't sure if she could afford to break herself open again.

2

Fiona

County Kildare, Ireland
Fall 1984

Fiona checked herself in the mirror repeatedly, adjusting her too-big hand-me-down kilt and polo shirt. Her older sister, Elenora, was much taller than Fiona was, and the clothes she passed down were often too long and wide in the shoulders. Fiona stared at her reflection and saw what everyone else would see, another Grisham in secondhand clothing. The only small relief she felt was that now, if she rolled her kilt enough and tucked in her shirt just so, she could start to see a feminine shape take place in her silhouette.

Despite the ill-fitting uniform, Fiona still looked pretty for her first day of school. She was a petite girl with fiery red hair that fell in curls down her back. She had bright green eyes that flashed emerald in the sunlight. Fiona's eyes were the kind of rare green that people noticed and commented on when they met her for the first time. She'd grown so used to the compliment she'd forgotten to notice them in the mirror most days. Instead, she focused on the small imperfections. She gave the blemish on her cheek and the slightest bump on her nose, which her mother assured her gave character to her face, far more attention than they deserved. She never allowed herself to consider that she was beautiful but rather compared herself with endless scrutiny to Elenora.

"Stop fussing, would you?" Elenora was now standing behind Fiona, who was still fidgeting with her outfit in the mirror. Elenora grabbed her school bag from the line of hooks screwed into the wall at the back door of the farmhouse and slung it over one shoulder.

"I can't, Nor. None of these fits right," Fiona complained, tugging at her uniform.

"Well, maybe if you would have spent less time with your nose in a book this summer, you might have learned how to do alterations by now," Elenora said, frowning. "Come on now. We're going to be late," she said pulling Fiona's arm, dragging her away from the mirror.

Fiona followed begrudgingly, pulling her own bag off the hook and slinging it over her shoulder as she trailed her sister out the door.

"Bye, Ma," the girls called in unison as they let the door swing shut behind them, not waiting for a response. Their mother, Aoife, was likely too busy to notice them coming and going anyways. Fiona and Elenora had four younger siblings that were between the ages of two and ten years old who required all of Aoife's attention. Fiona didn't mind though. It gave her more time to do what she wanted without scrutiny. Fiona and Elenora had watched their two older brothers carefully in their teen years and had learned from their careless mistakes. While the Fiona and Elenora were good, responsible girls, they still knew how to sidestep the rules when necessary.

The girls ran up the long gravel drive to the road to wait for their bus to arrive. They could see it bumping along the dirt road in the distance, arriving in a cloud of dust. The bus squealed to a stop and the hinged door groaned open. The two girls climbed aboard and found a spot together near the front. Fiona opened her book and started reading, her last chance to escape somewhere far away before starting a new school year.

The buses queued in one long line of yellow tin outside the school as hundreds of students unloaded down the steps and flooded in through the front doors. Newbridge Secondary School was the catchall school for everyone within a fifty-mile radius, and its walls were bulging with the uniform-clad students from the surrounding counties.

"Fi!" Mary yelled and ran toward Fiona, wrapping her in a hug.

"Oh, thank god!" Fiona replied, squeezing her tightly. Elenora gave Fiona a quick wave and walked off. Now that Fiona was safely in the arms of her best friend, she no longer cared if her sister was there or not.

"I'm so excited," Mary squealed under her breath.

"For what?" Fiona asked as they walked down the hall together, their arms linked as if they were heading down the yellow brick road and not a school corridor.

"I don't know, a new beginning. New faces, people who aren't the same four people we spent the summer with. I was starting to suffocate," Mary said dramatically.

Fiona nodded; she understood the feeling. Although, more people weren't necessarily what she longed for. She yearned for quiet places away from the obnoxious brood in her house, but Fiona was excited for new experiences. Living on a nonworking farm out in the countryside, Fiona often felt isolated and that she lived a mundane existence. She did the same thing every week that she had her entire life. The only thing that changed was she grew older, and her ma kept having more babies. What she really wanted was to have a life of her own.

Mary and Fiona walked until they reached the row of lockers they had been assigned: Fiona's near the front, and Mary's halfway down the hall. Fiona was thankful for this, because she knew they would see each other at least a few times a day. The school bell rang, sounding off one long buzz, and the girls slammed their lockers shut and gave each other a wave before heading off in opposite directions.

Fiona's first class was homeroom, which after the first fifteen minutes transitioned to an English class that she knew she'd excel in. Reading and writing consumed her entirely most days when she didn't have any other obligations. She often lost herself in the plots to her favorite novels, muddling up her real life with those of the characters she was reading about. She'd even been trying her own hand at writing a novel, intoxicated by the idea she could create another world for herself.

Fiona found her class, slid into her seat and dropped her bag on the floor beside her. The teacher stood at the front of the class with her back turned to the students as she scratched her name across the chalkboard. *Miss Hemmingway*, the sprawling cursive read. How apt for an English class, Fiona thought. The woman turned, assessing the new cohort of homeroom students with her piercing eyes. She was a tall woman in a long dress, and she had a certain no-nonsense look about her. Her honey-colored hair was pulled back into a utilitarian bun and her chin tilted up with the utmost affectedness.

"Good morning, class. Welcome to your

homeroom. My name is Miss Hemmingway, and you will be learning English literature this semester." She stopped for dramatic pause." As your homeroom teacher," she continued, "I will be responsible for updating you on any and all school news and happenings. Look to your left and look to your right. These will be the people you spend the rest of the year with."

Everyone swiveled their heads, inspecting their peers.

To Fiona's left was a mousy girl called Jo who offered a half smile, which Fiona returned. She had been in classes with Jo before, and they got along well. To her right was a tall broad young man with jet-black hair and deep blue eyes. He smiled a toothy smile and extended his hand to her.

"Garret," he said.

Fiona took his hand, using the firm grip her father taught her to shake it. "Fiona," she said, her heart fluttering.

"How was the first day?" Elenora asked as she sidled up to Fiona after the last bell. The hordes that walked in this morning were now retreating in a mass exodus, forking off expertly into lines leading to the appropriate buses. Fiona, ever lost in a daydream, never remembered which bus to load onto. She relied on Elenora to lead the way until they had found a seat together on the bus that would take them back home.

"It was good," Fiona replied cooly.

"That's all I get?" Elenora asked.

Fiona laughed. "I have Miss Hemmingway for homeroom."

"Ah, she's tough. I had her last year," Elenora said.

"So, I heard," Fiona said, raising a brow toward her sister.

"Yeah, she wasn't fond of me," Elenora said with a chuckle.

"She was not." Fiona laughed again. She looked out the window and spotted Garret loading onto another bus. She sighed dramatically.

Elenora narrowed her eyes at her sister. "Who is he?"

"There's no 'he'!" Fiona squawked defensively.

"Mm-hmm, I know that look. There is definitely a 'he,'" she said, rolling her eyes.

Fiona's blush deepened. "There was a guy in my homeroom who was … nice," Fiona offered.

"Name?" Elenora asked.

"Garret something. Didn't catch the last name,"

Fiona said, still watching out the window for a glimpse of him.

"Tall, dark and handsome?" Elenora's brows creeped up her forehead suspiciously.

"That's the one," Fiona said. "Do you know him?"

"Of him," Elenora said. "All the girls were talking about the family who just moved to town from Dublin: the O'Tooles.

"What about them?" Fiona asked, curious.

"Just that they moved here over the summer and have a very handsome son who would be a good addition to the rugby team, mostly. All the girls were talking about him today once they got eyes on him."

Fiona blushed again. Her fair complexion offered her no mercy when it came to hiding her emotions. Everything was always laid out for the world to see.

"Get in line, Fi," her sister said, sensing her crush, "or better yet, stay away from him."

3

Maeve

Guelph, Ontario, Canada
Summer 2011

It was dark out and Maeve still hadn't left the office. The vertigo she'd suffered earlier in the day still lingered, and she hadn't eaten anything all day apart from the lozenge Natalie had offered her and an old granola bar she found in her desk drawer. Maeve, instead of eating, had drowned herself in endless cups of coffee, tea and water. Once she was immersed in the world of maternity homes and adoption scandals, she couldn't bring herself to leave the office in search of food. The only breaks she allowed herself away from her desk were to the bathroom and break room to refill her favorite mug.

Maeve had gone from anxious and eager to entirely fixated in a matter of hours. Waves of anger and excitement coursed through her as she uncovered new bits of information. Unfolding in front of her was the outline of an elaborate puzzle, with each new piece that she unearthed urging her to dig deeper. Even if Maeve wasn't personally invested in the matter, the information in front of her would have been enough to keep her hooked from a journalistic perspective. Investigative journalism was like skydiving or spelunking. It was for adrenaline junkies who got their high off chasing a thrill with an unknown outcome, often putting their physical or emotional state at risk. The infuriating misuse of government power to keep mothers away from their children had set off a rage-fueled fire in Maeve's belly for all the mothers and children who had never had the chance to be together.

"Knock, knock," Natalie said, lightly rapping on Maeve's felted cubicle wall.

Maeve looked up and smiled tiredly at Natalie. Her eyes were dry and stinging from the hours spent glued to her computer screen. Maeve glanced past Natalie's head and saw it was already four o'clock, almost time to wrap up for the day.

"What's up?" Maeve asked, pushing her chair away from her computer to give Natalie her full attention.

"I just wanted to come check in on you and see how the rest of your day went." Natalie folded her arm over the top of the cubicle wall and leaned on it, signaling she wasn't going to leave until she was sure Maeve was okay.

"Oh, thanks. I'm okay. Well, some of this stuff is terrible," Maeve confessed.

"How so?" Natalie asked, peering over the little cubicle wall to try to sneak a glance at Maeve's screen.

"Have you ever heard about the Sixties Scoop?" Maeve asked.

"Is that some sort of group dance?" Natalie asked jokingly.

"No," Maeve replied seriously, shaking her head.

"The Sixties Scoop was the mass roundup of Indigenous children who were born into the welfare system from their mothers in the 1960s. The Canadian government literally took these children out of their homes and put them up for adoption, placing them in predominately nonindigenous middle-class families."

"That is terrible," Natalie said, frowning. "How many children were involved in this?"

"Twenty thousand." Maeve met Natalie's eyes, which reflected her own alarm. "And that's not the worst of it. Some of these children were sent to other countries. Some went to the United States, and some children were moved as far as New Zealand. They were scooped off the reservation and sent away, just for being born poor and on welfare."

Natalie's gaze hardened. "You know what? Forget what I said earlier. If you can handle keeping yourself emotionally distant, you have my go-ahead to dig into this Maeve. I'll have someone else cover your regular beat."

"Really?" Maeve asked.

"Really," Natalie replied.

"Thank you." Maeve turned back to her computer and kept searching, while Natalie walked back to her office.

Another couple of hours passed before Maeve finally hit a wall. She checked her phone and saw numerous notifications from Ethan attempting to get a hold of her. She sighed and turned her phone off. If he asked, she could pretend it died earlier in the day. All she wanted to do was go home and lay down. Her stomach had taken to gnawing on itself out of protest, and she needed to get some rest after what she'd discovered today. She turned the lights out and locked up the office, her body buzzing the way it did when she had a new investigation underway. Maeve loved the feeling of being the first in and first out of the office when she was working hard on a story. There was something powerful about being alone with nothing but her thoughts and the story brewing.

She walked along the lamppost-lined streets of the downtown Guelph core, watching people through the windows of shops and restaurants. She needed to walk off the adrenaline- and caffeine-induced swell in her chest. She took her time walking up and down each street in a zigzag pattern, drawing out her commute. It was eight o'clock before she had worked herself up enough to put the key in the front door. The lights were on, and Maeve could see in through the front window to the kitchen. Dinner was on the stove, and Ethan was sitting at the kitchen table on his laptop, sipping on a whiskey and deep in concentration. She felt a wave of guilt for ignoring his calls and texts all day. Maeve pushed the front door open and took a deep inhale. The smell of garlic and oregano greeted her warmly.

"I'm home," she called out.

At the sound of her voice, Ethan turned around in his chair to face the door and stood up. He walked toward Maeve with his face twisted in concern. He stayed quiet as he searched Maeve's face for an answer to his unspoken questions, like he was unable to get a clear read on her. He took her bag and hung it up in the front hall closet before turning to face her and wrapping her into a hug. Maeve stood stiffly at first, feeling guilty for her behavior, but slowly her tense muscles started to soften. His familiar scent of sandalwood and Ivory soap relaxed her, and she allowed him to pull her closer and laid her head on his shoulder, wrapping her arms around his back.

With a jolt, Maeve pushed back, grabbed his forearms and her green eyes flashed wide. "Your parents! We were supposed to go to your parents. Oh, Ethan, I'm so sorry," Maeve said, wincing.

Ethan offered a sad half smile. "Yes. That's why I was trying to call you all day."

"Ugh, no," Maeve groaned, burying her face in her hands. Maeve hated to disappoint Rose. She was the closest thing to a Mother Maeve had, and Rose had done everything she could to help Maeve over the last fifteen years.

"It's okay," Ethan said, rubbing Maeve's back and ushering her to the kitchen table where he was stationed. "I told her everything and she understands. Don't worry."

"Ethan!" Maeve snapped, spinning around to face him. "I wasn't ready to tell them!"

Ethan threw his hands up in surrender. "What was I supposed to do? You went completely MIA. I had no idea if you were even coming home tonight." Ethan paused to steady himself before continuing. "I understand this is a lot for you, but I need support too, and she deserves to know." Ethan's chin jutted out in defense as he avoided Maeve's glare.

"This isn't about you, Ethan," Maeve said in a huff and marched upstairs, unable to breathe the same air as him right now.

She was overstimulated and unraveling. Her pulse was beating in her ears so loudly she couldn't hear anything Ethan was muttering from below. When she got to her room, she sat on the end of the bed and buried her face in her hands. She was exhausted and angry, and she wasn't sure who she was mad at anymore. She slithered her way up to the headboard from the foot of the bed and spun herself around so she could put her legs up the wall. Something about letting the blood drain out of her feet and into her head at the end of the day reset her nervous system, and she desperately needed to calm down right now. She stared sat the ceiling and noticed a new water stain in the corner and made a mental note to tell Ethan about it later.

When she had settled down and the guilt of her outburst set in, she flipped herself back right side up on the bed. What she found was Ethan leaning in the doorway, holding a bowl of spaghetti and meatballs, his version of a peace offering.

"Hungry?" he asked, offering the bowl with an arched brow.

"Yes, thank you," she replied, taking the bowl from him with a weak smile. She was embarrassed, but not enough to reject his meatballs.

Ethan pulled the side table around to the end of the bed, arranging her bowl, napkin and utensils for her before sitting beside her while she ate.

When she finished, Maeve said, "Everything feels upside down right now." She still couldn't bring herself to meet his eyes but found his presence beside her comforting.

"Everything is the same as it was yesterday," Ethan said in an effort to put her at ease, but instead, that just agitated her further. He didn't understand.

"I think I just need to be alone right now," Maeve replied. She didn't look up at him, knowing that his face would fall, and he'd look like a sad puppy, and she'd give in.

"Honey, we have been through this before," Ethan said calmly. "Alone is not what you need." Ethan waited, staring at the side of Maeve's head expectantly.

He wanted her to meet his eyes and give him reassurance that they would get through this together, but she couldn't do that yet. She knew he was just as scared as she was that this could break open their perfectly curated life and planned future. Maeve had barely dipped her toe into this, and she already knew there would be a lot of turbulence ahead. After what felt like a stiflingly long moment of silence between them, Maeve lifted her gaze to meet his.

"I'm spinning and I have barely scratched the surface," she said, picking at the last bits of spaghetti that were stuck to the bowl.

"Okay. Let's play Facts and start from the beginning," Ethan said, jumping at the chance to try and make things better. "This morning you were informed that you were able to put in a request to obtain your mother's birth certificate. Fact?"

"Fact," Maeve said, smiling for the first time since this morning.

Facts was a game they played when either one of them was getting too emotional about something to the point they couldn't be logical. It was a lot easier to de-escalate a situation if they removed all feelings and assumptions and stripped it down to the facts. It wasn't always a welcomed game, but it always worked.

"And you went to work today and spent the entire day doing research. Fact?" Ethan asked, raising an eyebrow her way.

"Guilty," Maeve replied, nodding.

"What did you learn?" Ethan asked. He wanted her to break down the information she gathered into cold, hard facts, stripping all of her attachment from it.

"I learned that there were thousands of women—not even women—girls between the 1940s and the 1980s who were placed in homes for unwed mothers, where they were forced to stay, give birth and surrender their children to 'better homes,'" Maeve said, looking Ethan in the eyes now.

His face twisted in that way it did when she talked about her childhood. It was a look of pity and discomfort.

"I learned," Maeve went on, "that as part of this setup, the government set out protective laws that guaranteed the mother and child could never find each other, even if they wanted to. The adoptions were closed, any information sealed and unavailable to the adoptive family or child. These children had no way to learn about where they came from or even their mother's name." Tears started to stream down Maeve's cheeks, her feelings creeping right in with the facts when they weren't supposed to.

"It's all so wildly fucked up," Maeve said, wiping her eyes with the back of her hand. She used the corner of her sleeve to wipe at her nose. "Part of me wants to know, to finally have some answers, but the other part of me is terrified that whatever I find will be worse than I could have imagined myself." Maeve took a deep breath after releasing all of her thoughts out loud.

Ethan took Maeve's face in his hands and looked her in the eyes, "whatever happens, you are still you, I am still me, and we are still us. Your life as you know it will remain the same. It's your choice. You can go looking for your mother or not. Either way, I am here to support you."

Maeve nodded, ending the conversation. She knew he was just trying to be supportive, but his words cut into her. She didn't want things to just go on being the same if she had the chance to know her mother.

"I'm really tired. I think I'm just going to shower and go to bed." Maeve gave Ethan a half-hearted smile. She needed more time to process before she could handle any more pity from him.

Ethan took the cue and nodded back, scooping up her dishes on his way out and walking back downstairs alone.

Maeve turned on the shower as hot as it would go and waited until the room filled with steam to step in. The heat hit her shoulders, forcing them to slowly release away from the position they were frozen in by her ears. She stayed in there until the water turned from hot to tepid and her fingers and toes pruned from the moisture. Maeve had read that pruning was an evolutionary process designed to give the human body grip underwater, or to keep you safe in a slippery situation. She thought about that as she examined her fingertips and wrapped a big towel around herself, finally calming down from the day she had.

Maeve slipped into her pajamas and sat at the small desk they had in the corner of their bedroom. She booted her laptop back up and, a few moments later, opened the browser to type in www.adoption.on.gov into the search bar. With a few clicks of her mouse, she was on the website outlined in the letter she received that morning. She wasn't sure what to expect when she reached the website, which she had avoided looking at all day, but there was no clear call to action for adopted children looking to find their mothers. After clicking through the website pages for several minutes and repeatedly being redirected to the home page, she finally found the registration page. It was a fairly simple electronic form asking for no more information than her name, gender, date of birth, Social Security number and her contact information. She checked the box at the bottom of the page, giving them permission to contact her via phone or email and clicked Submit. The screen closed, and a secondary window popped up that said, thank you for your inquiry, we will be in touch in 14–28 business days.

Maeve's heart dropped into her stomach. The entire thing was so anticlimactic after a day wrung with stress. She was functioning solely off the adrenaline she was getting from the quick progress, only to be stymied by bureaucracy. She was defeated by the reality of long government processing times as she waited to learn about her past and how that might impact her future. She rubbed her temples, closed her laptop and placed it on the side table, which Ethan had moved back into place when she was in the shower. She turned off the light, rolled over into her pillow and fell into a deep sleep.

4

Fiona

County Kildare, Ireland
Fall 1984

It didn't take long for Fiona's crush on Garret to turn into a full-blown obsession. She spent an extra hour getting ready in the morning for school and made the effort to take in her sister's old uniform clothes so that they fit her better, showing off her petite figure. Garret O'Toole did something to her that she couldn't quite explain. It wasn't just his thick black hair or his piercing blue eyes; it was all of that and the way he looked at her. At sixteen, she had never felt truly seen before and the confidence it gave her was addicting. When they were in the same proximity, Garret made her feel like she was the only person in the world, even if they were standing in a crowded school hallway.

Every morning Fiona arrived in her homeroom class, and the anticipation of sitting beside Garret was enough to give her heart a case of the flutters. They had been getting to know each other in fragments, sneaking in conversations when there was a lull in the lesson. She woke up before her alarm every morning to get ready, looking forward to school to indulge in these small moments.

One morning Fiona arrived in class and took her seat, waiting for the second bell to buzz and the remainder of the class to arrive, except this morning, Garret didn't show up. Fiona sulked for the entirety of the class, having spent extra time primping this morning just for him. Her sour mood lasted the entire morning and through to lunch. Before now, she hadn't realized her emotional well-being entirely depended on their small bits of conversation to set the tone for her day. When Fiona was walking from her third-period class to her fourth, she sensed someone behind her.

"Hey, Fi," a deep voice said.

Fiona turned around and saw Garret standing in the hall smiling at her. "Hey," she said almost too enthusiastically as her entire spirit lifted, "where were you this morning?"

"Did you miss me?" he asked, those blue eyes crinkling.

Fiona blushed. "No, I just—"

"I'm teasing," he said, cutting her off. "Our rugby game went late out of town. I slept in, and my ma drove me in for second period," he said with a shrug.

"If I slept in, I'd be told to walk to school," Fiona said, shaking her head. "My ma would never wrestle the four little ones into the car to drive me forty-five minutes."

"Where do you live?" he asked.

"Kildare," Fiona said. As much as she longed for a bigger life, she was proud of where she came from.

"Ah, I'm just a bit past there," he said.

Fiona nodded. Everyone knew where the O'Toole's lived. It was big news around here when people moved down from Dublin.

"How are you enjoying County Kildare," she

asked, waving her arms as if she were presenting the land to him.

"Well, it's a bit different than Dublin, I suppose, but not all bad. Theres a really cute lass I've been making eyes at."

Fiona blushed, losing all the composure she'd momentarily gained.

"I'd be happy to show you around a bit," Fiona said, surprising herself when it came out of her mouth.

"I'd love that." Garret smiled brightly. "Are you free after school today?"

"I am." Fiona was nervous now, picking at the skin around her nails. "I'll meet you in the foyer after last bell." Fiona checked her watch. She was already late for her next class, and she wanted to avoid a tongue lashing from her teacher. "I have to run. See you then!" she said taking off in an awkward gallop down the hall, hoping she wasn't embarrassing herself.

"See you then!" Garret's voice boomed down the hall behind her with a chuckle.

The last bell of the day rang, and Fiona's stomach twisted in knots. She'd promised Garret to show him around caught up in the moment, but she wasn't going to be much of a tour guide herself, having grown up a few towns over. She took a deep breath as she stood in the foyer fidgeting with the hem of her kilt. She would have to wing it.

Fiona stood watching the hordes of students pass through the halls and out the front doors. The noise was deafening as hundreds of them all talked at once, excited for the fresh air after a long day of sitting still indoors. She started to worry Garret had forgotten or changed his mind as the halls emptied and there was only a handful of students roaming about. It always felt eerie once school had let out, the noise of the day waning, and except for the students waiting for their rides or after-school activities to start, the halls and classrooms were empty.

Most days after school, Fiona participated in a school sport, but today was her one day off. Usually, she spent the time exploring the library or wandering through the shops downtown before taking the city bus back home, but today she was going to spend it with someone new. Fiona checked her watch, agitated. She had now been waiting twenty minutes for Garret, longer than she'd ever waited for her own sister before leaving. She was starting to feel foolish. She paced the foyer for another two minutes before deciding she wasn't going to waste her one day to herself waiting around for someone who wasn't going to show. She picked her schoolbag up of the floor, slung it over her shoulder and walked through the double glass doors out into the fresh, cool September air.

"Fiona!" Garret called just steps behind her, pushing his way through the glass doors.

Startled by the lumbering boy, Fiona turned around to face him, her face betraying the indifference she'd hoped to emanate with visible hurt. "Garret. I thought you'd changed your mind." She rolled her shoulders back, trying to appear unruffled.

"Sorry for the wait. I got held up by Mr. Dunne trying to recruit me for the basketball team," Garret said, nearly out of breath from trying to catch up to her. "He's a talker."

They both smiled and shared a knowing look. Mr. Dunne was indeed a talker. It could take what felt like a year off your life if you got into a conversation with him that he was passionate about.

"That's all right," Fiona said, softening. When her heart settled down to a steady beat, she said, "Now that you're here, let's go."

"Where are we off to Miss Grisham?" Garret asked.

"To my favorite place in any town: the library." Fiona grinned, grabbed his hand and dragged him down the road.

The Newbridge Library sat atop the hill on Main Street, just a five-minute walk from Newbridge Secondary School. Fiona loved the story of the old church, and every time she was inside it, she felt like she was a part of history too.

"Do you always do extracurricular reading when school lets out?" Garret asked.

Fiona rolled her eyes. "Well, yes, but this isn't just any library, Garret. This," she said, pointing to the beacon atop the hill, "is something special."

Garret looked to where Fiona was pointing and saw a cathedral perched over the Main Street, sitting high and pretty with stained glass windows and tall spires. He frowned, confused. "Are you taking me to church as penance for my tardiness?"

Fiona grinned and cleared her throat as they walked up the cobblestone path. "The Newbridge Library," she said in her best presentation voice, "was built inside of what was previously a Catholic Church built in the early 1500s."

"Ah," Garret said, visibly relieved.

Fiona continued. "During the Glorious Revolution, when the Irish Catholics were being persecuted and forced to reform to the Church of England, Catholic churches were being burned and destroyed as an act of finality for their religion. In an attempt to preserve the stunning landmark in their town," Fiona said, "members of the parish came together to try and save their beloved place of worship."

"So, they turned it into a library?" Garret asked, trying to understand.

"Yes, but not at first," Fiona said. "At first, the Catholic Church was turned into a place of study for the Protestant religion. Later, it was used to house books of all kinds and continued to be a great meeting place for people all over County Kildare. As the centuries passed, the old church stayed intact, undergoing many renovations and becoming the most well-known library in the county. Everyone knew if they couldn't find books in their town, the Newbridge Library would have what you were looking for.

"It was rumored that in the late 1700s, groups of Irish rebels chose this church as the gathering place for all fellow rebels across County Kildare. They held secret meetings in the basement and plotted against the English, spending weeks holed up underground while library goers trotted above their heads," Fiona said excitedly. It was this bit of history that she felt so deeply connected to and part of why she wanted to share it with Garret. The library was a shapeshifter, a place that appeared as one thing, but when you stepped inside, you realized it was something else entirely.

"Wow" was all Garret could say as they kept walking up to the top of the hill.

As they stood at the steps of the church, Fiona's mind quieted for the first time all day.

"Come on, let's go inside," Fiona said, smiling, and she tugged gently on Garret's hand.

Garret looked down at where she grabbed him, surprised by her touch, and squeezed back.

5

Maeve

Guelph, Ontario, Canada
Summer 2011

"Maeve can you come into my office when you get a chance?" Natalie said, appearing as if by magic at Maeve's cubicle.

Maeve jumped at the sound of her voice. She had her headphones over her ears pumping classical music in to block everything else out, so she hadn't heard her footsteps approaching. Maeve turned around to find her boss hovering above her so closely she would be touching Maeve if not for the cubicle wall. Maeve took her headphones off.

"Sorry, I didn't catch that. What's up?" Maeve asked, forcing a smile despite her annoyance at the disruption to her workflow.

"Can you come to my office?" Natalie tapped her nails impatiently on the cubicle wall now. She wasn't leaving until Maeve came with her.

"Sure thing," Maeve replied, closing her laptop. She stood up and followed Natalie through the newsroom and into her office.

The newsroom was packed today. Most of the staff were in the office, and the place was buzzing with a frantic energy. That was one of the first things that drew Maeve to journalism: the feel of the newsroom when people were passionately writing away and breaking stories. The excitement that bubbled up among the other writers when a big story came in or they were working on a deadline was infectious.

Natalie opened her office door ushering Maeve in. Maeve took her usual seat in one of the faux leather chairs across the desk as Natalie plopped down into her seat and brushed her dark hair away from her face with the back of her hand. "It's a hot one," she said, looking around her desk in search of something. Maeve sat and watched Natalie fumble around and sweat started to prickle at her scalp. Maeve shed her lightweight cardigan and was down to a sleeveless turtleneck, which still felt like too much fabric. Her arms were sweaty, and she could feel them sticking to her chair every time she leaned back. The only reprieve was the slight breeze from the standing fan whenever it rotated her way. "Ah, here it is." She pulled a sheet from the top of the pile of papers trapped beneath the paperweight.

"I wanted to get an update on the new piece you're working on. I've seen you in here early every morning and after hours most nights. How are you getting on?" Natalie said, finally looking comfortable in her seat.

Maeve smiled, it was true, she had thrown herself into it to keep her mind busy. The anticipation of receiving information about her own adoption was eating at her.

"I've been working on a lead I found. I posted on some forums to try and gather any personal experiences from either mothers or children separated at birth."

"What's the lead?" Natalie asked.

"A woman contacted me about her sister, who, when she was just twelve, was sexually abused by a friend of her family. She was sent away to a maternity home for unwed mothers and kicked out two days after the baby was born."

Natalie just nodded while listening to Maeve speak, her face unflappable.

"When she came out of the home, her family shunned her. They didn't believe her story of the abuse. They blamed her. This poor girl had to go to a church shelter, as she had nowhere else to go.

"She was just a kid trying to return to normal life, and she was ostracized from her school and community as well. She was left with very little options and very little hope. So, she turned to the church, the very place that held her hostage, and became a nun. She stayed there until she was sixty years old and died of cancer." Maeve shook her head; this was only one-half of the story of the two people taken away from another.

Natalie steepled her fingers and pressed them to her lips, thinking. "That's a very sad story," she finally said.

"This is just one story of thousands. You wouldn't believe the recorded number of women who were taken away from their families and put in institutions for unwed mothers to carry out their pregnancies. The women were essentially kidnapped, forced to deliver the babies, only for the babies to be taken away from their mothers once they were born and sold for adoption. And this unwed mother, she was just put back out into the world, a shell of herself and alone." Maeve was upset now, her own feelings creeping back into the conversation.

"Maeve," Natalie said, stopping her, "while this is sad, one woman's story isn't going to cut it here. If you want to do this you have to tell a bigger story, do the research, use the numbers to prove the effect it's had on these women. You can't get caught up in everyone's sad story."

Maeve pulled back, offended. "It's not just a sad story. This is about people's lives. Lives that were ruined because someone decided that they knew better than a child's own mother." Maeve stood up; her face red now.

Natalie held a hand up, gesturing for Maeve to stop. "Sit down, please."

Maeve hesitated before she sat back down

begrudgingly.

"If you want to do this and you can separate your story from your feelings, you have the go-ahead, like I said. But writing other people's stories as you yearn for your own mother is not going to help you, and it's not going to sell newspapers." Natalie met Maeve's eyes. "I am happy to let you run with something you're passionate about—you are an amazing journalist, Maeve—but I'm not going to let you just run yourself into the ground because you feel a connection to these women. You need to talk to the experts, learn more about the systems that put these women in these positions and how they are remedying them now, if they are."

Maeve nodded, understanding now. Natalie was her friend, but she was also her boss, and the job came first.

"Of course," Maeve said. "Sorry," she added as the shame washed in in the wake of her outburst.

Natalie reached across the table to put her hand on Maeve's. "It's okay," she said, giving it a little pat. "I found someone I think would be good for you to speak with. He's a professor at the University of Toronto who spent the last several years doing research on human development and adoption psychology." Natalie handed her the paper she was holding.

"Dr. John Horner, PhD, English literature?" Maeve asked more as a question than a statement.

"Yes, he has been an English professor for the last thirty years, but he took an interest in human development and adoption. He's been teaching courses and writing academic papers for years. I thought he might be a good person for you to talk to get some background for your article."

"Okay," Maeve said, nodding. "I'll get in touch with him. Thank you." She stood to leave.

"Are you sure you're going to be okay with all of this?" Natalie asked, a look of concern creeping over her face.

"I'm positive," Maeve said, dismissing herself from the stuffy office.

Maeve typed **Dr. John Horner** into her search engine to see what she could find on this lead from Natalie. She found his university profile, which included a short biography, the classes he taught and his contact information. The headshot on his faculty page looked fifteen years too young to be him at his current age, but he was handsome, with kind eyes and a wide smile. She read about the work he was focused on, which included literature, women's studies and family life, specifically related to adoption.

Maeve typed his address into the bar and contemplated how to start the email. Cold emailing was Maeve's least favorite part of her job. She could write for days, but somehow a four-sentence email trying to summarize who she was and what she needed always induced writer's block. After typing and erasing the message several times, Maeve finally settled on a message.

Dear Dr. Horner,

My name is Maeve Grisham. I am a journalist who works for the Toronto Star group of papers, specifically for the Guelph Tribune. I am currently working on an exposé about the treatment of unwed mothers and children between 1940 and 1980 and was hoping you'd be willing to offer your expertise. Your name was brought to my attention as an expert in women's and adoption rights, and I was hoping you might have some time to speak with me about your research.

Thank you in advance,

Maeve

She pressed Send and checked her watch. It was nearly four o'clock, and today she wouldn't miss dinner at Ethan's parents. She had been avoiding his mother's calls and texts about the wedding ever since, unsure how to put into words why she had no headspace for such a thing. She and Ethan were starting to grow distant, and while she felt guilty, her pursuit of answers for this piece seemed urgently more pressing. Nevertheless, she packed up her things, slipped out the door and headed directly home.

Maeve walked through the front door and called as cheerfully as she could, "I'm home!" She put her bag down and walked around to the kitchen, listening for Ethan. When she didn't see him or hear a response, she walked the base of the staircase, tilting her ear up to listen for sounds from above. She heard the trickle of the shower running. Ethan was getting ready. Pleased she had a bit more time to work before they left, Maeve settled in at the kitchen table and opened her laptop back up. To Maeve's surprise, there was already an email waiting in her inbox from Dr. John

Horner.

> Maeve,
>
> Nice to e-meet you. I'd be happy to talk.
> Do you have availability tomorrow to come
> down to Toronto and chat?
>
> John

Maeve's heart beat in double time as adrenaline flooded her body. With shaky hands, she typed out a response.

> John,
>
> I'd be delighted to. How does 1 pm work
> for you?
>
> Maeve

Maeve held her breath as she hit Send and felt her body tingle in anticipation. This was her first real lead on her story, and it was someone who might be more passionate about it than she was. As she began to shut her laptop, she heard Ethan creaking down those old stairs when another message arrived in her inbox. His response was just one word: **Perfect.**

Maeve took Ethan's hand and forced a smile on her face. Despite her mind being elsewhere, she owed him this: an evening dedicated to their future. The sun was setting, and the heat of the day was tapering off. Maeve's bare arms now felt cool to the touch, and she wished she'd brought a sweater. They walked the few blocks over to the Clarkes' home in a comfortable silence as Maeve was distracted with thoughts of her meeting with the professor tomorrow.

The house that Rose and Callum Clarke lived in was the same home Ethan grew up in. It was the home Maeve moved into at fourteen and what inspired her own happy family fantasies. When Maeve and Ethan started dating, she was between foster homes. The Clarkes were kind and let her stay for a few weeks, compassionate for the poor girl with no family. They invited regular visits from Child Protective Services and soon became qualified foster parents, taking Maeve in for good. The Clarkes were kind to take her in, and they even came to love her like one of their own. They provided for her and protected her for the last ten years, folding her into their family unit. Yet, even after a decade and an impending wedding, somehow, Maeve still didn't quite feel like she fit in with them.

Ethan and Maeve walked up the front steps and swung the front door open without so much as a courtesy knock. At the sound of the security chime, Rose rushed toward the door, her eyes bright.

"Maeve! Ethan!" Rose pulled both of them into a tight embrace.

Maeve hugged her back with one arm and squeezed Ethan's hand with her other while they were all entwined in an awkward group hug.

"Come in, come in," Rose said, ushering them into the living room. She was always so excited to see her children. This particular quality, the unwavering love, had made Maeve uncomfortable as a teenager. She always thought something must be wrong with this woman, but now it was one of the things she loved about Rose the most.

The smell of a roast chicken cooking in the oven greeted them as they rounded the corner into the kitchen. Ethan's dad, Callum, was bent over the open oven, wearing Rose's bright pink apron as he basted the chicken.

Maeve let out a belly laugh for the first time in what felt like weeks.

"What's so funny?" Callum asked as he stood up and walked over to give her a hug. "How are you doing, sweetheart?" He looked in her eyes.

"I'm okay, staying busy," Maeve replied, "feeling rather impatient, in all honesty."

Ethan stared at Maeve from the other side of the room with his mouth slightly open. That was the first honest answer Maeve had given about how she was feeling in weeks. She saw him shut his mouth as he tried to act normal, but his face betrayed him.

"We all have our fingers and toes crossed for you, Maeve," Rose said, shooting Ethan a look.

Callum pulled the roasting pan out of the oven and placed it on the stove. He clapped his silicon oven mitt–clad hands together with a *thwap*. "Hungry?" he asked the group, proud of his golden bird.

"Mmm, yes, let's eat," Rose said enthusiastically, ushering them all to sit down around the table.

Perched on the corner between Maeve's and Rose's seats was a white binder with gold embossing that announced it as the *Wedding Plans*. This was the second wedding the Clarke family had planned in the last few years after Ethan's sister married her husband, Jack, three summers earlier. Rose was thrilled that this time around, she had complete control without another set of in-laws to consider. Ethan and Maeve's wedding would be the party of the season, and Rose wanted to make sure everything would be just so. It was planned to happen in three months' time at the Lakeview Club, the country club the Clarkes were members at. This meant, invited or not, any number of his parents' friends would be able to peek in at the wedding if they happened to be at the club that day playing tennis or golf. For this reason, Rose required everything to be perfect. The wedding would be her shining moment to show off her beautiful family.

The four of them ate the roast chicken Callum had carefully prepared for tonight and finalized plans for the wedding like a normal, happy family. It was the first time in weeks Maeve was able to allow herself to be in the moment.

"Cheers to the Clarkes," Maeve said, toasting the group.

"Cheers to the newest Clarke joining the bunch," Rose said, holding up her glass as the boys raised theirs, saying in unison, "Hear! Hear!"

6

Fiona

County Kildare, Ireland
Winter 1984

It was almost Christmastime. The air had cooled dramatically, as if it were in a hurry one day. The warmth of the autumn air disappeared and damp cold set in overnight. Across the county, there were Christmas carols playing in the shops and there were decorated trees propped up in store windows. This time of year, Fiona's mother would prepare hot apple cider for sipping when they got home from school. Every time Fiona walked through the door, she loved how the spices filled the air of their home, bringing a wash of nostalgia over her of Christmases past.

Fiona and Garret were going steady now, and she'd matured in the last few months. The confidence she felt knowing someone wanted her to be theirs made her stand straighter and hold herself taller.

Thursday had become their standing day to spend time together during the week. After the bell rang at the end of the day, Fiona looked around the halls for Garret, who was usually waiting in the foyer for her. When he wasn't there, she walked outside in the cold, shivering as she looked around the parking lot. A car honked and Fiona spun around. A burgundy station wagon pulled up along the curb and stopped where she was standing. Fiona squinted to see inside, but the windows were tinted. The passenger window rolled down, and she saw Garret's head emerge from behind the glass as he manually cranked the window open.

"Well, what do we have here?" Fiona asked, beaming. She walked around the car to open the passenger side door and slid into the front seat. The heater blasted warm air through the vents, a welcome reprieve from the frigid wind whipping around outside. Garret leaned across the center console to kiss Fiona eagerly. When he pulled away, he gave her a little squeeze on the knee that shot goose bumps up her bare legs.

"My parents went on holiday to the Highlands for the weekend. I have a car and the house to myself, if you're up for it?" Garret asked, staring straight out ahead over the dash.

Fiona's hands went clammy. She had been eager to get some time alone with Garret, ached for it really. But the good Catholic girl inside her urged her against it, knowing it was strongly frowned up to be unsupervised like that with a boy. Garret sensed her change in demeanor even before she said anything. She watched as his face shifted from eager excitement to disappointment.

"Oh. We can go somewhere else. I don't mind," he said, his eyes still fixed on the dashboard.

"No, no, let's go." She forced a smile, patting his leg with encouragement.

It wasn't that she was uncomfortable with his proposition, she just didn't trust herself. Fiona wanted to be alone with Garret in his house more than anything. She wanted to see where he lived and catch a glimpse of his real life outside of school. She wanted to see his room and to hold him close. She was so sick of trying to contain herself in public with onlookers always casting judging looks their way.

"You sure?" He glanced over at her to see if she was serious. Fiona could see a smile twitch at the corner of his mouth.

"Yes!" she said more enthusiastically this time. Her anxiety waned as she talked herself into the idea. "You just surprised me, is all," she said giving his hand a firm squeeze. She leaned over the console and pecked him on the cheek.

At Fiona's go-ahead, they slowly rolled out of the parking lot and onto the road. Garret's house was past Fiona's on the outskirts of Kildare. She figured she could get home in time for supper if she left by five, which gave them just over two hours together. Garret turned on the radio to a local station that played American pop hits, and a crackly Tina Turner song played through the speakers, filling the silence between them. Without taking a bus that made frequent stops, the car trip on backcountry roads was only thirty minutes. Soon Garret pulled up the drive to a large estate surrounded by fields where Fiona could see a handful of goats roaming free. It reminded her of her own home, acres upon acres to roam free and explore.

"This is beautiful," Fiona finally said, breaking the long silence as they pulled up to the house.

Garret smiled and shrugged. "It's not much, but it's home," he said. "Would you like a tour?"

"I'd loved one," Fiona said as she stepped out of the car and walked toward the front door.

"I'll show you around outside first before the sun goes down," he said. "Here, take one of these. There's quite a chill in the air today." Garret wrapped Fiona's shoulders with a thick wool blanket he grabbed from inside the front door. Garret gave her shoulders a little rub, warming them up.

They walked around the property, and Fiona could sense the change in him right away. Seeing him here, at home, Garret was self-assured and carefree. She followed him around the estate, taking it in. The house sat among rolling hills surrounded by green grass and roaming animals. There was a little pond with two mossy boulders set up on the edge and the two of them wandered that way and sat together huddling for warmth. The sun started to lower closer to the horizon and cast a warm orange glow, and Fiona thought this was the most romantic thing she'd ever seen.

"I like to imagine the goats had traveled a long way before settling and deciding this would be their home," Garret said as he looked off into the distance.

Fiona laughed and wrapped her blanket tighter around her shoulders. With the sun gone, she was cold to the bone now.

Garret wrapped his arms around her, rubbing her shoulders to create some friction to warm her up again. "Let's get inside and warm up now before it gets too dark to find our way back," Garret said, hopping off the boulder and offering his hand to lower Fiona down safely. She took his hand with one of her own and used her other hand to secure the two edges of the blanket around her shoulders as a shawl. Holding hands, the two of them ran as fast as they could without toppling over one another back to the main house, racing against the evening sky.

7

Maeve

Guelph, Ontario, Canada
Summer 2011

Maeve was up and out the door early the next morning, eager to get to Toronto. She walked through the quiet streets of Guelph as the sun rose over the basilica to get to the train station. She was on her way to meet Dr. John Horner at the University of Toronto campus.

She sent Natalie an email before she left to let her know that she would be working on the road today and prayed she wouldn't be reprimanded for being out of office without warning. They had a strong working relationship, but Maeve knew she should have asked first. She was set to meet Dr. Horner at his office at 1:00 p.m., and while the train from Guelph to Toronto was only an hour-long commute, Maeve didn't travel into the city often, and she wanted to make sure she arrived on time with plenty to spare.

Dr. Horner taught at the University of Toronto, a campus Maeve had toured once upon a time before she'd opted to stay in Guelph and earn her degree alongside Ethan. In her careers class in high school, she was told she could attend any university if she had the grades, but reality set in when she saw what it would all cost. Even with her academic scholarships, she wouldn't be able to afford school, food and housing, so Rose and Callum graciously let her stay in their home past high school while she completed her degree. It was at the University of Guelph where Maeve studied journalism, built her group of friends with Ethan by her side and started to plan their life together after they were done with school. Everything was good, until Ethan met

Christine Jones in his Psychology 101 class in the second term of their first year.

Christine Jones was a goddess. She was leggy, blond and one of the most beautiful girls Maeve had ever seen in real life. She looked like one of those Victorias Secret Angels, tall, lean, perfect hair and a seemingly unflawed face. Maeve had seen her around campus and heard some of her friends talking about her, the way teenagers talked about beautiful people behind their backs. There were whispers of juvenile plastic surgery and an eating disorder, and she'd even heard a rumor she was an escort, but Maeve knew all that gossip was just female jealousy. Maeve didn't have time for gossip, so she never paid any attention to it, until it was Ethan saying her name. One day he'd come home and started talking about his new lab partner, and he had that look in his eyes that he got when he was excited about something. Maeve had brushed it off for a while, not wanting to cause a stir in their unruffled home life and let the feeling settle at the back of her mind, where it only nagged occasionally.

Six months passed before Christine Jones surfaced in her life again at their friend Graydon Dorchester's Halloween party. Maeve and Ethan got ready and pre-drank separately, he with their guy friends, and she with the girlfriends, all of which had participated in a group costume for the party. There were five of them, and they opted to go as the Spice Girls. Maeve, of course, was Ginger Spice because of her wild red hair, and she, Posh, Baby, Sporty and Scary were all dressed in platform boots and tiny dresses for the occasion. Maeve felt sexy and she was excited for Ethan to see her. When she walked into the party that night, the music was blasting, the lights were low, and it smelled like stale beer and sweat. Maeve accepted the red Solo cup filled with keg draft beer and sipped it slowly, taking in her surroundings. She liked going out and drinking with her friends, but she never allowed herself to get really drunk, like most of the people here would get tonight. Maeve always stayed sober enough to get home and take care of her friends, always scanning the crowd for danger. While she had managed to get out of the foster system into a safe home, she still found it hard to trust anyone. Maeve looked for Ethan. He had texted her when they left the pre-drink, and he would have been there already, but she couldn't see him. She excused herself from the group to look for him. She tried the kitchen, the bathroom, the backyard—he was nowhere to be found. A sick feeling twisted Maeve's stomach then, and she stood at the base of the stairs for a while, willing herself to go up and check the bedrooms. Someone bumped into her from behind, spilling her beer, and she took that as the nudge she needed to climb to the second floor.

There were three doors to the left, and two on the right. All of them were open except for the last one on the left. Maeve walked to the end of the hall and opened the door slowly, looking inside the room. There were two people having sex on the bed. She could see the back of the girl and the long blond hair flowing down her back, but she couldn't see who was underneath her. Maeve waited another few seconds before closing the door, feeling guilty and ashamed for what she'd done. She didn't know if it was Ethan, but if it wasn't, she'd just intruded on someone and felt sick about it. Maeve sat at the top of the stairs to steady herself for a few moments before returning to the party. She sipped on her beer and ran her hands through her hair, hating herself for even thinking Ethan would do something like that. As she stood to walk downstairs, she heard the door open behind her. She turned to look as Christine Jones and Ethan stepped out of the bedroom.

"Maeve," Ethan said, and his face went white.

Maeve looked between him and Christine as her own face lost color. She bent over and puked up her belly full of keg beer onto her white pleather platform boots.

Ethan rushed over to help her, and Maeve pushed him away. "Get off me," she said, wiping her mouth with the back of her arm.

She locked herself in the bathroom to get cleaned up. She stayed in there for an hour as Ethan pleaded for her to come out from the other side of the door. She sat on the edge of the filthy tub while the party raged on below, considering her options. She could break up with Ethan, but then her life as she knew it would evaporate. She would have to find somewhere to live, a job that could pay for rent and bills and food to survive. Or she could give him a chance to explain himself and apologize, leaving intact the life she had. She didn't really have an option to leave, not a real one anyways, not yet.

So, Maeve walked out of the frat-house bathroom and said, "Get your things. We are going home." And they did.

It wasn't long after they had graduated and secured steady jobs that Maeve and Ethan bought their house. The deal was that they had to earn enough to cover the mortgage, but it was thanks to a generous gift of a down payment from Ethan's parents that they were able to afford it. Callum owned a real estate development company, which would one day be Ethan's, so they felt it was important for their children to own their own homes as early as they could to really get a sense of how a home worked. Callum always said it was one thing to live somewhere but another to truly understand what made a house a home. Maeve understood this when they bought their house, and that home was more of a promise for a future home than a home at the time. It had "good bones," Rose had said as they walked through the old house, just streets over from where Maeve had lived with the Clarkes all these years. Bones it had, but not much else. Ethan and Callum ripped the walls back to the studs and tore the carpets up from the floors to reveal the original hardwood, which was worse for wear. They had to get a plumber to run new lines, an electrician to install new wiring and a drywaller to build up the new walls. Ethan had rented a floor sander from Home Depot to refinish the hardwood, which took weeks to grind off a hundred years of water damage and carpet glue. But when they were done, they were beautiful, and Maeve couldn't look at those floors without thinking about how much work went into restoring that small part of history. It took over a year for the renovations to be complete, and when Maeve and Ethan finally moved their furniture in, it felt like the start of a new chapter, just the two of them.

Technically, the house was in Ethan's name, but no one ever made Maeve feel that way. They were a pair, Maeve and Ethan, Ethan and Maeve, and they had been that way for so long that Maeve felt like she wasn't her own singular person anymore. Maeve's friends were Ethan's childhood friends and their girlfriends. Some came and went, so Maeve would befriend them and take them in, as the Clarkes had done so graciously for her. Her boss, Natalie, was Maeve's first real adult friendship outside of her life with Ethan. It was the first relationship she made away from everywhere else that their lives were intertwined. Maeve was just Maeve at work. She loved her job not only for the work but for the freedom to be herself, and not what was expected of her everywhere else. Being an investigative journalist was thrilling to her. It combined all of her passions: writing, research, storytelling and cracking clues. She had gone through phases in her childhood when she thought she might want to be a detective or a forensic analyst. She loved piecing together puzzles. However, she discovered rather traumatically during a biology class in the eleventh grade that she was too faint of heart to ever pursue a career that involved blood or dead bodies. So, instead, Maeve stuck to the research component of her passions and found a path that suited her queasy stomach better.

The train ride downtown was in no way a scenic one. This ride was a commuter train that made many stops along the way, picking up businesspeople from Guelph to Toronto who would rather sit and work than sit in traffic all morning. Driving into the city was never something Maeve had even considered enduring. She much preferred a slow morning, sitting in a seat with a hot coffee either reading or writing, blissfully tuning out the crowd around her. When she arrived at Union Station, her quiet commute was abruptly ended by the loud buzz of the station, thousands of people coming in and out on buses and trains. Maeve packed up her things securely in her bag before exiting briskly through the station out into the open air.

Judging by the traffic, Maeve decided a walk would be better than trying to catch a taxi or ride the underground train to the university campus. She walked along the crowded streets of the city, abuzz with commuters heading to work, coffee in hand, phones pressed to their ears, already on calls. She walked past the skyscraping business towers alongside lanes of traffic as she headed toward the part of the city the campus was tucked away in. She bypassed all sorts of people from businessmen to artists to people who lived on the streets to tourists snapping pictures as they leaned back to try to capture the entirety of the tall buildings.

She walked until she descended upon the campus, which was almost otherworldly in contrast to the concrete-and-glass buildings that made up the downtown core. Stepping onto grounds of the University of Toronto was like stepping back in time.

The academic buildings were erected in the early 1800s, almost two hundred years before Maeve was born. She walked along the paved paths that wove through the campus with her eyes fixed upward so she could take in each building she passed. The architectural styles were a mix of Romanesque and Gothic Revival, and looked eerily similar to those she'd seen at the Oxford and Cambridge campuses she'd visited the summer she went traveling with Ethan to England. They were the type of buildings that took time to build, that used brick, stones and lumber of a much higher integrity than anything you could buy today.

Maeve wandered the campus and checked her watch. It was noon, one hour until it was time to meet with Dr. Horner. She'd had the foresight to pack a lunch for her journey and found a nice spot under a shady tree to sit and eat. Maeve was too distracted today to do any sort of valuable work, so she just sat and picked at her lunch as she watched the students walk by, imagining how her life might have been under different circumstances.

"Maeve?" She heard a voice call above her.

She looked up to find a large shadow of a man lumbering over her. Maeve put a hand up to shield her eyes from the sun to get a better look at him. While he wasn't as young as his photo, as she'd suspected, she was sure the man standing above her was Dr. John Horner. He tilted his head and stared at her with a curious look she couldn't quite read. Nervous she'd lost track of time, she checked her watch—12:45 p.m. She wasn't late. Relieved, she stood up to face him.

"Hi, are you Dr. Horner?" she asked, finally at eye level. Maeve held out her hand as a professional courtesy, noticing too late that there were remnants of her peanut butter sandwich pasted to her hand. He took it anyways.

"Sorry to startle you. I recognized you from the photo on the website. I was just walking to my office to prepare for our meeting," he said, pumping her hand enthusiastically. He was still staring at her in a way that slightly unsettled her, but Maeve forced a smile.

"No worries at all, it's a pleasure to meet you. I was just admiring the campus. It's beautiful," Maeve said, making a point to glance around again.

"It certainly is," Dr. Horner agreed. "I've been here since I started university many, many years ago. They can't get rid of me." He winked. "My office is just this way. Let's walk," he said as they ducked under the low-hanging branch that was providing the shade and back onto the path.

Maeve fell into step beside him. They walked past a building covered in ivy with arched windows. Maeve paused for a moment to take in its timeless regality and had to run to catch up with Dr. Horner, who was now giving her an impromptu campus tour.

"This building here is the gender studies facility," he said, and turned down a fork in the path. "I have spent lots of time there teaching lectures, but my office is in there," he said, pointing to a building a little farther down. "That is the literature building, where I spent the start of my career, and there my office remains."

The building wasn't as grand or gothic as the one she'd just stopped to admire. It was more modern, in a mid-century sort of way. It stuck out, its clean lines and concrete, plopped amid the gorgeous gardens and buildings that were covered with blankets of ivy. It looked cold and out of place. It was as if she'd been walking through a museum and had just left one exhibit in the 1800s into another one in the 1960s. So it took her brain a moment to switch gears and appreciate the art for what it was. Dr. Horner rambled on in the way older people do when their minds are filled with collected knowledge that they are eager to share. Maeve followed quietly behind him, keen to be a sponge here today.

Eventually, they approached the literature building and stepped inside. Its interior reflected the exterior style of clean lines and minimalistic features.

There were metal staircases and white walls that lined the wide corridor that ran two stories high. Maeve and Dr. Horner slipped down a winding hall and finally up a staircase to the second floor. The corridor was narrow and lined with doors. They stopped about halfway down on the left at one that had a small brass nameplate on the door that read, Dr. John Horner, PhD. He swung the door open and flicked on the light switch, then held his arm open, gesturing for Maeve to go in first.

"Please forgive the mess," he said in a way that made Maeve believe that it was never not a mess in here.

Maeve walked in the office and looked around, taking her seat across from the heavy leather chair behind the desk. Dr. Horner removed his hat and glasses and rubbed his eyes before looking back at Maeve. Without them, in this soft light, Dr. John Horner looked much younger, and to her surprise, she found him rather handsome. Without the cap and glasses, he'd transformed from looking like a stodgy fifty something professor to someone else entirely. His clean-shaven face was hardly lined, and his eyes were sharp with a flicker of intensity.

"So, Maeve Grisham," he said, folding his hands on

the desk between them, "what prompted you to reach out to me, of all people?" he asked, getting right down to business.

"Well," Maeve started, clearing her throat, "my boss actually found your name and suggested I reach out to you for the piece I'm working on."

"Ah," he said, raising his brows high on his forehead, "tell me about the story."

Maeve took a sharp inhale. She was expecting to be the one asking the questions today, and she felt put on the spot.

"I am writing an exposé on the failure of the Canadian government during 1940s to 1980s regarding the treatment of unwed mothers," Maeve said. She could feel the intensity of his gaze on her and started to feel out of her depth on the subject matter.

Dr. Horner steepled his fingers and pressed them to his lips thoughtfully. "And what led you there?"

Maeve flushed hotly. She instinctively brought her own fingers up to feel the burn of her cheeks, assessing the scarlet of her face by touch. She felt only a mild warmth against her fingertips. She relaxed only slightly. Something about Dr. Horner unsettled her. He looked at her as if he knew her and spoke to her with such a familiar comfort. His ease with asking the questions made Maeve feel obligated to answer honestly.

"Well, "Maeve started, "I have some personal stake in the matter and felt it was time to do what I could to get educated about it." *There*, she thought, that was enough to give him without completely baring her soul to this stranger.

Dr. Horner nodded knowingly. He could have pushed, and Maeve would have given him what he asked for, but instead he stayed quiet for a while, considering her words.

"Once upon a time I felt I had some stake in the matter too," he finally said. "So, that we have in common. Passion and ownership are the only two true drivers in life."

Maeve nodded, agreeing.

"I've spent the last twenty-five years doing research on this and trying to connect children and their mothers who were separated, and my research has been used as part of a recent legislation change," Dr. Horner said. "Most of my research is published, you can find it online. So, what I want to understand is what more I can do to help you?"

Maeve frowned, confused. "Well, I don't know

exactly. I've only started to scratch the surface," she replied, chewing at the inside of her cheek. She was starting to think she had requested this meeting prematurely.

Dr. Horner nodded, pursed his lips and leaned forward. "What is it you're looking for?" He searched her face for whatever she wasn't telling him.

"My mother," she replied, feeling the sting of tears burn her eyes.

8

Fiona

County Kildare, Ireland
Winter 1984

"Fi, what's going on with you? You're even more of a recluse than usual. I feel like we haven't talked in ages," Elenora said. The two girls were in the process of moving the living room furniture around to make space for the Christmas tree their father was out collecting with their brothers.

"Hmm?" Fiona looked up at her sister as if she hadn't noticed she was there. She'd been lost in a daydream somewhere far away. Garret had taken over a large amount of real estate in her brain as of late. If she wasn't thinking about him, she was writing about him or reading a book and pretending the characters were the two of them. She had fallen prey to the all-consuming obsession of a first love.

"Are you okay?" Elenora asked, stopping to stand and face Fiona with her hands on her hips. "You've been acting strange. I haven't heard you talk about anyone lately, not even Mary. Usually, you won't shut up about Mary, not that I'm complaining it's a nice break but it's... weird."

Fiona blushed and her stomach turned. Apparently, she hadn't done as good of a job staying under the radar as she'd thought. "Yes, of course, I'm fine. I just, well," Fiona paused and stood a little straighter, "I have a boyfriend," she confessed in part. She wasn't sure if she was willing to give more than that away just yet.

"Oh, have you now?" Elenora asked with a raised brow. There was a twinkle in those matching set of sparkly green eyes she shared with her sister.

Fiona froze in place. She began to suspect Elenora might know more than she was letting on. "I do. He's that new student at school who moved here from Dublin. I'd been showing him around on Thursdays, trying to make him feel welcome…" Fiona offered only some details, hoping to end this conversation, but by the look on Elenora's face, she had little chance of getting out of this comfortably now.

Elenora grinned. "So, it's true then. You have been kissing Garret O'Toole behind the library."

Fiona turned crimson. "Who told you that?"

"Everyone's been talking about it, Fi. Most girls in my year had their eye on him. They're all jealous." She laughed. She was teasing her little sister, not knowing how deep her feelings ran. "Good for you." She gave her an approving nod and continued pushing an armchair out of the way with her hip to make room for the tree.

"Oh god," Fiona moaned. She covered her face with her hands and felt the flush in her face travel down her neck and burn a hole in her belly.

"So, is he a good kisser then?" Elenora asked, grinning wider now.

"Nor! That's private," Fiona said defensively.

"What? I'd tell you if you asked." Elenora

shrugged, then gave her sister a nudge with her shoulder.

"I love him," Fiona whispered, tears welling in her eyes, surprising herself. She had been feeling much more out of control with her emotions lately, and it was scaring her. She was teary over happy things and became dizzy and sick to her stomach at the slightest exertion. She wondered if everyone felt like this when they were in love.

"And what do you know about love?" Elenora asked more seriously now. The tone of jest in her voce faded into parental concern that only an older sister can impart on their sibling.

"You wouldn't understand," Fiona said avoiding eye contact, uncomfortable with the turn the conversation had taken.

"You think I've never liked a lad before then?" Elenora pushed back, not easing up on her.

Fiona took a step back and Eleanor stepped forward. A dance of confrontation.

"Well, I've never heard you talk about one, so how would I know?" Fiona said.

Elenora took a deep breath. Fiona sensed she was trying to settle her temper and muster some patience for her little sister. Fiona often noticed this from her right before she softened. Elenora had a temper that would go off like fireworks when they were younger. But as she matured, she had learned to control it and channel it into more useful things. To channel her own emotions, Fiona turned to her writing. Elenora had her paintings as an outlet. Elenora's artwork scared her a few times when she was younger; it was angry and full of rage. As Fiona started to mature herself, she understood that letting out those pent-up feelings was better than holding them in, and art without emotion was not art at all.

"Come sit. I think we've done enough for Dad to get the tree in." Elenora grabbed Fiona's hand and sat her down on the couch beside her.

The thing about being the oldest daughter in the house, despite having two older brothers, was that Elenora often had to play mother to Fiona, while their mother was busy with the babies. They had grown apart since they began developing at different times, and Elenora started her own life with friends and activities outside of school. It had created a natural distance between the two of them. But even with the distance, Fiona still felt as safe and comforted by her older sister as she always had.

"I thought I was in love last year, with Willie,"

Elenora said.

Fiona looked up at her sister surprised. Willie Flannagan was their next-door neighbor, who they'd lived beside their entire lives. She and Elenora had grown up playing with Willie in the fields that connected the two family properties. The Grisham's and Flannagan's would have family cookouts together when the days got longer in the summertime, and Willie's mother watched the Grisham children every time Aoife went to the Dublin hospital to birth another child. They were a nice family, but Fiona had always thought of them like cousins, an extension of their own family. Fiona tried to see Willie through her sister's eyes. Willie was by no means a handsome lad, but he was kind and smart and always full of ideas.

"I had no idea you felt that way about him," Fiona said, still trying to imagine the two of them as a pair.

"I did. He and I had always had a little crush on each another, but it was never anything more than that. Then, last year, we started spending more time together after school. One thing led to another, and he kissed me. After that, I thought he was mine." Elenora looked wistfully into the distance.

Fiona turned her head to face her sister, surprised.

Elenora had her undivided attention now. "And then what happened?"

"We dated for a while and it was really nice," she said, smiling sadly at Fiona. "He was thoughtful and would bring me books and trinkets and flowers. I was completely smitten."

"So, what went wrong?" Fiona asked, frowning.

"All was well and fine until he started trying to pressure me into more than I was comfortable with. I tried to resist, but after a while I felt like if I didn't give in, I was going to lose him. So I lost my virginity to him, and he broke up with me a week later." Elenora looked at her hands now.

"What?" Fiona sprang up from her seat, outraged for her sister. "I'm so sorry, Nor. That's horrible. I'll go over and give him a proper smack in the face right now," Fiona said, ready to fight.

"Fi, it's okay. I'm fine now. I'm just trying to let you know that sometimes feelings at our age can feel like love, but sometimes people are just trying to get something from you, and they don't actually love you back." Elenora patted the seat beside her, gesturing for Fiona to sit back down. "All I'm saying is—be careful."

Fiona nodded. She appreciated the cautionary tale

and did feel bad for her sister, but what she had with Garret was different. They were really in love. Fiona had lost her virginity weeks ago, and he was still holding her hand, walking her to class and spending every Thursday with her. She knew, though, trying to explain that to Elenora now that she had a chip on her shoulder toward men wouldn't work.

"I will be," Fiona said, squeezing her sister's hand.

Christmas break went faster than expected. With her older brothers' home on holiday for two weeks, the Grisham household was busy and rife with laughter and activities. It was the first time they had all been together under one roof since last Christmas, and it felt wonderful to have everyone here. While she felt fluish and more tired than usual, Fiona had been distracted enough not to notice that she had skipped her period. It wasn't until she was back at school and enmeshed in her routine that she realized she was three weeks late.

While she felt a bit troubled by this, she considered the odds of her being pregnant after only have sex with Garret once to be fairly slim. Fiona had managed to push the thoughts aside during the day, but at night the worry crept in, and she spent hours bargaining with God. There had been a girl at her school two years ago who disappeared midway through the year after gaining a considerable amount of weight. While no one had confirmed anything to date, the rumor mill was hot with stories of her pregnancy and being shipped off to a home for unwed mothers to have the baby. When the girl returned to school last year, she was gaunt and barely recognizable. She dropped out just months before graduation. The thought of that girl whose name she couldn't remember sent another wave of nausea coursing through Fiona's stomach, and she couldn't keep it down this time. She ran to the bathroom and vomited up her lunch.

The week dragged on and Fiona's anxiety increased. She lost focus in her classes, and on more than one occasion when she was called on, she came up blank for an answer, not having heard a word of the lesson. Finally, Thursday came, and Garret was waiting for her in the foyer of the school after last bell. When she saw him, Fiona felt her stomach flutter in that newly familiar wave of nausea, different from the nervous butterflies of puppy love as she'd experienced the last time she saw him.

"Fi," Garret said, beaming at her as he walked

across the foyer to sweep her into his arms. She was long past hiding their togetherness, and it was freeing to be able to be with him in public now after her conversation with her sister. "I missed you," he said, bending down to kiss her.

"I missed you too." She smiled back. She held on to his embrace extra tight today as tears welled in her eyes.

"What's wrong?" Garret asked after he pulled away, noticing her watery eyes and pale complexion. "Are you feeling all right?"

"Mm-hmm" was the only response she could manage. The tears had covered her eyes and clouded her vision, and she knew she would unravel if she tried to speak. Garret wrapped his arm around her protectively and led her to the parking lot. They huddled close together as they made their way to his parents' car.

"Hop in. Why don't we go for a drive?" he said.

Fiona nodded as she wiped her tears and slid into the passenger seat.

They rode in silence as they drove out of town and along the back roads. Fiona kept her gaze straight ahead on the road, actively avoiding Garret, who kept turning to look at her, trying to meet her eyes.

She wasn't sure if she was pregnant, but she knew she had to tell him what was going on. Fiona sat in the uncomfortable silence for a long time. She didn't know if she was going to be able to actually speak the words out loud. The burning inside her chest and shaking in her hands made it almost impossible to move.

"I'm late," she eventually said after they bumped along the dirt road. She stared straight ahead, too afraid to even look at him.

"Late for what?" Garret asked, peering over at her quizzically.

"My time of the month. It was supposed to come three weeks ago, and it hasn't," Fiona said as fast as she could get the words out.

"Oh," Garret said. The air between them stilled as he held his breath, frozen in time. "Have you taken a test?"

"No, not yet. I was hoping it was just a fluke from being off routine over the holidays, but now I'm really starting to worry." Fiona picked at the skin around her nails.

"Well, let's go get a test then, and you can take it. Then you can either stop your worrying, or we will know if there is something to worry about," Garret said matter-of-factly. It was a logical answer for a simple problem, but Fiona hadn't managed to see it quite the same way. If it was positive, her whole world would change, and she wasn't sure she was ready for that just yet.

"Maybe we should wait a bit longer just in case it comes," Fiona said, bargaining again.

"That's not any way to deal with a problem," Garret said, sitting up straight, still keeping his eyes on the road. "We will go get a test, go back to my house and take it. My parents are out for the evening. They're heading to a dinner straight from work." Garret didn't wait for Fiona's reply as he navigated the roads back to his family home, stopping in the parking lot of the pharmacy closest to them. They stepped out of the car and walked in together, navigating the aisles silently until they found the one they were looking for.

Fiona kept her head down as they walked to the cashier and Garret checked them out. He paid for the test while neither of them made eye contact with the clerk. They walked back to the car, and Fiona focused on the squelching of their shoes on the wet pavement as drops of rain fell around them. In the car, the windshield wipers held her in a trance as Garret tried to grab her hand to calm her down. While he had been assertive before making a plan and taking action, she could tell he was worried now too.

They pulled up the long drive of his estate, and the rain was now pouring down. Garret turned off the ignition, grabbed his backpack from the back seat and the white paper bag that held the pregnancy test.

He turned to Fiona. "On my count, we run," Fiona nodded. "One, two, three- go!"

Fiona and Garret opened their doors and ran as fast as they could across the drive and up the front steps. They stood huddling underneath the stone overhang and pressed up against the front door, both now soaking wet. Garret fumbled for his keys and jammed them into the lock. With a click and a turn of the handle, he pushed his way inside, grabbing Fiona's hand and dragging her into the warm, dry house.

"Let's get you out of these wet clothes," Garret said, peeling off his jacket and then his uniform shirt, revealing his bare chest, which she'd only seen once before. Fiona looked away as she peeled off her soaking wet clothes and tossed them into a pile on the floor. Garret grabbed her and pulled her in close, covering her mouth with his warm kiss, instantly putting her back at ease as his body warmed her damp skin. Being here with him made her feel like nothing else in the world mattered. The harsh reality kicked back in as she spotted the corner of the white paper bag sticking out from the pile of Garret's wet clothes. She pulled away, walked over to the bag and picked it up.

"I'll be right back," Fiona said, and she walked toward the powder room.

"I'll come with you," Garret said in step behind her.

"No, I can do it alone. I'll bring the test right out. You won't miss a thing," Fiona said with a forced smile.

Garret nodded, shivering as he wrapped his arms around his shirtless body.

"I'll go grab us some dry clothes and throw ours in the dryer then," he said, nodding to himself as he tried to make himself useful.

Fiona went into the powder room and closed the door. She pulled the little cardboard box out of the paper bag, unwrapped the test and set it on the counter as she read the instructions. She had never done this before, and she wanted to make sure she did it exactly right. She sat down, urinated on the stick for five seconds and, when she was finished, laid it flat on the counter. It said to wait three minutes for accurate results, but by the time she had flushed and washed her hands, she could very clearly see two pink lines, which indicated a positive pregnancy test.

Stunned, she sat down on the bathroom floor and leaned against the wall, unsure how she was going to process this information. Her head was spinning, and she felt sick. Her mind raced with thoughts of her body during pregnancy, the act of childbirth, miscarriages and how she would possibly explain this to her parents. She hadn't even allowed herself to think about what her life what going to look like once a baby arrived.

Fiona started trembling from shock, which was compounded by the fact that she was wet and wearing nothing but her delicates. She hugged her knees and rocked back and forth for comfort, whimpering quietly. It felt like hours had passed before she heard a knock.

When she didn't answer, Garret let himself in, holding out an oversized sweatshirt and pants for her in his arms. "You're pregnant," he said, immediately understanding as he took in the state of her. "It's okay, Fi. We will figure this out, it's okay." He bent down and scooped her into his arms. He carried her to the couch, covered her in a blanket and sat beside her while she cried softly into the pillow.

9

Maeve

Guelph, Ontario, Canada
Summer 2011

Weeks passed as slowly as months while Maeve dug deeper into her research, waiting for her own piece of mail to arrive. After her first meeting with Dr. Horner, she was faced with a moral dilemma: continue her research or stop on account of her personal agenda overtaking the story. When she met with Dr. Horner, she felt as if he were looking right through her, which left her feeling unsettled and questioning her motives. She needed to decide if she could pursue the story even if she didn't get the answer she was hoping for. And she needed to decide what she'd do if she got the answers she'd waited her whole life for.

What John, as he insisted she call him, gave her were more questions to answer. She'd started this investigation with just one: What happened to these women? But that wasn't the only important question. She could lose herself for days, weeks even, as she had, reading heart-wrenching stories about young women forced to give up their children, never to see them again. If she wanted to create an impactful piece of journalism, she would have to answer more than that. She needed hard facts and data.

The first question John posed to her was "Why now?" Why, after all this time, was the government unwinding their carefully crafted regulations that had kept adoption records sealed for the last seventy years. This question piqued Maeve's interest, because in all her research thus far, she had not come across a clear answer. All the web pages and emails she received were polite explanations of sad misfortunes, often without apology to all those who were affected. The reason was hidden somewhere, and it was something she wanted to get to the bottom of.

The second question he asked her was "Who is going to care?" While this question stung at first, Maeve quickly came to terms with the fact that most people wouldn't care about the mothers and children who were torn apart and never reunited. Most people wouldn't care about the lack of identity these children had for their entire lives, not seeing a resemblance in the faces around the dinner table or holidays.

The third question John asked was "What will the redemption be? Will it be monetary? Is it as simple as reuniting children and their parents, or are you hoping to start a legal battle and provide a small sum for those who were affected?" (Not that any amount of money could repair a lifetime of trauma.) Maeve knew only what her redemption would be, and that was finding her mother. She needed to meet the woman and find out why she was here in Canada an ocean away, all alone.

Maeve thought about this as she sat on the hind legs of her desk chair nearly tipped back horizontally, chewing on the end of a pen. She spotted Natalie walking across the office toward her and righted herself, putting down the drool-covered pen.

"What's up?" she asked cheerfully, wiping at her mouth to ensure there was no drool remaining.

"Just checking in on your adoption piece and what your capacity is. I know I said I'd have someone take over your beat, but with everyone taking their summer holidays and your wedding and honeymoon coming up, I'm getting a bit worried about our output," Natalie said, grimacing for effect.

Maeve felt her stomach sink. She was upset for two reasons: first of all, she had zero interest in writing about anything else, and second, she'd pushed her wedding and honeymoon so far out of her mind, the thought of it all came crashing back in with a wave of guilt.

"Right, of course. What do you need me to cover?" Maeve owed Natalie this, even though it was the last thing she wanted to do right now.

"Just some local community stuff, I need a backfill of about ten to fifteen articles, just little puff pieces. Good news stories, good Samaritans you know. There's a whole slush pile of them in the info inbox for your choosing." Natalie offered a half smile.

"No problem, I'm on it. When do you want them by?" Maeve asked, stifling her sigh.

Natalie sucked in a breath. "Two by the end of this week and ten before you go get married?" She asked it as a question, but Maeve knew it was not.

She nodded obediently despite every fiber of her being rebelling against the idea of putting her attention anywhere else. "I'm on it," Maeve said, turning back to her laptop.

"Thanks, Maeve." Natalie tapped the top of her cubicle twice before walking back to her office.

Maeve checked the time on her laptop screen. It was just after one o'clock, which gave her plenty of time to dig into the community leads and pump out a few puff piece drafts before the end of the day. She would, of course, have to fact-check and reach out to the senders for quotes, but she was confident she could have more than two stories done by the end of the week. While they weren't her favorite type of articles to write, they were easy, and after weeks of research without much to show for it, it felt good to work on something she could complete in full.

As the wedding approached, Maeve was feeling more and more distant from Ethan. Instead of making final changes to seating charts and floral arrangements, Maeve was working as hard as she could to get the articles for Natalie done so she could get back to her research. She had completed fifteen pieces in two weeks, enough to give her time to focus on her own investigation without being sidetracked again. Somehow, the biggest day of her life was becoming something she dreaded rather than looked forward to. With Maeve spending so much time at the office, Ethan and his mother had taken over all wedding related tasks, and for that she was grateful, but still, a lingering feeling of distress grew like a pit in her stomach. She had no one to talk to about this, of course, since her entire family was Ethan's family, and her friends were their friends, so she packed the feelings away as deep as she could manage and carried on.

Maeve woke up one Tuesday and began her day in the same way she started every other day. She rolled out of bed quietly and tiptoed out of the room so she didn't wake Ethan. Then she showered and walked down the old creaky steps, careful to avoid the loud ones, before starting her pot of coffee. As she waited for her morning brew, she padded toward the front door and peeked out the window to see if the mail had arrived yet. To her surprise, Maeve saw a stack of envelopes jutting up out of the metal box on the front porch. Without wasting a breath, she unlocked the door, swung it open and reached out to the mailbox. She kept her feet planted on the threshold as she stretched her arm as far as it would go. She performed this acrobatic feat each day, seeing if she could retrieve packages and mail from the porch without dirtying her socks. She wrapped her hand around the stack of mail triumphantly and slinked back inside the house.

Maeve walked into the kitchen with the stack of envelopes and sorted them onto the counter in front of her as she waited beside the gurgling coffee pot. Junk, junk, junk, bill, and then she stopped. The fifth envelope in her hand was addressed to her without a clear mark to identify where it came from. Her heart quickened as she shakily turned the envelope over to open it. Before she slipped her finger under the flap to break the seal, she strained to listen for any sounds indicating Ethan might be awake upstairs. After a few moments hearing only silence above her, Maeve sat down at the kitchen table to steady herself and tore open the envelope.

It contained three sheets of loose paper folded in

thirds on government letterhead. Maeve read the first page; a letter addressed to her.

> Dear Maeve Grisham,
>
> Please find enclosed the official birth certificate of your birth mother. If you have any questions or concerns, please visit www.adoption.on.gov.
>
> Sincerely,
>
> Bill Amos,
>
> Head of Adoption Services Ontario

Maeve turned the letter over in her hand a few times and then turned her attention to the pages behind it. The second two were photocopies of birth certificates, hers and her mother's. She scanned her mother's eagerly first.

> **Name:** Fiona Grisham
> **Date of birth:** May 14, 1968
> **Birthplace:** Kildare, Ireland
> **Parents:** Ronan and Aoife Grisham (née Doyle)

Maeve read it over a few times before putting it down and scanning her own for any additional information. There was no mother or father listed on hers. Disappointed, she turned back to her mother's, reading and rereading the four short lines that gave away more information than she'd ever had. This was the first real lead she had on her mother. Before now, the only other formal documentation she had was limited to a two-page outline of her mother's height, weight, eye and hair color. It was a caricature of a person, an idea left for the reader's mind to fill in the gaps. There was no information on age, who she was or who she came to be.

Now that Maeve had more to factor in, her heart raced as she started doing the mental math. If Maeve was born in 1985, that meant her mother was only seventeen years old when she gave birth. She was a child. Maeve's stomach roiled at the thought as she tried to piece together the missing information. She scanned the birth certificate over and over, looking for something to give her a clue. Her mind was hardwired to pick up details, and she was searching for pieces that would lead her to more answers.

Maeve's sleuthing began after a summer of devouring junior detective novels. She had spent the majority of her childhood with her nose in a book, and she became obsessed with the Nancy Drew series. Once she had read every book, she graduated to every thriller and mystery book she could get her hands on. She was obsessed with inserting herself into another world, escaping her own reality and looking for puzzles to solve.

She became more obsessed with investigating when she was in college studying English literature. Their class had read an investigative reporting piece written by Clifford J. Levy for *The New York Times*, and it exposed the abuse of mentally ill adults in state-regulated homes. It was incredibly moving and had won the *Pulitzer Prize*. That story gripped onto a part of Maeve deep inside that felt important to pay attention to. She herself had been a part of a government-regulated system and suffered. In that moment, she knew she wanted to do what that reporter did, find important stories and share them with the world so that the circumstances might change if people knew what was going on behind closed doors.

Maeve heard a *thump* above her head as Ethan stood up out of bed and walked toward the bathroom. She heard the toilet flush and the familiar creak of the stairs as he descended toward the smell of coffee.

"Good morning." He sleepily rubbed his eyes as he padded toward her, stopping to kiss her on top of her head.

"Morning. How'd you sleep?" Maeve asked, turning the papers over on the table, trying not to alert him to their presence. She wasn't ready to talk about it.

"Like a log," he said, pouring his coffee and bending over slightly to take a nice long sip. When he looked back up from the mug and over to Maeve, he registered that something was amiss and frowned. "Is everything okay?" he asked, walking back toward the table.

Ethan leaned over Maeve's shoulder to look at the stack of papers under her hand and reached down to take them from her to look for himself. Her instinct was to hold on to them tightly, but she let them slip through her fingers and into Ethan's hands. He raised the letter up to eye level as he took another sip of his coffee. Maeve watched his eyes grow wide over the top of the mug.

"Wow," he said after he'd swallowed his sip, "you got it."

"I did," Maeve said, nodding, still in disbelief herself.

"Do you feel... relieved?"

Maeve frowned, she didn't know what she felt

other than a nagging sense that something felt off. She picked up her mother's birth certificate again and spotted it.

Maeve placed the two birth certificates in front of her on the table, and her heart pounded so loudly that the blood *whooshing* in her ears silenced everything else around her. A thousand thoughts ran through her mind as she tried to make sense of it all.

"I have to go," Maeve said, standing from the kitchen table, ready to run from Ethan and the comfort of their home once again.

Ethan's brows knit together in concern. He set the coffee on the counter and reached his arms out for Maeve, trying to pull her into a hug. "Hey, come here."

"I'm sorry, Ethan. I just can't right now," Maeve said, brushing him off as she made her way toward the front door.

"What am I supposed to do here?" he asked, his concern turning to anger. She sensed Ethan had been frustrated with the distance she'd put between them lately, but she'd hoped he'd been too busy with the wedding to make it into a problem. She could see now that she was wrong.

"I just need some space," Maeve said as she laced

up her tennis shoes at the front door.

"All we've had is space. It's like I don't even know you anymore. You're gone at the crack of dawn and come home after I've gone to bed. I don't even know where you go."

"I'm at work. Where do you think I am?" Maeve asked, her voice rising in defense.

"How the hell am I supposed to know?" he yelled. "I don't know the last time we had a real conversation. I've been working my ass off getting ready for this wedding that you seem to have zero interest in being a part of!" Ethan's face was red and he was angry.

"I have a lot of work to do!" Maeve yelled back. She had one hand on the door handle, ready to run now. She had no interest in dealing with Ethan's feelings on today of all days. "You're so selfish," she muttered under her breath.

"Me? Selfish?" Ethan's voice rose in pitch as he let out a laugh. "I've taken care of you since you were fourteen years old. You haven't had to do anything. We just took you in. How is that selfish?"

"Oh, am I just some charity case to you then?" Maeve said. They had had variations of this fight for years, and it was too easy to slip into right now.

"No! Seriously, Maeve, get a grip! You do what you want, when you want, and you don't care what I want or how I feel. Ever!" He was yelling and his face had twisted into a mean scowl.

Maeve didn't have a retort to that; he was right. But Ethan had always expected Maeve to fit neatly into his life. She was suffocated by the production of it all. But she worked hard to be what he needed her to be because she didn't have anyone else. All that work for neither of them to be happy.

"I have to go," Maeve said again, and she turned her back on Ethan, opened the door and walked down their front steps toward a house she'd once called home.

10

Fiona

County Kildare, Ireland
Spring 1985

As it turned out, in Ireland, you are not considered to
be an adult and in charge of your own medical
decisions until you are eighteen years of age. This fact
made Fiona's pregnancy her parent's problem to
solve, not hers. At only sixteen years old she had very

little say over her own life, let alone the life of another human. To make matters more complicated, the legal age for sexual consent was seventeen, which Fiona also was not. To say her parents were outraged was a gross understatement, but they were not mad at her; they were mad at themselves for not worrying enough about her. They had trusted her to make good decisions, and they had let her slip through the cracks, too busy with work and focused on her younger brother and sisters. The trouble with thinking a child isn't one to worry about is that you're always wrong. Even the strong, independent and responsible ones need someone to look out for them. Because they, too, are just children.

While the Grisham's placed blame on themselves, they also turned their anger toward the O'Toole's and their parenting. The O'Toole's had responded in kind, equally outraged at the situation, which left two angry sets of parents and two very distressed teenagers, one of whom was pregnant.

Garret and Fiona secluded themselves from others at school and slowly and quietly slipped away whenever they found an opportunity. The stress of their home life brought them closer together, and they vowed to each other that they would get married as soon as they were able to and move away to have their own life. They talked endlessly about the right thing to do and how to move forward. They hadn't planned to have a baby, but they were prepared to do whatever they had to do to stay together

Fiona was an athletic young girl, so her belly didn't swell in the way that she'd expected it to, like she'd seen her mother's do over and over. Svelte and petite, Fiona hid her belly with ease beneath her school uniform. The boxy polo shirt and tartan kilt concealed her shame from her classmates, family and friends until spring, when she was more than six months pregnant. Then one day her belly showed up in all of its glory, refusing to hide any longer.

Fiona walked down the creaky farmhouse stairs in tears, searching for Aoife. The two of them had not been on good terms since the pregnancy, but Fiona still needed her mother, and today she was sure she couldn't go to school looking like this.

"Mum," Fiona said, looking at the ground as she approached her in the kitchen.

Aoife stood over the sink with her back to Fiona, washing a bowl of berries she'd freshly picked from the garden. She turned around to face Fiona and scanned her body, lingering on her now protruding belly.

"Oh dear. I was waiting for this to happen," Aoife said more calmly than Fiona expected. She set the bowl of berries at the edge of the sink, wiped her wet hands on a tea towel, walked over to the kitchen table and pulled out a chair for Fiona. "Come sit down. We need to talk."

Fiona nodded and walked over to her, her stomach now grumbling at the smell of bacon cooking in the oven.

"I can't go to school like this, Mum. People will talk," Fiona blubbered, covering her face with her hands. Up until this point, the only confirmation that she was pregnant had been those two pink lines and the horrible morning sickness that had taken away her pleasure for all food and smells for the first third of her pregnancy. This big round protrusion would label her to everyone and confirm she would indeed have a baby. Until now, "pregnancy" had just been a concept she'd had months to think about as her body showed no clues how it might change and adapt for the child growing inside. At sixteen, she was keenly attuned to her changing body and hadn't minded the extra fullness in her breasts. But this bump, this roundness that stopped her clothes from fitting, was going to be a problem that Fiona didn't see a way around.

"What am I going to do?" Fiona sobbed.

Aoife wrapped her arms around her daughter stiffly.

Fiona had been in denial for so long it felt like a sudden shock to her system all over again. "I can't deal with this," she said, nuzzling her face into the space between her mother's neck and shoulder.

"I know, dear. That's why we need to talk." Aoife sat down across the table from Fiona and met her eyes. "We tried to talk about this with you a few times, but you've shut your father and I out." Aoife sat with her back straight and her hands folded on the counter in front of her.

Fiona was unable to collect herself and continued to cry into her hands.

"I've spoken with your Aunt Orla, who lives in Canada. My older sister, do you remember her?"

Fiona shook her head without looking up.

"You would have met her when you were a child. She used to come home to visit more often."

Fiona tried to place Orla in her mind, but she couldn't.

Aoife continued. "She has agreed to take you in

until you have the child, and you can put it up for adoption in Canada. It will make everything easier for your transition back home and back to school. We can tell everyone you've gone to do some schooling abroad. We have it all worked out. With the baby due in September, you can come back and start the school year a month late, but you won't have missed much at all." Aoife said it all so matter-of-factly, like there was no discussion left to be had.

"You want to send me off to Canada?" Fiona roared with outrage as she pushed back from the table. "I'm not going to Canada! I'm staying here with Garret."

"Fiona, dear," her mother said, standing to lock eyes with her for the first time in what felt like years. "I understand you are upset, and this is not what you planned—it's not what any of us planned—but your father and I have decided it's for the best that you go to Canada to finish out your pregnancy and give your child up for adoption there."

Fiona looked at her mother with horror. In her naivete, she hadn't even considered what was going to happen once the baby got here. She was so preoccupied with how she was feeling and her changing body and trying to conceal it from everyone around her. She knew she didn't have many options now that her belly had started to show, but she couldn't imagine a life outside of Kildare or being alone in another country pregnant. It was a horrible thought. She couldn't believe her mother would abandon her at a time like this.

"So, you're sending me away to be alone to have a baby, and then I have to give it away and come home and pretend like nothing ever happened?" Fiona was now screaming at her mother with tears streaming down her face. Her pregnancy had heightened her emotions, but the fierceness she felt to protect this little baby in her belly surprised her. She hadn't planned this and hadn't prepared to be a mother, but she knew she would never be the same after this, whether she kept the baby or not.

"Something like that, yes." Aoife stood her ground and remained steady. "You are just a girl, Fiona. You have your whole life ahead of you, and raising children is a very, very hard thing to do. You should not have to do it at sixteen years old. It's hard enough to do it at twenty-five … or thirty." Her mother placed her hand on Fiona's shoulder and guided her back to the kitchen table, "You're lucky we have somewhere nice you can go. A lot of girls in your situation don't have that choice, Fi."

Fiona sat down and slumped, resting on her elbows, tired and losing her fight. This might be the only plan that made sense, but she didn't like it. She and Garret didn't know how to raise a baby, they didn't have jobs or an education, but they would have loved this baby.

Aoife took the lull of Fiona's outburst as an opportunity to continue reasoning with her daughter. "I want you to be able to finish high school, go to university and have a career. You'll barely be able to manage finishing high school with a baby, and I'm not going to take care of it for you. I have eight of my own."

Fiona nodded, knowing her mother had the experience and authority to tell her what was right in this situation, but it didn't stop her from feeling completely helpless.

Fiona did not return to school that week, or at all for that matter. Over the course of the next few days, her parents arranged for her to fly from Dublin to Toronto, where she would live with her Aunt Orla. It was final, she was leaving, and she had no say in the matter.

Fiona and her father sat outside the airport in his car. Neither of them was able to look at each other, nor were they willing to begin their goodbyes. Ronan cleared his throat as he reached into his inner jacket pocket. When his hand emerged, it was holding an envelope thick with cash.

Fiona was surprised enough to break the silence. "What's that for?"

"This is for you, Fi. I took out some Canadian money for your little trip." Ronan looked tired, his own tumble of curls had grown shaggy and the lines on his forehead looked deeper than usual. Fiona suspected she was the reason behind it.

She looked between Ronan and the envelope, analyzing the moment. "Thank you," she finally said, taking it from her father. Somehow, she was even more uncomfortable now than before. She slipped her finger under the fold and peeked inside. There was five hundred Canadian dollars in cash. Her eyes widened at the stack of bills. "What am I to do with all of this?"

"This is for you, a gift to spend on yourself while you're traveling abroad," he said, clearing his throat.

Fiona winced. This was how they were going to frame it—a summer abroad for Fiona and no one would be the wiser. The money was his penance for sending her away.

"Thank you, Dad," she said as she unbuckled her seat belt and maneuvered her bump awkwardly around the center console to hug him.

He wrapped his arms around her tightly, and Fiona felt something drip onto the top of her head. She looked up as she touched her head, feeling the wetness and saw that her father was crying quietly, tears dripping down his rough face.

"I'm so sorry, love. Everything will go back to normal when you come home," he said, wiping the tears from his cheeks.

Fiona nodded hopefully, now with tears of her own stinging her eyes, but she knew nothing would ever be normal again.

Fiona wandered the airport corridor, lugging her overstuffed backpack and a wide canvas tote slung over her shoulder. She still had an hour until she boarded the plane, so she continued to walk, inspecting each shop, kiosk and restaurant. She watched strangers board their flights and take off into the sky, and she started to feel like maybe she wanted more from this world, and perhaps she could see this trip to Canada as a great adventure after all.

11

Maeve

Guelph, Ontario, Canada
Summer 2011

What Maeve had spotted on the birth certificate that sent her running was a name: Aoife Doyle, her grandmother. The only other Doyle she'd ever known was Orla Doyle, her foster mother. Orla's house wasn't far from where she lived; in fact, it was only a ten-minute walk from where she spent the last decade or so. Orla's home was technically in the same neighborhood as the Clarkes family home and now her own, but it was just far enough out of the way from where she lived and worked that she didn't walk by it regularly. Standing in front of it now, she was reminded of how beautiful the old house was. With its grand limestone exterior and old-world charm, it stood out along a row of smaller cottage-like homes that had been slowly renovated into modern dwellings over the years. A wave of nostalgia washed over her as she spotted the ash tree in the front yard where she used to climb up and sit on the branches to read.

As Maeve stood anxiously on the stoop of her childhood home, it felt familiar, but she noticed things that happened to a home that was long uncared for. The grout in the exterior stone was worn away and the hinges on the shutters had loosened, causing them to hang slightly askew. The Orla she knew never would have let that happen. Maeve felt the urge to run in the opposite direction, afraid of what she might find inside.

There was an unfamiliar car in the drive, brown and nondescript, but that offered no clues to Maeve if the home still belonged to Orla or not. Maeve had waited much too long to visit to be able to discern if any changes had been made by Orla or new owners. Nonetheless, she was here now. She took a deep breath and rang the bell, then held her breath while she waited. Maeve allowed some air to escape when she heard footsteps approaching. She took a step back, remembering the storm door swung outward onto the porch.

A tall man with brown skin wearing nurse's scrubs opened the interior door with a smile. "Hello, may I help you?" he asked kindly.

"Oh," Maeve said, exhaling with relief, "I think I've come to the wrong house." She began to back away clumsily, then turned to leave, not ready for whatever she was going to encounter inside the house.

"Who are you looking for?" he called after her.

"Orla Doyle," Maeve said, her name sounding foreign on her tongue now. "She … I … well, actually, we both used to live here. I thought she still might." Maeve stumbled through her answer. Heat rose in her cheeks as she regretted her decision to show up here without warning.

"Ah, you must be Maeve," the man said. "I thought

you looked familiar. I recognize you from the photos. Please come in. Orla is in the kitchen having her tea." The man swung the door open and invited her in.

Maeve stood there frozen in surprise for a moment before she followed him into the house she'd once spent half her life in. She stepped across the threshold into the familiar entryway of her childhood. There was still the upholstered stool with a shoehorn next to it and the umbrella holder stationed beside the door, just as it always had been. The antique brass mirror still hung in the entryway for last-minute checks before leaving the house, and the small shelf that had little hooks on it for your keys was still mounted beneath it.

Maeve walked slowly through the front hall, taking in the familiar photographs and works of art hanging along the wall. It was a straight path from the front door to the kitchen, where she spied Orla sitting at the kitchen table sipping Barry's breakfast tea, just as she always had.

"Fiona, dear, what are you doing here?" Orla asked, and her face lit up with delight.

Maeve's face turned white.

The man, who she now understood to be Orla's nurse, came up behind Maeve and placed a hand on her shoulder.

"I haven't worked out who Fiona is yet, but she talks about her often," he whispered. "She's in and out of lucidity these days. Sometimes we get a few hours a day where she knows where she is and what day it is, and other times she slips away into another time and place."

Maeve nodded, understanding. When a mind has Alzheimer's, the logic and reasoning skills disintegrate, and the brain makes up for it by swapping memories and time periods trying to make sense of what's in front of it. She knew it would be hard to get to the truth of anything here, even though it was so close to the surface.

Maeve walked closer to Orla and took her hand, holding on to the very small bit of hope that the nurse had given her. To hear that Orla was still experiencing moments of clarity meant that Maeve might be able to get some answers. Still, seeing Orla in this state, confused and ten years older than the last time she had seen her, unsettled Maeve. She looked over to the nurse for direction.

"It's okay. Just talk to her as you would if she remembered you. It might spark something in her mind that will bring her to clarity." He smiled and backed up out of view to give Maeve the room, while still keeping a careful eye on his patient.

Maeve nodded absentmindedly as she assessed the woman in front of her. While Orla looked older, she still was perfectly groomed. Her black hair was now shades of gray, styled with not one hair out of place. She sat tall with a straight back as she sipped her tea delicately. Maeve felt lightheaded as her memories of being taken from this home flooded in.

Maeve stood unspeaking as she mentally compared the now and then of it all. The familiar smells of lavender and eucalyptus still faintly lingered in the air, but now the smell was mixed with a harsh citrus scent of an industrial-strength cleaner. Judging by the male nurse at attention, Maeve assumed that Orla had round-the-clock care at this point. Most people in her condition would be in a nursing home or be cared for by a spouse or a child, neither of which Orla had. All she had was Maeve, and they were forced apart, leaving them both lost and alone.

"Hi, Orla, it's Maeve." She sat down beside the frail woman at the kitchen table and took Orla's hand in her own. "It's been a long time."

Orla smiled as she held Maeve's hands between

hers in a warm grasp. "You look so much like your mother, Maeve. I thought you were Fiona."

It took all of Maeve's strength not rear back in her seat. This information, all of which had been kept from her, was now out in the open. Orla's memories were all jumbled up, and she'd forgotten that big secret she was keeping from Maeve all this time as if it were nothing.

"How did you know my mother?" Maeve asked when she'd composed herself. She knew she was crossing a line that verged on exploitation, but she was desperate for answers.

"Fiona? She's my niece." Orla still smiled cheerfully as she looked deep into Maeve's green eyes. "You really are the spitting image of her." Orla reached out to touch Maeve's hair in the same way she used to stroke it when she was a child. Maeve fought back tears that were stinging at her eyes. "How is she doing? I haven't seen in her a long time," Orla said as she turned her gaze out the window, lost in a memory.

"Well," Maeve said, choking back her tears. Each innocent question that came out of Orla's mouth was another cut to her already open wound. "I'm not sure, I'm trying to find her. Do you know where she is?"

"Oh, she's up in her room, she's always in her room." Orla said distantly, waving a hand toward the upstairs. Maeve's hope deflated; her chance vanishing just as quickly as it had arrived.

"Fiona's quite introverted, I just leave her be." Orla tutted. She had slipped backwards into another time.

Maeve's shoulders slumped in disappointment. The moment had passed, and she lost her lead. She turned to the tall nurse expectantly, hoping for direction.

"I'm sorry. I'm sure this isn't what you were expecting from your visit today," he said. "Maybe try again tomorrow."

"Can I stay? Maybe look around a bit?" Maeve needed more answers.

With that, the nurse stiffened. "That wouldn't be appropriate. You're welcome to come back tomorrow." He shifted his body to form a wall between her and Orla. "My name is Gerald. I am Orla's day nurse. I am here every day from seven to five. She has two night nurses, one from five to eleven and another from eleven to five." He started to walk forward as he spoke, ushering her from the kitchen back into the front hall. Once they were out of Orla's earshot, he softened. "Try again tomorrow. It will take some time."

Maeve nodded and thanked Gerald, then walked out the door.

Maeve arrived at her office shaky and pale. It was only 10:00 a.m., and she'd had more excitement today than the entire last year of her life. She wasn't sure what she was going to accomplish at her desk today, but she knew she couldn't go home. She walked to the kitchen to pour herself a cup of bitter office coffee. She nodded and mumbled hellos to her colleagues, who were also waiting to fill their mugs, before retreating back to her desk.

She opened her laptop and checked her email. The articles she'd written were all scheduled to be published over the next month. She'd filled her quota on the puff pieces Natalie had requested, so all she had to do now was continue on with her exposé. She had a long list of follow-ups to do and needed to get back in touch with John, who had some data to give her, but she didn't quite know how to move forward on that when she had so many unanswered questions about her mother. Instead, she opened Google and typed in her mother's name and her birthplace to see if it brought up any results. Maeve pressed Enter and closed her eyes, nervous to see what would appear on the screen once she opened them. As she expected, the screen presented no clear answers. Google spat out fragmented information on unrelated people and places, none of which pointed her toward her own mother. She spent hours trying different search combinations, trying to get a hit on something that would give her a lead. She searched **Orla Doyle + Aoife Doyle + Fiona Grisham** to see if any obituary or newspaper article that contained a family lineage connecting them all would come up. When that search turned up nothing valuable, she tried another: **Fiona Grisham + Kildare Ireland**. Still nothing.

They were in a time of digital transformation, where things were becoming increasingly more available online, but the majority of records and data still existed on paper. The internet was a growing place to spend time searching for information, but it was most valuable as a means of communication. Websites displayed meager information, such as location and contact information and instant messaging, and social media sites were opening the lines of the communication across the globe in new ways. Maeve, who was always in search of ways to find new information, frequented a site called Reddit, which was a forum she used when she had questions that she couldn't find answers through her own network, or she needed to ask anonymously. Maeve used a cryptic username as not to mar her reporter's reputation and took to the site to see if anyone could help her out. She logged on and posted a question to see if she could crowdsource useful tips from others out there in a similar situation.

> Copperhead234: Looking to find my birth mother. I was given up as a baby and recently found out my mother's name and birthplace but have no idea where to start. Has anyone else had success finding their birth mother? Any tips?

Maeve left her post on Reddit, knowing it could take hours or days for a response. She had a smattering of followers, but she had never posted about adoption before. With the new subject matter, she wasn't sure if anyone would respond.

She stood up to use the restroom, feeling shaky on her feet. She wasn't sure if it was from the coffee or the stress, but she made a mental note to switch to herbal tea for the rest of the day. When she got back to her desk with a fresh mug, she heard a familiar ping that signaled someone had responded to her post. Maeve leapt into her seat so fast the tea sloshed up out of her mug. With quick reflexes, she jumped back out of the way, barely escaping a burn. Her heart was beating out of her chest now as she approached her computer, seeing the response bubble beneath her query.

> Graphicdude32: @copperhead234 I found my birth mother through Facebook, have you tried there yet?

Maeve flushed with embarrassment. In her anxiety-ridden haste, she hadn't thought to start there. She opened up Facebook and typed **Fiona Grisham**. Instantly, hundreds of results appeared, ticking down her screen. Two hundred Fiona Grisham's stared back at her, a daunting number of potential mothers. Maeve had to fight to overthrow her emotional response and put on her investigative journalist hat. She scanned the screen for options to narrow down the search results. She could filter by city, work or education, none of which she had an answer to. Maeve tried another search to see if there was an easier way. She typed in **Orla Doyle** to see if there was any way she had set up a profile for herself over the last few years. A few profiles came up of women who shared a name with Orla, but it was just a handful, and none of them were her Orla.

Maeve was starting to get agitated now that the excitement had worn off, and a headache settled in its place. Still, she was determined to make some headway, so she kept trying. She knew these social media sites were meant for a younger generation, but Rose had one, and even Ethan's grandmother, so she tried a search for Aoife Grisham, hoping that the North American obsession with sharing photos online translated overseas.

Twenty-five Aoife Grisham's popped up on her screen. This was a more manageable number, she thought. The first fifteen were not the right age; they looked to be twenty to forty years old. She assumed Fiona's mother had to be at least sixty by now, so she was able to narrow down her search quite quickly. The remaining ten Aoife's lived across the globe between Australia, Canada, USA and Ireland. Maeve started with the Irish ones, trying to look through their friend lists to see if anyone else in her life had known her mother and forgot to mention it.

At last, she found a lead. There was an Aoife

Grisham from Kildare, Ireland, who was sixty-five years old and had a husband named Ronan. Maeve felt a physical pain stabbing at the left side of her chest as she clicked through the pictures on her profile, trying to catch a glimpse of someone who looked like her. She came across a photo of about thirty people that was captioned Christmas with the Family. Orla had said she looked just like her mother, so she scanned it wildly for her own face. The people looked so tiny and grainy on her screen, but after a few passes, she spotted her. In the back row with her arms around two teenage-looking boys, Maeve saw a woman who clearly resembled her: long copper hair, the same skin tone and delicate face … She could tell even in this pixelated photo that this was her mother. She had to be.

Maeve put her cursor over the woman in the picture, hoping a tag would pop up and identify her. When it didn't, Maeve let out the breath she'd been holding in a loud sigh. She moved the cursor to the left to one of the boys, and a tag popped up, Aiden O'Toole, and to his right, another boy was tagged as Finn O'Toole. Maeve's heart beat wildly out of her chest, and she felt like she was going to be sick. Could these boys be her brothers? Maeve opened a new tab and went back to her Google browser, taking a deep breath she typed in Fiona O'Toole.

Instantly, thousands of results flooded her page.

> Fiona O'Toole's New Book on The New York Times Bestseller List
>
> An Honest Review of Fiona O'Toole's Latest, Deep River.
>
> Fiona O'Toole is *The New York Times* bestselling author of five novels, including *Running Free*, *A Gracious Host* and *Deep River*. She lives in Kildare, Ireland with her husband and their two sons.

Of the thousands of results that flooded her page, all the relevant information she found about her mother was synopsized into two sentences. Most of the photos that appeared were the same headshot from her author bio, a still shot of a stunning woman with an uncanny likeness to her. She saw Fiona's copper hair tumbled in waves over her left shoulder and she offered a kind smile. Maeve searched her expression for any meaning. Did she look like she was mournful over a lost daughter? Did she look like she regretted leaving Maeve behind? But she couldn't see anything past the expertly Photoshopped headshot. She needed to get back to Orla's house and see if she could find some more answers.

12

Fiona

Toronto, Ontario, Canada
Spring 1985

Fiona stepped into the arrivals terminal with all of
her luggage and scanned the crowd for her ride. She
stopped when her eyes came upon a tall, lean woman
with thick black hair tied neatly into a low ponytail,
holding a little cardboard sign that read, *Fiona*

Grisham. The woman she assumed to be Orla bore a strong resemblance to her mother, just slightly older, taller, leaner. She stood erect with her shoulders back and her chin up, signs of a confident woman. Fiona watched her for a few minutes before Orla was able to spot her. While she may have been older than Aoife, she was certainly better kept. A light touch of makeup with a trim figure, Orla donned an outfit that looked professional yet casual. She wore a white button-down blouse that fanned out at the neck and a high-waisted pair of black wide-bottom trousers. She looked otherworldly to the women Fiona knew. Fiona was used to the mothers of her friends and neighbors, hair unkept, apron donning mothers who spent their lives caring for their hordes of children. But Orla looked nothing like them. Fiona had only seen outfits like this in fashion magazines that she stole from Elenora, but she'd never seen much of it in person, she was mesmerized.

Fiona took in Orla's outfit from head to toe, and when her gaze settled back on Orla's face, their eyes locked. Fiona smiled and gave a half-hearted wave as she shuffled in Orla's direction, wheeling her two suitcases clumsily on a luggage cart.

"You must be Fiona." Orla smiled and offered her

hand. They shook hands, and the formal gesture felt strange for the intimate arrangement they had. When she pulled her hand away, she folded up her sign, tucked it into her purse and reached for Fiona's luggage. "Let me help you with that bag."

Fiona nodded, suddenly having lost her tongue.

"How was the flight?" Orla asked, now in motion. She walked ahead of Fiona down the corridor.

Fiona fell into step behind her, following the confident woman blindly, already fully trusting her. "Not bad actually, I read a book cover to cover. I don't often get that much quiet time to myself."

Orla laughed. "I remember that feeling well. That's how I ended up over here all by myself. I had to fly across the world to get some peace and quiet."

Fiona smiled, already feeling familiar with this woman. Orla turned and walked through a set of doors that opened to the parking lot as Fiona walked quickly, trying to keep pace.

"While it's a noisy city compared to living out in the country, you'll find you can get more quiet time here."

Fiona looked up trying to understand what she could possibly mean as the planes rumbled noisily overhead. They walked farther and Fiona kept her gaze skyward. She created a shield with her hand to soften the light, but she couldn't look away. It was beautiful. "Is it always so bright here?" she asked, standing in the middle of the parking lot now as she stared into the sky.

Orla stopped to look up; she had smartly worn sunglasses. "Much more so than home, yes. It doesn't get to be the same type of gray you're accustomed to. That's one of the things I love most about living here. Even when it's so cold it hurts to breathe, the sun shines bright, and the sky is blue."

"That sounds wonderful," Fiona said, still looking up. She almost bumped into Orla, who was opening the trunk of a car.

"This is us. Here, pass me your bags and go hop in the front," Orla said.

Fiona did as she was told. She walked around the wrong side of the car first, noticing the steering wheel was where the passenger side should have been, and then walked back around again to get in the other door. She sat on the cool leather seat of a car that would never pass muster to drive the back roads of County Kildare.

She waited while Orla fussed about in the trunk of the car, arranging the luggage to fit, and thought about how Canadian Orla sounded. There was hardly a trace of Irish lilt left in her voice. Perhaps it was the outcome of time spent immersed in this country or the result of trying to fit in. Either way, Orla fascinated her.

They drove in traffic along the highway, and Fiona watched out the window as cars whizzed by and they approached the city. There were towering buildings in front of her and a large body of water to her right. Entranced, she took in this great new city in a country she had not yet learned much about.

Until recently, Fiona had never cared much about what was going on outside of her small corner of the world. The farthest she ventured was diving deep into another realm in one of her fantasy books. Now, as a seventeen-year-old girl, for the first time she was truly getting to expand her horizons from what she knew of her homeland and the people who inhabited it.

They drove into the city, taking the long winding streets this way and that. From her window, she saw shops and restaurants alongside tall apartment buildings and offices. She couldn't see the water anymore and there was certainly no grass, which puzzled Fiona greatly. Where would the children play? she thought as she rubbed her belly absentmindedly.

"We are almost home," Orla said, bringing Fiona back from her thoughts and into the present. Fiona could feel Orla watching her with concern as they drove together in silence. Occasionally, Orla tried to engage in small talk, but Fiona kept her gaze set on the streets rolling by outside the window, fascinated by this new world she was thrust into.

The car slowed as it turned down a street that appeared to be more residential, the feel of the city shifting from a place cold with business to warm and full of family life. Fiona's shoulders dropped in relief. She was starting to worry they were heading to a windowed box in the sky, and she wasn't sure she would fare well there. She was used to rolling hills and endless land, she didn't think she could manage in an apartment building. To her great relief Orla pulled into the driveway of a two-story detached home that had a yard, and grass. On the boulevard there was a young maple tree that didn't quite offer much shade, but it bore the signature Canadian maple leaves hanging from its branches.

"We're home," Orla said, turning her head to look over at Fiona with a little smile.

Fiona smiled back for the first time since she arrived. "It's a lovely home, Aunt Orla." And it really was. While it was not grand in size, it had airs of familiarity with its small, covered porch and rocking chair, just like they had at her house. Orla unpacked the trunk as Fiona quietly took in her surroundings. She could feel the sun on her face and the spring air on her skin. It was drier and warmer here from the sun.

"Oh, I can help with that," Fiona said as she heard the wheels roll against the asphalt driveway, snapping out of her daydream. She rushed to help her aunt, who was hauling all three of Fiona's bags.

"Thank you, dear," Orla said, passing over the bags for Fiona to hold while she turned her attention to the keypad on the garage. She punched in a four-digit code, and the door rose with a whir. No one had automatic garages like this at home, just long driveways and sometimes a sheltered carport. Everything she had seen so far since landing in Canada felt futuristic and fascinating. The two women walked through the garage and worked together to hoist the luggage up two steps, ascending into a mudroom.

Fiona felt Orla's eyes on her as she wandered

through the main floor, silently assessing her new pregnant houseguest. Her slim but muscular figure hid the bump well, but Fiona could see Orla trying to sneak a glance of her little mound poking out beneath her T-shirt. Orla had never wanted children of her own, according to Aoife, but based on their interactions so far, Fiona thought she would have been a good mum.

"Come on, let me show you to your room," Orla said, hoisting the large suitcase up the first step and slowly shuffling it one step at a time. Lift, thrust, step. Lift, thrust, step.

Thirteen stairs later, they made it to the landing. To her left, there was a bathroom, then a master bedroom, and to the right two more smaller ones. One with a bed and the other with a desk, presumably Orla's home office.

"Over there to the right," Orla said, nodding her head in the direction of a room with a bed. She wiped her brow with the back of her hand, then rolled the suitcase behind Fiona and watched her inspect her new space.

"It's beautiful, thank you," Fiona said after looking around at the large bedroom.

The bed sat in the middle of the room below a

vaulted ceiling and against a large window overlooking the backyard. Fiona paused to look out the window and tried not to cry. She was working very hard to see this trip as an adventure and not the shunning and punishment it was.

She turned back to her aunt and said, "I think I'll unpack now."

"Of course," Orla said, taking that as her cue to leave. She backed out and shut the door behind her, leaving Fiona alone to settle in.

The phone rang in long echoes, with that characteristic long-distance tone as Fiona tried to phone home to speak with Garret. It was proving to be more difficult than she'd expected to connect with him and her parents, them being five hours ahead. By the time she woke up in the morning, Garret was off to school, and by the time he got home from his activities, there was only a small window when they could catch each other before he went to bed. Her mother was more available, but as Fiona knew quite well, she was busy at home with the youngest of her siblings, and getting everyone out the door and home again, fed and washed was a race. It felt as though the phone rang for ages as she sat there listing to the extended ring until there was finally a break, and she heard a faraway-sounding voice.

"Hello?" Mrs. O'Toole said.

"Hello, Mrs. O'Toole, is Garret home?" Fiona asked, bracing herself for the woman's inevitable exasperation. Even though Fiona knew Orla's line was taking the bulk of the charges for the long-distance calls, Mrs. O'Toole had not hidden her frustration about the frequent phone calls to her son. She had undoubtedly been relieved to hear of Fiona's trip to her aunts and likely thought she was rid of her for good. But Fiona and Garret were in love, and an ocean between them was not going to keep them apart forever.

"Fiona, dear," Mrs. O'Toole said in a kinder voice than she'd expected. "Garret's out with some friends tonight, but I'll certainly tell him you called."

Fiona slumped into her down-filled queen bed that she was now becoming accustomed to having all to herself. Before now, she had always had to share a room with her sister Eleonora, and long ago they had pushed their single beds together to talk late at night and kept them that way. All it took was a few weeks, and she was already very comfortable acting as an only child with her own room.

"Oh, all right then. I'm sorry to bother you," Fiona said, sniffling into her sleeve, trying to hold back her tears. Lately, these calls to home seemed to be the only conversations she had outside of Orla, who worked endless hours, and Fiona was beginning to feel lonely.

"How are you holding up?" Mrs. O'Toole asked, sensing Fiona's despair. "Pregnancy can be a very trying time. I'm so sorry you're having to do it all alone and away from everyone." Her small bit of kindness broke Fiona down from a sniffle to a sob.

"It's been very hard," she said as tears streamed down her cheeks. Fiona let herself cry hard into the phone for the first time. "The only thing getting me through these days is feeling the baby kick. It helps me to remember I'm not ever really alone."

"Oh, love," Mrs. O'Toole said, now crying on the other end of the line. "You are a very strong lass. We are all thinking about you, and I know Garret can't wait for you to come back home. I'll tell him to ring you when he's in. Take care of yourself, Fiona."

"Thank you," Fiona said as the line clicked dead. While that was not who she'd hoped to speak with, Mrs. O'Toole did somehow make her feel better.

Fiona rolled herself ungracefully out of bed. Her

belly made that one of the more trying tasks in her day lately. Once she was upright, she padded down the hall to the bathroom. A shower would help turn things around, and then she planned to get outside and enjoy the fresh air. She had had enough of sitting around in her room waiting for time to pass. Clean and dressed, she went downstairs to locate the trail map she'd spotted a few days back in the sitting room. She found it tucked in a basket, along with magazines and newspapers. Satisfied with herself, she sat at the counter munching on an apple while she studied it. She unfolded the map watching it grow from the size of a pamphlet to the size of the countertop. She located Orla's house on the map amid the multicolored lines that crisscrossed and overlapped on the page and the trail network behind it, charting her route with a pink highlighter. She circled major intersections and wrote down important landmarks in her notebook in case she got lost along the way. After an hour or so of going over her plan, Fiona felt confident. She packed her knapsack with her map, water, snacks and notebook and headed out on an adventure.

A gate in Orla's backyard opened into a forest. Fiona hadn't yet tried to navigate it, but based on the map, and Orla's advice, she knew that just a few meters past the gate there would be a trail. Orla mentioned the forest to her when she first arrived, but Fiona hadn't felt up for much exploring until now. As she'd looked out into the deep forest, she considered that if she ventured out alone, she might not find her way back. However, the alternative was sitting alone in her room, ruminating over every detail of her life, so she decided to walk into the forest and see.

The trails were wide and the trees were tall, and it helped Fiona escape from the familiar buzz of the city she had quickly become accustomed to. Cars whizzing by neighbors chattering while they cooked in their backyard, people walking down the street on their way somewhere. These were all noises she was unfamiliar with hearing when she first arrived and had set her on edge. But now the chaos had become the noise-laden background of her life. Walking through the forest brought back the quiet of her past life, and it settled over her like a warm blanket. The quiet allowed her mind to wander to a pleasant place filled with daydreams, just as she was accustomed to spending most of her time back home. Here in the city, where she was greeted with friendly hellos on the street and polite small talk in the cafés and shops, Fiona had been too busy getting acclimated to the culture of this new country and its people to slip into her natural rhythm.

Back home in Ireland, Fiona wandered away from the noise of her house and into the fields to find a quiet place to read or write. With Orla being at work all day, Fiona was surprisingly deafened by the silence and had instead gone in search of the noise. When she'd felt up to it, she began walking the streets to explore little coffee shops, museums and bakeries. Her father had given her more money than she knew what to do with, so she just spent a little each day trying new foods, seeing new movies and exhibits, and she tried to make the most of her time alone in a new place. But now, being in nature and feeling the quiet around her, Fiona felt like she was home again.

She wandered down the narrow path in the forest that started at the end of the street and led to a stream at the bottom of the hill. Holding on to trees so she wouldn't lose her footing, Fiona kept going even when she was unsure she would be able to make it back up that steep hill in her current state. She followed the flow of the stream until she reached an underpass that was covered with graffiti. She paused to admire the spray-painted artwork before ascending a set of metal stairs that led to what looked like a field above. Hauling her now eight-month pregnant body up a steep set of stairs proved to be hard work, but Fiona panted with accomplishment at the top. She stood and looked around enchanted. It was not a field at all but Mount Pleasant Cemetery.

Cemeteries were like books to Fiona. Each one told its own story, and she had always loved wandering through them, reading the headstones and imagining the lives of those beneath her feet. She liked to make up stories about their lives and imagine who they were with only the small details from their tombstones providing context. From the epitaphs she could impart if they had lived alone or had a family, and often the line inscribed on the tomb was a very clear insight to who they were as a person. The rest of the story was up to her imagination. Fiona wandered for a while with her head down, reading each stone she passed. When she had made her way across the grass to a dirt path, she finally looked up to see how far she'd wandered. Her eyes scanned the wide expanse of the cemetery, taking in all the lives and stories buried beneath her feet. Hot and tired, she sat on the bench dedicated to a couple by the names of James and Grace Weaver. Fiona reached into her knapsack to pull out her water bottle, granola bar and map. After chugging back her entire water bottle, she located the cemetery with her finger and realized it was part of an intricate system of trails, graves, shrines and buildings. She saw on the map that there was a chapel, and Fiona decided that was where she would go to next. She finished her granola bar and hauled herself back up on her feet. Her lack of abdominal strength and shifting center of gravity was really becoming a nuisance.

Because of the size of the cemetery, it took her nearly fifteen minutes to walk from where she had entered through the Moore Park Ravine across to the Chapel of Mount Pleasant Cemetery. The chapel was not in any way what Fiona had expected to find here in this old cemetery. The building was modern, made of brick with clean lines and clear windows. The churches in Ireland were centuries old and made of limestone and stained glass, and you could feel the history of the people who had passed through leaving their mark. This building was nothing more than a new world gathering place, and it made Fiona feel like the foreigner she was for the first time since coming to Canada.

She wandered back out of the building and looked around for a place to rest that felt more comfortable. It was a beautiful summer day, so she found a large oak tree and settled beneath it in the shade, then pulled out her notebook and pen and let the pent-up words inside her flow onto the paper.

13

Maeve

Guelph, Ontario, Canada
Summer 2011

Gerald, Orla's nurse, said his shift began at 7:00 a.m., so that's when Maeve planned to get there. She figured if she arrived at the top of the day, it would be her best chance of catching a lucid moment with Orla. The sun was already up when she began her trek, and the heat was burning the morning dew off the grass. It was going to be another wickedly hot day. Maeve climbed the few steps to Orla's front stoop, opened the storm door and knocked gently. She heard footsteps approaching, and with a swoosh of the inside door, she met Gerald once again, standing there in scrubs.

"Good morning, Maeve." He smiled. "It's nice to see you again." Gerald stepped aside to let her through the threshold into the foyer. "Orla is in the sitting room doing a crossword puzzle. Feel free to join her."

"Thanks, Gerald," Maeve said.

She set her bag down near the front hall and tucked her phone into her pocket, then walked down the hall toward the sitting room, which sat adjacent to the kitchen, and the sight of it brought back another flood of emotion. Every single piece of furniture, art and decor was frozen in time, along with Orla's disease. There was a TV above the fireplace along the far wall, with two overstuffed reading chairs flanking it on either side. Tucked up along the inside of the big bay window was a writing desk that overlooked the lush garden, which someone had clearly been maintaining. That desk saw her through years of homework. Many nights before bed, Maeve would cozy up on the sofa and watch television while Orla would take her turn at the desk, paying bills, doing crosswords or reading newspapers. A pang shot through Maeve's chest as she watched the still elegant Orla, once a force of a woman who lived her life independently, now reduced to spending her days at home, cared for by a nurse twenty-four hours a day. She watched Orla from her place in the doorway for a few minutes, not quite ready to get her heart broken again this morning. Yesterday was tough. Just when she had worked up enough courage to step into the sitting room, Maeve felt her phone buzzing in her pocket. She pulled it out and saw Ethan's number flash across her caller ID.

Maeve had no intention of answering her phone. She knew it was unfair to Ethan to shut him out like this, but there was a shiny bright light in front of her, pulling her further and further away from him. The thought of what could be overtook her desire for the way things were. Maeve hit the big red Decline button and went to slip her phone back into her pocket when it started to buzz again. Maeve sighed a heavy exhale and answered it.

"Hey, hon. Sorry I left without saying goodbye. I

was up early and didn't want to wake you," Maeve said with a false cheerfulness. She was trying to get ahead of what she knew would be an anger-fueled lecture.

"Maeve, I feel like I haven't seen you in weeks, and then you came home and pass out without waking me up or saying hello and then leave again without saying goodbye. What is going on?" She was right. Ethan was angry. He was yelling, and Maeve winced reactively despite him being on the other end of the phone.

"I know, I know. I'm sorry." She was trying to dampen the fire in Ethan before he had a chance to really blow up. He had a right to blow up at her, she thought. She just didn't want to deal with it.

"This isn't something a half-hearted apology is going to fix," Ethan started, not willing to back down this time. "We are supposed to be getting married, and I feel like I don't even know you anymore. You're acting strange, blowing off commitments, and you're barely home. We need to talk about this." His voice was angry, but she could hear a plea in it too. He missed her.

"I know. I'm sorry," she said again, unable to say the real and more important words that were running through her head like a full narration of her innermost thoughts and fears. "I just have some things I need to do, and I need the space to do it."

"I understand that's what you need, and I've been giving it to you, but what about what I need?" Maeve pressed her eyes shut. He was shouting louder now, and she knew there would be no calming Ethan down. His stance on the matter had officially changed from a concerned partner to scorned fiancé, abandoned by his betrothed weeks away from their wedding.

"Ethan, you're being an ass," Maeve said with a firm tone, holding her ground. "This is the one thing I've wanted my entire life, to find my birth mother, and you are being completely unsupportive." Maeve was growing angry at him now for being so selfish.

"I thought the one thing you wanted was to be married and have a family together, because that's what you always told me." Maeve heard his voice crack as he tried to reason with her. "You never once even tried looking for your birth mother before. You hated the person who abandoned you. This person you are turning into while you look for answers is not the person I have lived with for the last ten years."

Ethan was throwing punches now, and while they

stung, Maeve knew that it meant he was hurting more than Maeve had cared to notice while she was off on her pursuit of answers.

"I did," Maeve said as her eyes flooded with tears. She stood pressed against the wall out of sight between the front door and the sitting room tucked out of sight. She could easily turn around, walk back out the door, go home to Ethan and put this to rest. Or she could just as easily walk through to the sitting room and possibly get some answers from Orla.

"You did? And now you don't?" Ethan said.

"I didn't say that" Maeve said sniffing.

"But you meant it," Ethan said.

"No, that's not what I meant. I just need some time here to find some answers. It's important," Maeve said pleadingly. She was willing him to put his own feelings aside and understand why she needed to do this.

"Can't you do this after the wedding?" Ethan asked, his voice settling back into an even-tempered tone. "You've waited twenty-five years. What's another few weeks? Why do you have to cause this chaos in our lives right now? Can't you see how selfish you're being?"

"Are you kidding me?" Maeve snapped back,

angry now. "I have done everything your family has wanted for this wedding. I haven't made a single decision; I've kept my mouth shut for months and have been happily going along with everything." Maeve took a breath, tried to calm herself down, and spoke in a whisper: "I don't even have a family to invite, and I have like three friends. This wedding is only for you and your family."

"You mean the family that took you in, fed you, clothed you and gave you a home when you didn't have one? The family that bought you a house and gave you access to every resource available? You're going to tell me I'm selfish? What about my mom and dad? My sister? Our family, who has poured their hearts into building a home around you. What? You're going to just walk away from all of that at a drop of the hat to go see if you can find something better?"

That hit Maeve like a punch to the gut. She left the line silent, unable to find a comeback. He was right. That was what she was doing, and unfortunately for him, she needed to see it through. She needed to find the answers before she got married and committed to this for the rest of her life.

"Where are you? It's seven a.m." Ethan was

practically spitting his words out now.

"I'm at Orla's house."

"Your foster mom?" Ethan asked, confused.

"Yeah," Maeve said hesitantly. She suddenly felt hyperaware that Orla was sitting in the next room, and she hadn't even said hello yet. "I was hoping I might find some answers here."

"Why would she have any answers?" Ethan asked, now completely bewildered.

Maeve took this turn in the conversation as her chance to pivot. "I can't really talk about that right now, but let's sit down and talk tonight, and I'll tell you everything." Maeve hoped this would buy her some time.

Ethan sucked in a breath on the other end of the line but said nothing.

"I promise," Maeve said, and she meant it.

"Okay, five o'clock, and don't be late," Ethan said.

"Okay," Maeve agreed. She just didn't know if she was going to be able to give him everything he wanted right now. She hung up the phone and walked toward the sitting room.

Orla looked up when Maeve walked in, and a look of surprise flickered across her face. "Maeve, dear. What a nice surprise. It's been ages," she said, staring at her in disbelief, like she hadn't just seen her yesterday.

Maeve's heart practically leapt out of her chest. She was lucid. "Orla, hi." Maeve teetered on the metal seam in the floor where the tile and carpet met, unable to move an inch. She feared even the slightest misstep would burst this lucid bubble.

Orla stood slowly from her chair, removed her glasses and placed her crossword on the table beside her. "Get over here," she said, opening her arms wide. "I heard a rumor you were getting married." She took Maeve's left hand gently in her own to inspect the stone on her ring finger. Even after years apart, her hands felt as long and slender as the always did, and Maeve fought back tears.

"Wow, Maeve," Orla said with a low whistle, "would you look at that?"

Maeve felt a tear fall at the mention of her impending marriage. The undoing of her and Ethan paired with being so close to Orla she could smell her familiar scent was too much.

"Oh, honey," Orla said holding Maeve out in front of her at arm's length. "I've heard marriage isn't that bad!"

The two women burst out in a laugh that broke the

tension, and Maeve wiped her eyes with the sleeve of her shirt.

"It's good to see you," Maeve said, straightening herself in the stiff-backed way Orla had taught her to hold herself.

The women sat in armchairs on either side of the fireplace and caught up on the last thirteen years of their lives. Maeve told Orla about all of her adventures and milestones, and Orla apologized over and over about having to let her go and confided in her the struggles of her disease. She said they had tried some experimental treatments over the years, but they were still fifteen to twenty years away from developing better drugs and protocols. After a long while of catching up on the things you do when years of time has passed, Orla leaned in and squeezed Maeve's hand.

"So, why are you here today, after all this time?"

"It's my mother," Maeve said, looking Orla straight in the eyes, watching for her reaction. "A legislation recently passed that allowed me access to my mother's birth certificate." Maeve paused to take a breath. "I have figured out who she is, where she lives and that you"—Maeve looked at Orla expectantly— "are her aunt."

Maeve left out the part where she had come to visit yesterday, because she didn't want to confuse or embarrass Orla.

"Ahh," Orla said, leaning back in her chair. "I thought she would have reached out to you by now." Orla frowned in the way she did when she was thinking hard, considering her words. "What do you want to know?"

"Anything, everything." Maeve stumbled, disarmed by Orla's openness to the direct question. "Who is my mother? How did I come to live with you? Did she want to keep me? Does she know where I am now? To start." Maeve felt restless now, knowing the answers were right there on the tip of Orla's tongue.

"I haven't talked to your mother in a long time," Orla said, shifting in her chair uncomfortably. "It was very complicated with my disease and the time change. It got to a point where we couldn't communicate anymore after you left."

Maeve tried to make sense of what she was saying. "So, you were in touch my mother when I was living with you?" she asked eagerly, trying to work out the timeline.

"Yes." Orla nodded, and her eyebrows knit

together, trying to think back and remember the facts clearly. "Fiona came to live with me for a while when she was pregnant. My youngest sister, Aoife, your grandmother, sent Fiona away to have the baby. She was only sixteen when she got pregnant, and Aoife had eight children at home."

"Oh, wow, that's a big family." Maeve frowned, trying to take this all in.

"Yes, I was the oldest of nine myself," Orla said. "Aoife and I are twenty years apart. I am the eldest, and Aoife is the youngest of my family. As soon as I could, I moved away from the never-ending parade of babies in my house. I preferred the quiet to the chaos, so having so many people around all of the time was exhausting for me. I wanted to have my own life," Orla said, and she smiled at Maeve, then added, "but you were the greatest gift, dear."

"Why don't you have an accent? I don't remember you talking about your family or where you came from at all."

"The accent was something I tried very hard to lose when I first came over. I was pestered a lot about it, and I wanted to be taken seriously in my line of business." Orla nodded as if she were just remembering this now. "I didn't mention it because it all seemed so close to the surface and intertwined. Your mother and I made the decision to wait until you were a bit older to tell you the truth of it all. We were planning to tell you when you turned sixteen. We didn't think you were ready to hear the whole story yet. You were so young."

"Why did no one ever tell me?" Maeve asked, her voice cracking as tears streamed down her face.

"I'm so sorry, dear," Orla said, tears now welling in her eyes. "When I got sick, I couldn't care for you any longer, and because I had no living family in the country, it was up to Child Protective Services to take you in and make you a ward of the province."

"Why couldn't my mother come get me?"

"Your mother surrendered you when she went back home to Ireland. Legally, she had no right to you once she was out of the country. The way the laws worked meant that she couldn't find you, and you couldn't find her. We had skirted the rules for a while by having an arrangement where I was technically your foster parent and not the adoptive parent, but once I got sick, we were out of options."

Maeve sobbed silently into her hands. She had been so close to having a real family. Orla stood up slowly, walked over to Maeve's chair and pulled her in close to hold her like she did when she was a child. They stayed like this for a long time, and when Orla pulled away, something shifted in her gaze, and Maeve could tell she was slipping away, back into another time.

14

Fiona

Toronto, Ontario, Canada
Summer 1985

Fiona and Orla made a point to have dinner together every Friday night. Orla was working long hours, but she always made it home in time on Fridays to cook and eat together. Fiona had protested at first, ensuring Orla there was no need to do such a thing;

she would be out of her hair soon. But Orla insisted. While the first few weeks were clumsy and awkward as they go to know each other, the dinners became something that Fiona looked forward to at the end of the week. Tonight, they dined alfresco, which they did when the weather allowed, and Fiona donned a long linen tunic, one of the only things that fit her comfortably these days.

"Are there any churches around here that look like the churches back home?" Fiona asked Orla as she took a bite of her roast chicken.

The two women were seated at the patio table on Orla's back deck overlooking the pear trees. It was late, but the evening was warm, and the sun was still high. The days seemed to stretch on forever this time of year.

"Hmm." Orla pondered as she chewed her chicken thoroughly, "it's been so long since I attended service. Were you attending regularly back home?"

"I stopped going as soon as I started to show," she said, looking down at her swollen belly that was weeks away from producing a real live baby. "There's a library near my school that I used to go to every Thursday. It's in an old church, and it is a favorite place of mine. I used to go to read and write, and then Garret and I would go together. It became a very special place for us. I think I just want to feel that feeling again," Fiona said, pausing to take a long gulp of her water.

Orla smiled fondly. "Newbridge Library, one of my favorite places as a teenager as well. I loved the history it carried through its walls and that I could be there learning about science in a place of religion. I found the contradiction fascinating." Orla got that faraway look in her eye she did when she was reminiscing about home. Although she said she didn't miss it, Fiona felt like there was a small part of Orla that longed for home as much as she did.

"Me too." Fiona smiled. She was starting to feel a connection strengthen between her and her aunt. While they hadn't spent much time together with Orla working so much, Fiona felt very comfortable with the woman, and she was going to be sad to leave her when the time came. They still hadn't spoken much about what was going to happen when the baby came, but Orla had been present for all of Fiona's obstetrical appointments. She ensured Fiona she would be with her every step of the way. Part of her was nervous that neither of them knew anything about having a baby, but the other part of her was grateful for an ally who was experiencing this for the first time as well. Fiona felt confident they would be able navigate it together.

"Well, there is St. Paul's Basilica downtown, which was built in the early 1800s," Orla mused. "It would certainly be more reminiscent of what you're used to. However, it's in quite a busy area, so it may not feel quite like home."

Fiona's shoulders dropped, disappointed. She was starting to become quite homesick.

"I have an idea," Orla said with a twinkle in her eye. "Why don't we take a little road trip this weekend, and I can show you a little town that might remind you of Kildare."

That got Fiona's attention, and she popped her head up from where her chin had sagged down to her chest. "Where might that be?"

"It's a little town called Guelph, about an hour train ride from here. We can go Saturday morning and spend the day there. They have the most beautiful church, called Our Lady Immaculate, that sits at the top of the hill in the center of the city. In fact," Orla said, leaning in, "the whole town is filled with old churches, it has the most churches per capita in any city in Ontario. But this church, Our Lady

Immaculate, is the grandest. So grand that the city enforced a set of bylaws that state no sight lines to the church are to be blocked from various vantage points in the downtown core. Nothing must obscure the view of the church, and no new building can be built higher than it."

"That sounds absolutely perfect!" Fiona's excitement bubbled to surface level for the first time in what felt like months, maybe longer. "I'll go to the library and do some research before we go."

"That sounds like a great plan." Orla smiled, and she looked excited too. Fiona was looking forward to an outing together.

The next day Fiona woke up energized with purpose. It had been a long time since she woke up excited with somewhere to be. Lately, all her days bled together as she waited out the last few weeks of her pregnancy. Today, however, was different. Today Fiona was intent on learning as much as she could about her and Orla's adventure to Guelph. This morning, she rose early and put on one of her nicer maternity frocks and a bit of makeup. She brushed her hair and was downstairs before Orla for the first time since she'd arrived.

"Good morning, Fiona," Orla said with an amused look as she entered the kitchen, her eyebrows high up in her forehead, surprised at the sight of Fiona up and dressed before 8:00 a.m. with a full breakfast in front of her. Along with Fiona's lack of desire to get up and dress in the morning, she'd lost her appetite over the last several months. She felt large and sluggish and didn't feel much desire to eat lately. The doctors had told her it was important to feed her body when the weight on the scale plateaued as her belly grew larger, but Fiona couldn't force herself to eat when it made her feel so full and sick.

"Good morning." Fiona smiled up at her aunt, her cheeks filled with buttery toast.

"Where are you off to this morning, bright and early?"

"I'm eager to get to the library to learn more about that church you mentioned before our adventure tomorrow," Fiona said. She was grinning so hard her cheeks actually hurt a little.

"That's a great idea," Orla said. "Do you need a hand?"

"No, I think I'll go on my own. I need to figure out these streets somehow," Fiona said, stuffing another hunk of toast in her mouth.

"All right then," Orla said. "Can I pack you a lunch?"

"Sure!" Fiona said, nodding enthusiastically.

Orla prepared some fresh fruit, cheese and a peanut butter sandwich. Fiona had never heard of peanut butter before moving here and had become a big fan of it over the last few months.

"Thank you," Fiona said, taking the brown paper bag from her aunt and giving her a kiss on the cheek. "I'll be home later."

"All right, have fun now," Orla said with a chuckle. The meek timid, girl Orla picked up from the airport was a far cry from the girl she was sure her mother had told Orla about. Fiona was finally starting to find a bit of herself again.

Fiona headed outside, pleased to encounter a blue-skied breezy day. It had been a hot Canadian summer, something Fiona wasn't accustomed to, and the smog of the city mixed with the stifling heat had forced her indoors most days. Today, however, the skies offered a breeze that cooled her skin ever so gently, allowing her to walk the twenty minutes to the closest public library. As she approached, the disappointment she'd felt at the chapel yesterday washed over her again. This wasn't anything like the reformed church library she was used to. Instead, it was made of clean modern lines, new brick and glass, and was temperature controlled.

It didn't get hot enough in Ireland for them to need air-conditioning, but here in Toronto, every building she walked into off the street pumped out cold air through the vents. Fiona shuddered, feeling the cold air against her sticky skin as she looked for a librarian. She spotted a woman near the stacks and approached her.

"Excuse me," Fiona said to a woman wearing a name tag, who she assumed to be library staff, "would you happen to have any books on Guelph, Ontario?" She stood up straighter once she had the woman's attention. "I'm specifically looking for information on the churches there." Fiona's Irish lilt sounded especially strong in the quiet of the library.

"I'm sorry, miss. We don't carry that here. Let me check the logs for you. I'm sure there's a branch around here that carries what you're looking for." The woman smiled sweetly, avoiding eye contact with Fiona's swollen belly. She was close enough now that Fiona could read her name tag: June.

"Thank you, June," Fiona said, following in pace behind the kind librarian.

June disappeared into a back room while Fiona stood waiting. Her belly had started to drop, and it made standing still uncomfortable. She preferred being in motion at this point, both to ease the discomfort and avoid thinking about what was coming. She had started to feel twinges recently that felt cramp-like and tightening in her lower belly. When she asked Orla what that meant, she shrugged and said they would ask the doctor at their appointment next week. She was equally in the dark as Fiona, but she was still the adult in this relationship. Orla had tried not to press Fiona about finding an adoptive family for her baby but instead chose to leave pamphlets and books on her bed, outlining her choices. While her parents took the choices out of her hands, Orla was kind enough to make her feel like she was in control again, and she was grateful for that.

June emerged from the back room triumphant. "It says that any books on Guelph will be located at the library at the University of Toronto on campus. Have you been there before?" June asked.

"No, I haven't," Fiona said, shaking her head, disappointed. "Can I walk there?" she asked hopefully.

June chuckled kindly. "Well, I'm not sure I'd advise it in your state and this heat," she said, addressing the bump that had introduced itself from beneath Fiona's maxi dress.

"Is there a bus then?" Fiona asked, growing impatient.

"Yes, there is," June replied, sensing Fiona's tone and returning to a serious one herself. "Take the number six bus at the corner of King and Jarvis and get off when you reach Queen Street. You'll be right on the outskirts of campus then and can find your way to the library."

June disappeared under the desk for a moment, making a racket of drawers slamming open and closed and papers rustling around. She came up for air and wiped dark brown hair out of her eyes with a triumphant smile.

"Here," she said eagerly, thrusting a paper at Fiona. "This should help."

Fiona took the paper from June and held a map of the University of Toronto. She could tell by the sketches of the buildings sprinkled around the campus map that she was going to feel at home here.

"You look a bit young to be a student here." Fiona

heard a voice behind her, and she turned around, nearly knocking into the man behind her with her belly. "Ah, there are two of you, I see," he said, smiling down at her, his eyes crinkling with kindness. He stood around six feet tall, with deep brown eyes and hair that was just starting to gray at the temples. He looked older than her brothers but younger than her father and had a pair of glasses perched on his nose that he peered over to look at her.

"I'm not a student," Fiona said, assessing the man, who she deemed safe enough to speak with. "I'm just here looking for some books."

"Ah, well, this library has the finest collection in the city, so I'm sure you'll find what you're looking for," he said tapping the stack in his arms and turning to walk away.

"Would you know who I could speak with to help me find a book?" Fiona asked, the first person who hadn't judged her for her pregnant state almost out of reach.

"Of course," the man said, turning back around. "My name is John, but around here I'm known as Professor Horner," John said sticking his hand out for Fiona to shake.

"Fiona Grisham," she said sticking her hand out

and gripping his firmly, like her father taught her. "Also known around here as the pregnant Irish teenager." She smiled, and John let out a howl of laughter.

"And she has a sense of humor. Wonderful!" he said, walking toward a computer. "This is what you need to find what you're looking for, just type in the author's name or the subject you're looking for and hit Enter, and a list of titles will pop up with the corresponding code to where you can find it in the stacks."

Fiona stepped up to the keyboard as John stepped aside and typed in her information. The computer whirred and the screen filled with book titles that matched her query. She turned to thank John, who was peering over her shoulder at the screen.

"What has you interested in Guelph?" he asked, overstepping their newly formed rapport.

"My Aunt Orla says it's more like home there, not so big and busy, like the city," Fiona said, embarrassed as tears started to sting at her eyes.

"Care to take a seat?" John asked kindly, ushering her over to a long table with some open seats.

Fiona obliged and followed him, then sat down willingly, her feet aching from a day of walking.

"Where's home?" John asked, starting with a softball, clearly knowing the young girl needed someone to listen right now.

"County Kildare, Ireland," Fiona said with a sniff, trying to keep her composure. While she didn't often talk to strangers, especially not strange men in foreign countries, she felt safe here with John and sometimes it was easier to confide in a stranger than someone who held a stake in your life. "My parents sent me here to live with my mother's older sister until I have the baby, and then I'm meant to return home like nothing happened," Fiona said, her frankness surprising even herself.

"Ah, I see," said John, his face twisting with concern. "I'm guessing that didn't make you feel very good."

"No! They just sent me away to deal with all of this alone. Aunt Orla is lovely, but she's old and works a lot. I've just been alone all day every day, left with my own thoughts, waiting this out," Fiona said, pointing at her belly.

"That has to be tough," John said, nodding. He stayed quiet and allowed Fiona to continue.

"It is. I spend most of my time reading and writing. It's all I can manage to do," Fiona said as she pulled out her notebook.

John eyed it, and his eyes lit up, intrigued. "What are you writing about?" he asked eagerly.

"Oh!" Fiona said, her focus now on her notebook. "I'm writing a novel. I used to just write short stories, but I've had so much time on my hands lately," Fiona said, shrugging. "I've been writing about my favorite church back home. It's a mystery," she said excitedly. "I've heard there is a lovely church in Guelph as well, and I wanted to see for research's sake."

At this, John smiled broadly. "May I?" he asked and picked up the notebook.

Fiona nodded. No one ever seemed interested in what she was writing, so she was happy to finally share it with someone.

John flipped through for a while quietly.

When he looked up at Fiona, there was a look of curiosity on his face. He paused before speaking again. You are a fantastic writer, Fiona Grisham," he said, his face serious. "Promise me you won't ever stop."

Fiona flushed a hot red. She was suddenly tongue-tied and unable to form a proper thank-you, so instead she offered an embarrassed smile.

"Have you thought of studying English and

writing in university?" John paused before correcting himself. "Sorry, I don't even know how old you are." Now it was his turn to be embarrassed.

"I'm seventeen." Fiona had one year left of school before university. "I've considered it, but I thought maybe to be a teacher. I hadn't thought to make a career of writing." Fiona still felt too young to really be making any important decisions in her life. She absently rubbed her belly.

"You could do both, like me," John said.

Fiona cringed with embarrassment. She hadn't asked John a single thing about himself as she had rambled on.

"Are you a writer as well, Professor Horner?" Fiona inspected the titles on the spines of his stack of books on the table in front of them: *The Sun Also Rises* by Ernest Hemingway, *Don Quixote* by Miguel de Cervantes and *Tales of the Alhambra* by Washington Irving. Fiona had read Don Quixote, but not the other two.

John followed her eyes to the stack as she picked up the book atop the pile, *Tales of the Alhambra*. "I am, and an English professor. And these books," he said, tapping the stack in his arm, "are for a bit of research I'm doing on Spain for the novel *I'm* writing." He handed the book to Fiona, who skimmed the back cover for a clue to what was inside this seemingly historic novel.

"Research is one of my favorite parts of writing," Fiona said, skimming through the book.

"Mine as well," John replied with a laugh. "Sometimes I do too much research, and I completely lose the plot, but it sure is fun getting lost along the way."

Fiona smiled knowingly. She had yet to figure out an ending to her novel; she was having too much fun inside the conflicts along the way that she couldn't seem to write herself out of.

John looked down at his watch, checking the time. "I'm afraid I have to go, Miss Fiona Grisham, but it was pleasure meeting you." John reached into his messenger bag and pulled out a business card. "I do hope you find what you're looking for. Please stay in touch. I'd love to read your novel when it's finished."

With that, John was gone, and Fiona was left with a strange tingle of hope in her stomach as she watched him walk away.

15

Maeve

Guelph, Ontario, Canada
Summer 2011

Maeve walked through the front door of her home, the home she built with Ethan, feeling like a visitor. She didn't say a word as she quietly closed the door behind her. She felt exhausted and empty. After meeting with Orla and grasping at pieces of information she'd been longing to hear, she had cried on the curb outside her childhood home for a long time before she managed to compose herself and walk to work. Her face had been red and puffy, and her throat was sore, but she'd pushed through and put her day's work in before going back home. Now, all she wanted to do was curl up into a little ball and go to sleep. She had just spent days building up hope that she might possibly find some answers. And now that she had them, she was mourning the loss of a life she could have had. Her mother had wanted her; she had just been a child herself when Maeve was born. She was ruminating over the what-ifs and what-could-have-beens. She'd lost out on a life she deserved to have. Maeve knew there was still so much she didn't know, so many answers that would be locked away in Orla's mind, possibly forever.

Ethan had heard the door and walked out from the den, where he saw what state Maeve was in and paused before approaching further. Their phone call earlier had been tense, leaving them both uneasy.

Maeve looked up when she heard him round the corner and offered a weak smile. "Hey."

"Rough day?" Ethan asked from his position at the other end of the hall. His hands were stuffed into his pockets nervously.

"You could say that, yeah." Maeve tried to keep a light smile, which felt wrong on her blotchy and swollen face.

"Want to talk about it?" Ethan asked.

"Yes, I owe you an explanation," Maeve said hesitantly. She slowly shed her purse and shoes at the door.

She walked down the hallway toward Ethan and wrapped her arms around his stiff body. She knew that's what he needed right now, even though his touch made her skin crawl. In times of stress, the person she loved the most she pushed away the hardest, but she wasn't sure how to get past it. It appeared that the only way forward was to plow through the intense discomfort. Ethan softened and hugged her back, took her hand and led her to the couch to sit down.

They sat on the small love seat, side by side, either their shoulders or knees touching depending on how they angled themselves. In their frugality during renovations, they decided they didn't need more than one couch, because they didn't host, and they didn't usually mind being this close. However, it was in this moment Maeve kicked herself for not getting a sitting chair or footstool—anything so they didn't have to be touching for this conversation.

Maeve took a deep breath before speaking first. "I'm not sure where to start." Maeve picked at the skin around her thumbnail, a nervous habit she'd had since childhood that had lain dormant for years until the stress of the day brought it back out.

"Why don't you start with what you learned today," Ethan suggested.

"Okay," Maeve said, running her hand through her mass of curls. "My mother's name is Fiona Grisham. She was born in Ireland and got pregnant at sixteen." Maeve took a breath and shuffled her body back on the couch, so she was facing Ethan rather than being pressed in beside him. "She was sent to Canada to live with an estranged aunt to wait out her pregnancy and give birth to me and then return home."

Ethan frowned but stayed quiet.

"When I saw my grandmother's name on the birth certificate, Aoife Doyle, I got curious if it was just a coincidence or if Orla Doyle was somehow related to my mother. I knew it was a long shot to go see Orla based on her condition, but I felt like I had to at least see if she had any answers."

Ethan reached over and gave Maeve's hand a

squeeze. "What did she say?"

"When I walked in the house, she called me Fiona," Maeve said.

Ethan's eyes shot wide open. "So, she did know your mother."

Maeve nodded. "I figured out pretty quickly there was a lot I wasn't told as a child. As you know, Orla has dementia, so it was really hard to talk to her, knowing she knew something but couldn't communicate it. So, I left and searched on Facebook, trying to find a family member that might lead me to more information on where my mother is now." Maeve paused to take a breath and reached into her bag to pull out her mother's book that she'd stopped to purchase at the bookstore on the way home. It was called *Homers Point*, and she handed it to Ethan. "Look at the back flap" she said, nudging her head toward the book cover.

Ethan opened it to the author biography, and his brows rose. "Is this your mother?"

She nodded.

"Wow, you look just like her," Ethan said, studying the image for similarities just as she had.

"I know," Maeve whispered. "We really do look alike, don't we?"

"You really do." Ethan said, nodding, his eyes still transfixed on the picture.

"I found her family online," Maeve continued, still picking at the skin around her nails nervously. "She has twin boys. Fifteen-year-olds."

Ethan's face twisted in an uncomfortable expression of pity.

Maeve had to look away, embarrassed. "Its fine," she said, brushing off the feeling. "I needed more answers, so I went back to see Orla today, in hopes of trying to get some more clarity on the whole situation." Maeve tried to keep things moving along. She rolled her shoulders to work out the tension that was creeping up the back of her neck.

"And did you?"

"Not the whole story, but fragments. Orla told me that Fiona's parents sent her away here to Canada to wait out the pregnancy, in hopes of concealing the whole scandal. She was sent to live with Orla, who was her mother's older sister, who had never married, had no children and didn't talk to many people from home anymore. None of their family or friends knew Fiona was pregnant, and they told everyone she went to study abroad for a summer."

"Ahhh," Ethan said.

"Yeah. Orla was a single, childless financier in Toronto and agreed to take my mother for the summer. I guess she thought she could handle it for a few months. She had the space and didn't think a teenage girl would want much to do with her anyways, so she said yes."

"So, how did you end up with Orla?" Ethan asked, his curiosity piqued.

"I don't know," Maeve said, shrugging. "I didn't get much more out of her after that. She kind of went to a faraway place and started talking nonsense again, so I left."

"Did you mom ever come back?" Ethan asked.

"No," Maeve said, angry that she could actually see the life she could have had if things were different. The life that was taken from her before her first birthday. She slowly looked up to meet Ethan's eyes. "I need to go and find out what happened."

"Okay," Ethan said, nodding. "Why don't we go to Ireland on our honeymoon?" Ethan sounded earnest. "We've been struggling to pick a place. Ireland seems like the perfect spot to go."

"I need to go alone, Ethan," Maeve said more to herself than to him. "I need to go and find out who I am and where I came from." Maeve took a deep breath, trying to escape his gaze, because she knew what she was going to say next was going to hurt him deeply. "And I need to do it before we get married."

"What?" Ethan shot up out of his seat. He had not been expecting this. "Maeve, we are getting married in four weeks."

"I know," she said, nodding, "and I just can't get married without knowing who I really am first. I'm sorry. I think this is just something I need to do, and I need to do it alone."

"This is ridiculous. You can wait a month," Ethan said with a fire in his voice.

"No, I can't. We can postpone the wedding. We've been together for eleven years; we can wait a little longer," Maeve said matter-of-factly. She'd made her decision before the conversation even started.

Ethan walked out of the room, stormed up the stairs to their bedroom and slammed the door. Maeve contemplated giving him time to cool off, but she didn't want to give him time to get angrier with her. She felt bad enough that she had hurt his feelings that she needed to try and explain herself and dampen his temper. She paced up the stairs and opened the door to the bedroom to find him lying on the bed staring up at the ceiling angrily.

"Leave me alone." His words cut deep now that she was on the other end of being shut out.

"Ethan, please?" Maeve asked, taking a step closer to the bed.

"Stop," Ethan said, sitting up. "I told you to leave."

Maeve had pushed him too far. Her heart thumped quickly inside her chest, waiting for what she knew was going to be a berating.

"I have given you everything you have ever asked for. I've taken care of you, I've given you a home, a family—fuck! —even your job was because of me." Ethan was standing now, hovering over Maeve as she tried to keep her composure. "Where are you going to go when you leave me, and your family rejects you? You'll have no one."

Maeve reared back like she'd been slapped. "Ethan, stop!" Maeve put her hands up like a shield trying to block the words from hurting her.

"No, I won't stop, because you need to be realistic about this. What do you think is going to happen if you just show up in Ireland and present yourself to your mother? She gave you up to save her life, and she didn't come back for you. She has her own family now. As much as I know you're hoping for some sort of a reunion, I don't think it will be that simple. You said yourself the family didn't know you existed, except for Orla and your grandparents."

Ethan's face was twisted into an ugly scowl, and Maeve felt hatred toward him for the first time in her life. Despite the hard truths Ethan was laying out in front of her, she still believed there was a chance it was something worth fighting for.

"I still need to go. I'll never be able to move forward if I don't have answers," Maeve said, believing in her heart it was the only way to heal the broken girl inside.

"It's not going to make a difference. You just learned the answers from Orla. You know the truth. Showing up on your mother's doorstep is just going to create a lot more pain in your life," Ethan practically spat out his words.

"You don't know that. Orla isn't in her right mind. That's just her version of the truth," Maeve said, raising her voice defensively, and it was in that moment she made up her mind. "I'm going. I'll be back for the wedding, but I need to go." She crossed her arms over her chest as if punctuating the decision.

"I don't think you understand what's going on here." Ethan stood to face her and folded his arms across his chest. "You can't just take off to another continent with no return date in the middle of an argument and say you'll be back for our wedding. If you leave, there won't be a wedding."

"If you can't put aside the fact that a wedding is just a day, and a marriage is supposed to last a lifetime, then I don't think you're ready to get married," Maeve said, holding her composure. "I know I'm asking a lot right now, but I need this to move forward with my life. Throwing around hurtful words and ultimatums isn't making me want to stay."

Ethan glared at her, rage roiling behind his eyes. He had existed in a world where things had always been easy for him. This was not a part of his plan, and Maeve wasn't actually sure he would be able to get past it. But she needed this, and if he couldn't understand the intense need she had to find her mother, perhaps he wasn't ready to get married after all.

"I think we should postpone the wedding," Maeve said. "I don't think it's a good idea right now."

"Are you kidding me?" Ethan yelled.

"I'm serious," Maeve said, sure of herself. "I don't think we're ready." Maeve reached out and touched his arm gently. "I'm sorry, but this is something I have to do, and I hope one day you can understand."

Maeve took off her ring, placed it on the bedside table and took one last long look at Ethan.

There was no turning back now.

16

Fiona

Guelph, Ontario, Canada
Summer 1985

Early Sunday morning Fiona and Orla waited at the train station with their breakfast bagels and water bottles, ready to head out on their adventure. Fiona was excited to see the city and explore, and with her now nine full months pregnant, it felt as if time were running out. Orla had taken the liberty of organizing a walking tour for them so that Fiona could get the most out of their day as possible and hopefully feel that connection to home she was looking for. They boarded the train and found their seats, opposite each other for the journey. Orla sipped on her coffee and Fiona watched the world rumble by outside their window as the train left the station.

When the town of Guelph came into view from her window, Fiona craned her neck to spot the church that sat high above the city. It was a beacon calling them forth with a hundred steps leading from the road up to the church doors. The small town was sprinkled with low buildings made of limestone and red brick, spaced apart in neat rows, not like the cold urban buildings she'd come to know in Toronto that were crammed together tight and high toward the sky. The train screeched to a stop, and the two women shuffled off it, squinting into the arrivals area, looking for their tour guide. They spotted a woman clad in orthopedic running shoes and a large knapsack holding a sign high with their names on it. They walked toward her and offered a little wave when her eyes traveled toward them. She unapologetically looked Fiona up and down, silently assessing the young girl. Catching herself, she settled her gaze on Orla, who stood with her back straight and her eyes set with a sharpness that warned the tour guide to keep her mouth shut.

"Good morning, ladies!" the tour guide said enthusiastically, slipping the knapsack off her back to retrieve two water bottles. She handed them to Fiona and Orla. "Welcome to the Royal City Church Walking Tour!" she said as if she were announcing an act on stage. "My name is Alice, and I'll be your private tour guide today. We will start here in our downtown core doing a walk about to see the many churches we have in this six-block radius." Alice paused to wave her hand erratically, seemingly pointing out said six-block radius. "And then we will work our way up there." She paused again for effect and turned to point to the grand cathedral at the top of the hill. "To the basilica."

Fiona turned at the bottom of the hill, and they stood and stared open-mouthed at the beautiful sight. It stood in front of her in all its glory, just as it had been portrayed in the pictures. She'd caught a glimpse on the train, but being this close was another experience entirely. The basilica was a grand limestone structure with stained glass. There were tall spires that reached sky-high, and even where there were trees in the way, you could still see the building soaring above the treetops, standing proud as they overlooked the city.

Their tour guide, Alice, walked them through the streets of downtown, pointing out the sculptures and carvings intertwined within the stones that told stories of what the buildings had represented over the last two centuries. As they walked along the main road, MacDonnell, Alice pointed to a house on the corner.

"This house here is where the original blacksmith shop was built by an Irishman named John Owen Lynch who was recruited to come and be the city's blacksmith in 1827. Most of Guelph's Catholics at this time were Irish, and they were very poor. This early on in Guelph's settlement, there were no churches built yet, so John Owen Lynch opened his home up, and for many years, masses were held there."

Fiona looked at Orla, smiling broadly at this bit of history that felt like a part of her own. She wondered if Orla knew of the deep Irish history Guelph had or if she'd just made a lucky guess because the churches were so beautiful. Nonetheless, Fiona was feeling happy and relaxed for the first time since she had arrived in Canada.

"John Owen Lynch was a very influential part of Guelph's history and even helped bring in goods and horses," Alice said. "Before him, there was very little trade and merchandising happening in this town."

They continued to walk up and down the hilly streets of downtown Guelph, admiring the grand century homes wrapped in ivy. Between the hilly terrain, the old stone buildings and lush plant life that they were immersed in, Fiona was feeling quite at home. She watched Orla dab a tear from the corner of her eye at one point and wondered if she was feeling the strong connection to this town as well, even after being away from home for so long.

Fiona wiped her arm across her forehead, which was slick with sweat. The heat coupled with the hilly trek they had embarked on was causing her to become uncomfortable. In the past few, now weekly, obstetrical appointments, the doctors had urged Fiona to consider contacting an adoption agency to find suitable parents for her child. While early in her pregnancy they had been gentle about it, they seemed to be firmly implying that she was running out of options. Still, Fiona couldn't bear the idea of giving up a baby she hadn't even met yet. Logically there was no sense for a seventeen-year-old girl in a foreign country to raise a baby alone with no education or income, but logic held no weight to the feeling of her growing baby inside, flipping and fluttering around, poking and kicking her at all hours of the day and night. Even when she was alone, the baby kept her company, and Fiona often stayed up late at night reading the baby drafts of her novel as she worked through her writing. She rubbed her belly, waiting to feel a kick while Alice chattered on.

"In 1846, there was a great potato famine in Ireland. You might have heard of it." She leaned into Fiona and gave a wink, to which Fiona rolled her eyes. "And at that time, we saw another great influx of Irish settlers come to Guelph, enriching the Irish Catholic community. It was soon after that the churches started to make progress."

Fiona started to tune our Alice, who, while good at her job, was starting to get a bit irritating. Instead, she focused her attention on the greenery around her. The trees and shrubs that lined the street were different than the type of greenery in Toronto that she had become accustomed to. The young maples that lined the boulevards of the residential areas and downtown core were slim and tall, fitting in aesthetically alongside the high buildings that made up the Toronto skyline. Here in Guelph, the tree trunks were thick and wide, the tops growing into unruly canopying over lampposts. Homes were covered in ivy, and the grass on people's lawns were overrun with tiny wildflowers.

Fiona had sweat through her summer dress after an hour and a half of walking in the sun. Her feet were sore, and her belly was cramping in the way it had been recently when she was on her feet too long. While she wanted to rest, she was very eager to get to the basilica. She couldn't wait to see it up close.

"And now for the grand finale," Alice said as she threw her hands in the air for emphasis, presenting them to the church. "The Church of Our Lady Immaculate."

The three women stood together at the base of the church and craned their necks back as far as they could go to see the spectacle in its entirety. It was very grand indeed. Up close, the details were intricate and appeared to tell a story on every stone, window and archway.

"This church was designed by architect Joseph Connolly, and you guessed it," she said, winking at Fiona, "another Irishman!"

Fiona groaned. Alice's bit was getting old, but she kept listening this time.

"Joseph Connolly came to Canada from Limerick, Ireland, and was a prolific builder of churches here in Ontario. If you have ever visited St. Peter's Cathedral in London or St. Paul's in Toronto, you have been inside of a Joseph Connolly church before. However, Our Lady Immaculate is said to be his most impressive work."

Fiona could see why as they stepped inside. While the outside of the basilica was a thing of beauty, the inside had its own details to wow patrons. She finally felt at peace as she stood in this grand cathedral, built by her people, made of the same stones and glass that she saw in her dreams of Ireland at night. Fiona felt an overwhelming certainty in that moment that this town is where her baby was meant to live. It was as close to home as they could get while being an ocean away. She had come to accept that her parents would never let her bring the baby home, and she could not take care of the baby on her own.

Fiona found a pew to lean on as her pesky cramps turned quickly into debilitating ones. Her legs no longer able to hold her weight beneath her, she slid into a pew, frozen in pain and unable to move.

"Orla, help," Fiona whispered, barely able to speak and trying not to scream in this holy place.

Orla turned around quickly and went white at the sight of her. Orla's gaze traveled from Fiona's belly to the ground and stopped at the blood pooling between Fiona's legs.

"Call an ambulance," Orla whispered to Alice, trying not to alarm the other parishioners inside the church of the pregnant teenager in labor.

Alice turned around, took in the scene and gasped loudly. Heads turned to face them from all over the church, the acoustics of the building having been designed for voices to carry throughout so that the people at the back could hear the priest's sermon. Orla located a room off to the side and ushered Fiona in, where they would have some privacy. As Orla tried to assess Fiona, Alice went in search of someone who could give them access to a phone.

Within minutes they heard the sirens outside the cathedral. The paramedics rushed in, assessed the situation, strapped Fiona to a gurney and carried her down the steps as she writhed in pain. Once they were out of sight from the crowd and in the ambulance, they took Fiona's vitals as Orla answered their questions.

"This is Fiona Grisham … she's seventeen years old … forty weeks pregnant. She had some mild cramping over the last week, which our doctor told us was normal. We are currently here for a walking tour, but she is living with me in Toronto. No, we have no identification with us." Orla was trying to stay calm, but never having experienced a birth herself, she was rife with anxiety, unsure how this was going to proceed.

"All right, ma'am. Thank you for the thorough update," the paramedic said to Orla, then turned her attention to Fiona, who was experiencing momentary relief from the pain. "Can you tell us how you're feeling Fiona?"

"I'm okay. It's coming in waves. Seems to be getting more intense as they come." Fiona was able to speak clearly before another wave of contractions came on and she doubled over in pain.

"When did this start?" the paramedics asked.

Orla frowned, clearly frustrated after she had she had just given them all of the information she had.

Another contraction subsided and Fiona spoke again. "This morning the cramps started coming, but it wasn't this bad. It just started to get this bad in the last hour or so."

Orla turned to look at her with her lips slightly parted in disbelief. Fiona hadn't shared any of this with her. Fiona turned her attention to Orla and said, "I didn't want to worry you. The doctor had told us so much about false labor and first babies coming late, I just thought this was to be expected."

"Oh, honey," Orla said, squeezing her hand as they bumped along in the back of the ambulance driving up the hilly roads to the Guelph General Hospital.

In a *whoosh*, Fiona was whisked away down the hall with Orla running after them. Guttural noises escaped her as she felt the baby come. In a state of delirium, Fiona felt like she was watching herself from above as the baby came out and into the world, the pain and cramps instantly evaporating and endorphins flooding into their place.

The nurse held the up the naked baby, who had started to cry, and proclaimed, "It's a girl!" as she put her on Fiona's chest.

Fiona held her with tears streaming down her cheeks, a smile plastered across her face.

"Maeve," she said, smiling down at the baby girl with tufts of copper hair, just like her own. "I'll call her Maeve."

Part II

17

Maeve

Flight AC654 Toronto to Dublin, Ireland
Summer 2011

Maeve had all but run out the door to the airport, leaving Ethan behind in pursuit of her mother. While the guilt nagged at her, the excitement for what was in front of her was much stronger as she hopped on the plane. Sitting on the tarmac waiting to taxi, Maeve

sent off a few emails to let people know about her
sudden absence. First, she emailed Natalie.

> Natalie,
>
> I got a lead and had to take off to Ireland.
> We have postponed the wedding. I've
> attached eight articles that should get you
> through the next two weeks. I'll update you
> on the exposé as I have more information.
>
> Maeve

Maeve held her breath as she hit Send, praying she
wouldn't lose her job over this. She knew she'd
fulfilled her obligations, even surpassed them in
terms of output, but she was toeing the line of
unprofessionalism. It was bad etiquette to leave on
vacation without notifying your employer first, even
if that work could be done remotely.

The second email she sent was to John Horner. She
was supposed to meet with him tomorrow to go over
some of his research for her exposé and of course now
would be letting him down as well.

> John,
>
> I'm so sorry, but I've taken off to Ireland to
> go find my birth mother.

Maeve stopped typing and looked at the ridiculousness on her screen. She felt the pit in her stomach form as she started to doubt her rash decision to leave like this

"We are about to begin our ascent. Please turn all cell phones off for the duration of this flight," a voice crackled overhead.

Maeve looked around and saw all the flight attendants were occupied with other passengers, so she went back to her email and deleted the previous message. Maeve tried again.

John,

I've taken a last-minute trip to Ireland to try and learn about my heritage. Unfortunately I'll be unable to meet in person tomorrow. Can we reschedule?

Maeve

Before Maeve had a chance to read the message over for typos, a woman in a stewardess uniform approached, hovering over her seat. Maeve looked up guilty, pressing Send as she tried to hide her phone.

"Seat belt." The stewardess nodded at Maeve's lap.

"Yes, sorry," Maeve said, buckling the silver clasp around her waist.

She offered the stewardess a tense smile, which was retuned with a disapproving look. Maeve exhaled as the woman finally walked away, inspecting the next row of passengers for any ill behavior. Once she was out of eyeshot, Maeve pulled her phone out from between the armrest and the seat cushion where she'd stashed it and turned her phone off, hoping that when she turned it on again, she hadn't burned too many bridges.

The plane started to taxi on the runway, slowly at first and then faster, its nose rising into the sky. Maeve watched out the window as the world beneath her grew small and smaller until all she could see was sky around her. She pulled out her comfort novel, *Harry Potter and the Goblet of Fire*, tilted her seat back to a reclined position and settled in for her flight.

Maeve rubbed her eyes sleepily as she stood on the curb outside the Dublin Airport. The travel blogs she'd consulted all advised taking a red-eye flight on the way to Dublin to help combat the six-hour time difference she was about to endure. It seemed like a good idea at the time, presuming she'd been able to sleep on the plane, but she had not. Wearily, she hailed a taxi and hauled her luggage into the trunk before sliding into the back seat.

"Where to, miss?" the cabbie asked in a thick Irish lilt.

"Kildare. I'm staying at a bed-and-breakfast called Roundwood House—um, hold on, I'll find the address," Maeve said, rustling around in her purse to find the phone she'd pitched in there earlier.

"Ah, I know the place," the cabbie said, nodding. "Should be about forty-five minutes." Then he hit the gas and peeled out of the airport arrivals area.

Leaving on such short notice, Maeve hadn't had much time to plan her accommodations for her stay in Ireland. After a quick scour of available rooms in County Kildare, she booked the first bed-and-breakfast she could find that had decent reviews and fell well within her budget. Maeve tried to keep her eyes open, but they were heavy, and she fell asleep in the back of the cab, only to be woken by the cabbie slamming on his breaks and cursing.

"Damn heifer, move off the road!" he said, gesturing at the extremely large cow that was standing in front of the taxi, blocking the flow of traffic from both sides.

It just stared silently at them before letting out a deafening "Moooooooooooo" that practically shook the car.

"Jesus!" Maeve yelled, startled.

The cabbie laughed and peered back at her through the rearview mirror. "First time in a bovine traffic jam, I reckon?"

"Yes," Maeve said, laughing now. "Does this happen often?"

"More than I'd like," the cabbie said, removing his cap and scratching at his balding head. "Ah, here we go," he said, relieved as the cow started to move across the road to the other pasture.

Now that Maeve was up, she watched out the window as they drove along the rolling hills. She admired the lush green pastures and roaming sheep as she tried to imagine her mother growing up here and what her childhood had been like. It was a gray day, which Maeve had heard was to be expected, but even still, she could see the beauty of the country, the hills and old limestone estates peppered throughout, reminding her that she was no longer in the North America and her heritage lay deep within the countryside in old buildings and stories passed through generations.

After their forty-five minutes of driving along this scenic route were up, Maeve's driver turned a corner down a long gravel driveway with an open gate and announced they'd arrived at Roundwood House.

As the cab pulled in closer, Maeve took in the estate in real time. The first structure she spotted was a crumbling silo off to the left of them. Maeve tried to swallow, but her throat had gone dry fearful that the pictures she saw online had not be an accurate representation of her lodgings. As they drove around a corner, beyond the trees that protected the main building from view of the road, Maeve sighed a breath of relief. Roundwood House looked to be wholly intact.

The tires crunched to a stop on the gravel drive, and Maeve bid her farewells to the cabbie. She took a proper look at the house up close, in all of its limestone glory. It was a work in progress—that was for certain—but full of old-world charm. Apart from the clear need for some exterior repairs, Maeve could envision what the house once looked like. Standing here, she felt as if she had been transported back in time and landed on an 1800s-era farm. She spied a lively chicken coop off to her left as she approached the front door, and a vegetable garden to her right, a true farm-to-table experience, as it proclaimed on the website.

When she booked the reservation, Maeve had read that Roundwood House was an estate that had been passed down to the owner from a relative, and he had turned it into a bed-and-breakfast recently. It looked like the owner hadn't quite gotten around to fixing the outbuildings yet, but that's what Maeve got for booking last-minute accommodations.

Maeve walked up to the front door of the three-story stone estate house. There wasn't a doorbell or knocker to be found, so instead she rapped lightly on the door, hoping someone would hear her. She waited on the stoop for a few moments, leaning closer to listen for approaching footsteps. When she heard none, she tried the handle. The door swung open with ease into a quaint foyer, which Maeve let herself into. Upon entering, she was immediately greeted by the warmth of a wood burning fireplace, a welcome reprieve to the cool, damp air outside. While it was July, the temperature couldn't have been much warmer than fifty degrees Fahrenheit a sharp contrast to the heatwave back home. She left her luggage and wandered into the library with the fireplace that was heavily lined with shelves that were overflowing with books. Maeve perused the selection, already feeling at home in this foreign place.

"Hi, you all right there?" an Irish voice called out from behind her.

Maeve turned around, startled, to see a tall man with dark hair and blue eyes leaning in the doorway, a slight smirk playing at his lips. She stood there silently, unable to form a proper sentence in response.

"You must be the Canadian," he said, and the smirk turned into a smile. He stuck out his hand to introduce himself, "Colin Walsh. I run the place. Maeve, is it?"

Maeve's cheeks burned in embarrassment for her lack of social etiquette as she took his hand and shook it firmly. "Hi, yes, Maeve Grisham. Thank you for taking me in with such short notice," she said, smiling politely.

"Ah, no worries, lass. As you can see," he said, spreading his arms to display the home around him, "we still have lots of work to do. Roundwood House isn't exactly up to snuff just yet, are we?"

Maeve smiled; she was going to like it here. "I've never seen anything like it. It's wonderful."

"Thank you, ma'am. I've still a lot of work to do, but I have grand plans for this place." Colin looked up the winding staircase, smiling distantly at the chandelier, admiring his home. He shook his head and turned his attention back to Maeve. "Here, let me take that," he said, grabbing Maeve's' suitcase and hoisting it up onto his shoulders. "Follow me. I'll show you to your room."

Colin started up the grand stairs, and Maeve followed in step behind him. Just as it was outside, the inside, too, was a work in progress. Maeve could see the transformation taking place. There were repairs being made to the walls that hadn't yet been painted over, and she could tell the windows had all just been replaced, with little stickers freshly adhered to the corners. She could see paint peeling around the wide crown molding and a brown water spot on the ceiling. They turned right at the top of the steps and headed down a long hallway that looked to be freshly wallpapered in a pleasant putty-colored damask pattern. Each door along the hallway and its accompanying trim were painted different colors with intricate antique doorknobs that looked recently polished. They stopped at a sage-green door with an oblong gold knob. The little plaque beside the room identified it as the Garden Room.

"This is your room here," Colin said, giving the door a little knock in jest before entering.

Maeve looked around the little room, which had a large four-poster bed that sat up high, topped with a thick, full duvet printed in florals and what looked to be a handmade quilt laying along the bottom. The bed was adored in pillows that matched the tapestry of the heavy drapes that framed the bay window overlooking the front of the house where she'd entered. Maeve noticed all the fabrics here seemed thicker, as if they had been handmade, different than she was used to buying for her home. She ran her hand over the quilt absentmindedly. Past the bed and the window, there was another door, and Maeve opened it to find a small bathroom with a toilet, bath and shower. The floor was made if small pebble tiles that looked like it took days to complete.

"Thank you, this is beautiful," Maeve said turning back to face Colin, "I—"

"Dinner is at six," Colin said, cutting her off before she could say any more. "I cook and it's a family-style meal. Breakfast is at seven, same thing, so better be an early riser or you'll miss it. There is food in the kitchen you're free to snack on, but you'll likely have to venture into town for some lunch today. Feel free to roam the property and get a feel for the place, the library has tea and biscuits as well if you're just looking for a quiet place to sit." Colin scratched his forehead as if trying to make sure he'd covered all the bases.

Maeve nodded along as he spoke, trying to take mental notes of Colin's rapid-fire itinerary. "How do I get into town, and how far is it?" She was only now realizing that she was far outside of town with no car. Something she should have considered more thoroughly before she bought a ticket, packed her things and flew overseas on a day's notice.

"Ah," Colin said, assessing her from top to bottom with his hands on his hips. "I'm guessing you don't know how to drive stick, or on the right side of the road, do ye?"

Maeve reddened. He was correct in his assumptions; she did not know how to do either.

"Guilty," she said.

"That's all right then. Get unpacked and meet me downstairs in twenty minutes. I'll take you into town."

Before she had a chance to protest, he was off down the hall, whistling away to himself. Maeve peeked her head out the door and watched as he skipped down the stairs two at a time and disappeared around the corner somewhere. After he was gone, she wandered down the upstairs hall, peeking her head into the different rooms that laid behind the multicolored doors that were left ajar. While some rooms were under construction, some were empty, and there was only one room other than hers that looked to be complete and ready for guests. At the far end of the hall were two rooms side by side with the doors locked, and Maeve wondered who she would meet at dinner tonight.

She heard footsteps and hurried back to her room to unpack quickly so she could shower and freshen up before heading into town.

18

Roundwood House
County Kildare, Ireland
Summer 2011

Maeve and Colin drove into town in his beat-up pickup truck, bumping along the hilly country roads. Maeve had almost called for a taxi when she first saw Colin waiting for her in the old thing. The rusted-out machine looked like an ancient artifact.

"Oh, come on now," Colin said with a laugh. "It's

not going to bite."

Maeve opened the corroded door, feeling a bit better once she caught sight of the inside. There was a shiny vinyl bench seat that went all the way across the truck, and the inside was in far less a state of disrepair than the outside. She slid in, her bare legs sticking to the vinyl, and looked for the seat belt.

"No seat belts," Colin said with a shrug, and turned the key in the ignition. The truck let out a loud roar before the engine settled into its steady rumble. Colin spun the wheel and turned the truck around quickly to head down the bumpy gravel path, and Maeve grasped for handle above her head. She hung on tightly as they bounced down the road, and on some occasions, her rear bounced right of the seat with no belt to hold her down.

"So, what brings you to town on such short notice?" Colin asked in that indirectly direct way one only could when riding in a car with a stranger.

"Ah, well, that's … complicated." Maeve offered, not sure if she was ready to dive into her family drama with this stranger, regardless of how disarming he was.

"Needed a bit of adventure, did ye?" Colin took his eyes off the road momentarily to flash her a cheeky grin.

"Something like that," Maeve said, returning the smile. It was much too early to get into it all with him, but he certainly was charming. She shifted the conversation back to him. "How long have you been running the bed-and-breakfast for?" she asked, hoping he took the bait and saved the questioning for another time.

"Ah, I inherited Roundwood House from my grandfather's estate a few years back. I wasn't sure what to do with it at the time, but after my wife passed, I needed something to focus my energy on."

"Oh, I'm so sorry about your wife," Maeve said, turning her attention to nervously pick at a hangnail.

"Ah, thank you," Colin said with a sad smile. "It refocused me, you know? I couldn't work long hours at the accounting firm anymore. I needed a fresh start." Colin had laid all of his cards on the table.

"All right, here we go." Colin took a sharp turn into town. Maeve braced herself against the handle as the truck swerved and bounced. "Welcome to Newbridge."

Maeve watched out the window, grateful for the distraction as they drove slowly up the main drag. The road was narrow and flanked on either side by wide cobblestone walking paths that allowed patrons to peruse the shops along the way. It was lovely and quaint, and Maeve felt as if she were on the set off a movie.

They continued to drive up the street to the top of a hill, where they parked in front of a beautiful old church. It wasn't quite as grand as the cathedral she knew and loved from home in Guelph, but it had enough similarities to wash a calm comfort over her.

"What a beautiful church." Maeve marveled at it as they stepped out of the old truck and stood at the foot of the steps.

"Its's actually a library," Colin said, surprising Maeve. "Want to go and have a look around?"

"I'd love to," Maeve said, and they walked up the steps into the five-hundred-year-old building.

Maeve stepped into the Newbridge Library and was immediately struck by the grand ceilings and stained glass that lit up the floors with dancing bits of colored light. The library stacks ran from the floor to the ceiling and all around the perimeter of the open space. They were like colorful layers in a maze. In the center of the room sat a collection of tables gathered for patrons to work or read. Maeve walked slowly around the perimeter, taking it all in while avoiding the people deeply immersed in their books.

She had almost forgotten that Colin had come in behind her until he spoke. "Breathtaking, isn't it?" he said, following her eye up to the very top if the vaulted ceiling.

Maeve nodded.

"The whole of County Kildare was rife with us Irish Catholics until the revolution. When that happened, they all had to convert, or at least pretend to. In order to keep this place safe, they turned it into a library, but that was just a front." Colin leaned in close, trying to keep his voice soft out of respect for the smattering of patrons who sat at a table nearby reading. "As the legend goes, all of the men in town used to meet in this basement to plan rebellions and raids, even hiding fugitives for years inside these walls."

"Really?" Maeve said, her eyes wide as she scanned the building. "That's incredible."

"It really is! They wrote books on it. I think they're over there if you want to go take a look." Colin nodded his head toward the stacks in the back left corner of the room. "Now this library is known for its recordkeeping of the county. Despite its ancient bones, it's actually one of the first libraries around here to digitize all of its records. They had a TV show last year where people came here to do research on their family trees."

"Oh, I'd like to see that too," Maeve said, perking up.

"Go look around first, and then I'll show you how to work the computers," Colin said, checking his phone that was lit up with a call coming through. "I need to take this outside. I'll be back in a few."

He walked out the front door, leaving Maeve on her own to take this place in. She wandered back to the area of books Colin had suggested and took her time scanning each row for titles. Most books were in English, but many were Gaelic, reminding Maeve, who had started to feel comfortable here, that she was far away from home. It was the first pang of guilt she felt since arriving.

A young man came out of the stacks with his head down and bumped into her. Maeve was completely engulfed in a book on the history of the Newbridge Public Library. She looked up, ready to apologize. She was startled to see the green-eyed, black-haired teen who looked a lot like the boy Fiona had her arms wrapped around in the Facebook photo she had seen.

The boy stared back at Maeve and opened his

mouth to say something. He closed it again, deciding against it, but his eyes didn't look away from her.

"Sorry," she said, trying desperately to break the tension rising between them.

"Oh. No, my fault. Sorry." He shook his head, but he kept his green eyes locked on her matching set. "You look so similar to … someone I know."

"Ah, must be the hair," Maeve said with an awkward gesture, and pointed to her unruly mane. She cringed internally but didn't move. It seemed as if her feet were cemented to the ground.

"Yeah, maybe," he said walking away, taking one last glance over his shoulder before disappearing into the maze of stacks.

Finally, Maeve let out the breath she was holding. The moment passed, and the boy was gone, and Maeve was shaken.

"Psst...!" Maeve heard a voice call and turned around to see Colin standing at the other side of the library, causing not only her but the majority of the other patrons to turn their heads. He brushed them off with a wave of his hand and signaled to Maeve to come outside.

Relieved that she had a viable exit plan, Maeve put the book back and walked out from the stacks and toward the front of the library, where Colin was waiting for her.

"Everything all right?" she asked, clearing her throat, finally able to use her outside voice again.

"Yeah, sorry, I just need to go back to the house. The plumber I've been waiting to hear from finally said he can come by this afternoon. But I promised you lunch, so let me take you to the best pub in town, and we can grab some food to go," Colin said, guiding her down the steps.

As the two of them reached the bottom of the steps, she saw the boy standing near the sidewalk. She stopped to watch him a moment too long, and he looked back at her again. Their gazes locked as a black SUV with tinted windows pulled up to the curb next to him. The window rolled down halfway, and Maeve inhaled sharply. Inside the car, driving the SUV was a man who looked like a taller and broader version of the boy. He waved a quick hi to the man and opened the door to the car to get inside. He reached for the handle, pausing to take one last look back at Maeve, clearly unable to shake the resemblance. The man followed his son's gaze toward, and his eyes widened when he saw her.

Colin leaned over and waved, thinking they were

looking at him. The man behind the wheel waved in return before starting the ignition, finally looking away from Maeve and peeling away from the curb.

"Come on, let's get that lunch," Colin said, blissfully unaware of what was going on.

Maeve took his cue, nodded and followed him down the road to the pub, taking one last glance at the SUV driving away.

The pub wasn't far down the road, and just as fast as the moment had passed on the stoop of the church, they were inside an old musty pub that smelled of ale and fried fish. The atmosphere shift was a welcome change, and at the smell of the fried food, Maeve's stomach grumbled in response. Colin signaled to the barkeep which table they were headed to, and within seconds, a lean Irish man with a red beard showed up at the table with a dishcloth slung over one shoulder and two Guinness in hand.

"Colin," he said, nodding at her escort. "And who might this lovely lass be?"

"Afternoon, Paddy. This is Maeve Grisham. She's just arrived from Canada and is staying at the house on holiday."

"Welcome, Maeve. A good Irish name for a Canadian girl! Don't let this lad get you into any trouble now," he said with a wink. Paddy sat the ales down and wandered back to the bar.

Maeve was still too shaken from the encounter at the library to say much, and in response to her growling stomach, she drank the Guinness that sat in front of her greedily. The thick stout coated her stomach and soothed her nerves as it settled thought her body. After a few moments she almost felt tipsy from a large beer on an empty stomach, and a lopsided grin spread over her face as she looked around the pub and really took it in. There were antique Guinness ads hanging in frames along the wood-paneled walls lit up by the green pendant lights hanging over the cozy booth. Maeve sat in a leather button-tufted booth beside a stained-glass window that looked like it read Wine from the road. The bartender that had brought their Guinness was tall and bearded with wild-looking hair and a big grin on his face as he stood chatting with a customer as he pulled another draft.

"What do you want to eat? Colin asked, watching Maeve take in the place.

"What's good here?" she asked, looking around for a menu.

Colin nodded his head toward a blackboard with

today's specials written in chalk. "Cottage pie for me," he said flashing that toothy grin in her direction.

Maeve scanned the scant menu that offered bangers and mash, a stew, fish and chips, and cottage pie. "Make it two."

Colin nodded and stood up, then walked toward the bar to order their meals.

"Should be about ten minutes, and then we can get out of here." He slid back into the booth beside her so they could both see the entirety of the pub from their vantage point.

Maeve nodded absentmindedly. "Do you know most people around here?" she asked, wondering how well Colin knew the family from the library she suspected was Fionas. She knew this was a small town, and she hoped to get some insight on her family before meeting them.

"Ehm, not everyone, no. I worked in Dublin before opening up Roundwood House. But I've met some people now that I'm around more. Why do you ask?" Colin took a sip of his Guinness, which left a foamy mustache on his upper lip.

Maeve touched her own upper lip to make sure she wasn't wearing the same milky froth on her face. "Just wondering. You seemed to know the bartender

well, and you waved at those people at the library."
She ducked her head and tipped her glass to sip at the
last dregs of her ale.

"You mean the O'Toole's?" Colin asked, cocking
his head curiously at Maeve.

Maeve nodded, holding her breath. Her suspicions
had been correct.

"Garret's parents live up the road from
Roundwood House, I've met them a few times, just
being neighbors and all. And Fiona, his wife, is a
well-known author. She's pretty famous around here.
She does a lot for the schools and libraries, as I recall."
Colin looked down at his hands for a minute before
adding, "My wife used to be a teacher at Newbridge
Secondary down the hill there. That's where the
O'Toole boys go."

"When did she pass?" Maeve asked softly.

"Last year. Cancer. It was fast," he said, and Maeve
saw something shift in his face.

"I'm sorry," she said, trying to take a sip of her
Guinness to fill in the silence before remembering it
was empty.

"Why are you so interested in the O'Toole's?"
Colin asked, turning the conversation back to her. He
was looking at her in that way again that felt like he

knew more than he was letting on. Maeve didn't know if she was just being paranoid or if her intuition was off due to the jet lag.

"No reason," Maeve said, brushing him off. "Everyone seems friendly around here. It's nice." She smiled sweetly.

"Here you are," Paddy said as he stepped up to their table with their bag of food. "It's on the house," he said, giving Colin a wink as he walked away.

"What was that about?" Maeve asked as they stood to leave.

Colin rolled his eyes. "Paddy was in a bad way a few weeks ago, too many Guinness, and I had to take him home to sleep it off."

"Ah." Maeve laughed. "So, you're a caretaker."

"That I am, girly." Colin smiled, and Maeve felt that warmth rise in her chest again. She was in trouble with this one.

19

Maeve woke up with a jolt to the sound of her phone on the nightstand rattling beside her head. She checked the time. It was 5:00 a.m., which meant it was midnight back home. Maeve had missed dinner, retreating into her room when they got home and falling into a deep sleep. Ethan had clearly been out drinking and had spent the last several hours sending her text messages. The vibrations by her ear startled her out of a half sleep every time it happened. While the logical thing would have been to turn off her phone, for some reason in the dark of the night, she didn't feel enough willpower to shut him out. Maeve sat up bleary-eyed and looked at the fragmented messages.

It appeared as though Ethan had drunk himself free of all inhibitions and was unloading every feeling onto his phone and pressing Send. His messages oscillated from pleas for her return to telling her he never wanted to see her again. Maeve sighed and pressed her fingers into her eyes to relieve some of the pressure built up from jet lag and a sleepless night. She wasn't ready to answer him just yet, nor did she think a response would be welcome in his presumed state. She made a mental note to call him at a more reasonable hour and checked her email instead.

Her inbox was flooded with spam, as usual. Natalie had long ago set her inbox as the catch all for local queries when she was just starting out so she would be the first to catch wind of any incoming leads. It was greatly appreciated at the time and had helped Maeve build a strong portfolio of work, but her focus was on bigger things now. She forwarded the emails off to a few interns working at the paper for the summer, hoping they might find something to give them their first shining moment as a writer. Once she was through unclogging her inbox, she saw a note from Natalie. Maeve held her breath, afraid for the stern words of reprimand she was about to get. She knew it was a risk coming here before asking for time off, and it was probably the boldest thing she'd ever done, apart from leaving Ethan like that.

Maeve felt that something had cracked inside her, not in a way that made her feel fragile and broken but in a way that set her free. It was as if she had this hard shell of armor coating her and protecting her for all these years, a shelter from the pain of reality after she'd experienced so much loss and grief at a young age. But she'd felt more recently like she'd outgrown herself, and the armor she wore was more suffocating than protective.

So much had been hidden from her. She wanted change and answers and to uncover the truth of it all.

Maeve tapped on the email from Natalie and winced as she read the two-line response to her hasty note sent on the plane.

Maeve,

It is highly advised to follow protocol when

requesting time off. Please send me your
latest update on the adoption exposé by
end of week.

Natalie

"Ughh," Maeve groaned, "I'll be lucky to have a job by the end of this." She skimmed her inbox some more and found a response from John, which had a much lighter tone to it.

Maeve,

Safe travels and please let me know when you're back. Feel free to email me any questions you have in the meantime.

John

That made Maeve feel slightly better, and she turned her phone off and tucked it in the bedside drawer, putting everyone away and out of sight for now.

Somehow, in the span of the last forty-eight hours, her life with Ethan was gone and their time together felt like it had happened years ago, like the last decade of her life was another world entirely. She sat in bed and took in the room around her. There was a big wooden desk with a mirror above it, and she swung her legs around to the side of the bed and hopped off. The large four-poster Victorian-style bed was raised high, too high for her small stature to get up and down from easily, but it was very comfortable. She rearranged the duvet and quilts neatly on the bed and replaced the throw pillows as she'd found them. She wasn't sure what the protocol was for bed-and-breakfasts regarding maid service, but she had a sneaking suspicion if she wanted the room kept tidy, it was up to her.

She pulled out the small, upholstered chair from under the desk and sat down, then pulled her laptop out from her bag, which was leaning against the desk leg. As her computer took its time booting up, Maeve's thoughts traveled to Colin. There was something about him that caused her heart to quicken pace when they were near in a way that she hadn't felt the likes of since she was a teenager. He was handsome and he was easy to be around. Maeve felt comfortable with him, and that was something that didn't happen to her very often. She hadn't spent enough time here to decipher if the winks, cheeky grins and touchy-feely-ness was a cultural thing or not, but she was sure he was flirting with her.

Normally she wouldn't have noticed this sort of thing or paid any mind to it if she had. She'd been tied to Ethan for a long time and was enmeshed in the Clarke family unit. There had been no need to flirt and look elsewhere. Everything she wanted, she had, until one day a few weeks ago, she realized she didn't want it anymore.

Maybe she never wanted it, or maybe she just outgrew it, but it was like she woke up after receiving the letter that there was a possibility her mother was out there and had wanted a different outcome for their lives. She'd lived for so long wallowing in her own self-pity of abandonment and been the little victim the Clarke family saved, and she was done with that. She'd never be able to break free of that label with them; that's who she was to them and always would be. It was Maeve's time to find herself and the truth. Whether or not it worked out in her favor, she needed to grow up and move forward.

Maeve had read once that if you experience a major trauma in childhood, your brain gets stuck at that age and is unable to properly mature until you have processed your trauma and moved past it. This entire experience had caused her to consider that she had most likely been emotionally stuck at age twelve and was unable to move forward with her life. She had spent less than two days in Ireland, but she felt certain she couldn't go back to the life she had with Ethan.

She pulled out her notes on her unfolding story on adoption and read through them, trying to piece together a draft to send to Natalie. The stories she was digging up were tales of abuse, black-market adoptions and the twisted dealings of the church. Maeve was aghast learning that the very establishments that she was meant to put her trust in for safety and well-being were the very systems that were corrupt. There were nuns that were housing unwed mothers and selling their children to families they deemed suitable, and there were babies born on Indigenous land in reservations that were taken even if they were surrounded by family just because they fell well below the poverty line. These children and their mothers were all separated in a cruel and unjust manner, and Maeve wanted to paint the clearest picture of their stories so everyone could see what was hidden in plain sight for half a century.

She wrote furiously at her desk, each keystroke heavy and intentional. She was writing for herself, for her mother and for every mother and baby who never had the chance to be a family. Maeve saw a droplet of liquid on her keyboard and reached up to touch her face, realizing that she had been crying, the release of the words onto the page a catharsis for her soul. She sat back in her chair and stretched her arms over her head before giving her draft a read-through. She chewed anxiously on the side of her cheek as she read it, nodding along at the words. Sometimes when Maeve went into a state like that, the words flowed out heavily and with anger behind them, and what was left on the screen was not usable. It was important as a journalist for her to keep an even keel with her writing, exposing hard truths without too much emotion or bias. Today she had done that. The truth was there, raw and visual, but she'd managed to keep her personal feelings from creeping into the prose. Satisfied, if not proud of her work, she sent it off to Natalie.

Natalie,

My apologies for the unprofessionalism. Please find my latest draft attached. Let me know what you think.

Maeve

With that, she shut her laptop and got dressed, ready for a coffee and something to eat.

Despite it being July, Roundwood House had a chill to it that felt like late fall or early spring. There was a dampness in the air, and Maeve was grateful she'd packed a few sweaters and a pair of jeans for her trip. She padded down the grand staircase and saw the fire was burning in the den, and coffee was set out on the buffet with some pastries. Excited, she poured herself a steaming mug and stood by the fire as she perused the bookshelves for her next read. They were packed full of everything from Emily Brontë to the latest Jodi Picoult. There was Jeffrey Archer, Stephen King, John Grisham and Dan Brown. The shelves ran from the ground to the ceiling and were packed tight full of decades' worth of bestsellers all ready for her consumption. While Maeve had tried desperately over the years to read different kinds of fiction from indie publishers and small presses, she was an eternal sucker for a commercial bestseller. Maeve devoured books, sometimes in hours if she had the time. It was one of her favorite things to do, so she picked a Dan Brown book to start with, having finished her comfort novel on the plane. She sat and down in one of the worn wingback chairs and cracked the spine.

"You're up early," a voice called behind her.

Maeve jumped in her seat. She had been drawn into an intricate plot and had failed to hear the footsteps approaching. She looked up to see Colin leaning against one of the bookshelves, amused.

"You scared me," Maeve said.

Colin chuckled. "Sorry about that. I thought you'd have heard me coming."

Maeve reddened and held up the book in her defense.

"What are you reading?" he asked, then leaned in close to look at the cover.

Maeve tried not to breathe as Colin's face was nearly pressed up beside hers. She could smell his soap, something spicy with a hint of pine. Her heart quickened, and she silently cursed herself for not showering before coming downstairs this morning.

"*The Da Vinci Code*, a classic," Maeve said with a shrug. She'd read it and seen the movie, but that's what made reading it again so enjoyable. She could watch the scenes unfold in her mind as she read the words on the page.

"Hmm, never read it," Colin said with a shrug.

Maeve put the book down on her lap and looked

up at him quizzically. "How have you never read *The DaVinci Code*? Surely, you've seen the movie?"

"Mm, nope, don't think so," Colin said with a shake of his head.

"What do you like to read then?" Maeve asked, curious now what this man was made from. She herself was made from the books she'd read as a child, adolescent and adult, each story shaping the way she saw the world and herself.

"Me, nah, I'm not a big reader. I prefer to experience the world in real time," Colin said, and Maeve was almost offended. Just about every part of her was a reader, except for the parts that were a writer.

"Ah" was all she could say. She couldn't relate. She thumbed the pages in her lap absentmindedly. "Where did you get all these books then?"

"These were mostly my wife's collection, and then some are left over from people who came to stay. Some take one for the road, some leave books behind. The shelves weren't quite full when I started, so I picked up some from a car boot sale."

"I'm sorry, what?" Maeve asked, perplexed. "What on earth is a car boot sale?"

"You know, where you can buy and sell old

things?" Colin said, equally as confused now.

"Like a garage sale?" Maeve asked.

"Mm, not a garage, no. Like when people go sell things in a big field out the boot of their car," Colin said, sure Maeve would understand now.

Maeve frowned and shook her head.

"You know what? There's one this weekend up the road. I'll take you," Colin said matter-of-factly.

"Oh, really?" Maeve said with a laugh. "All right then, car boot sale it is."

"Wonderful," Colin said with that cheeky grin of his. "I'm heading out to collect eggs for breakfast. Would you care to join me?"

Maeve cocked her head in contemplation. She certainly was not dressed for mucking around in a chicken coop.

Sensing her hesitation, Colin added, "It will only take a few minutes."

"Sure, why not?" Maeve agreed with a false confidence. She stood up and replaced the book on the shelf before following Colin down the hall to the kitchen.

"You're going to want to put some wellies on," Colin said, pointing to a pair of rubber boots by the door. "Chicken shit is some nasty business."

Maeve scrunched up her face in disgust but did as she was told, slipping on the old rubber boots that came well up past her knees. She checked herself in the reflection of the glass door and smiled. She was completely out of place yet somehow felt right at home here.

"You do this every day?" she asked, giving Colin a once-over. He was clad in muck-caked coveralls and large rubber boots. She was standing close enough to smell him, and his spicy pine soap had been replaced by what she assumed was the chicken shit he'd referenced earlier. Maeve scrunched up her nose.

"You'll get used to the smell," he said with a laugh.

"I'm not entirely sure I will," Maeve said, pinching her nose so her voice sounded all nasally.

"Come on now," Colin said, leading her to the henhouse. "Time to pick your eggs." He handed Maeve a basket and held his hand out for Maeve to proceed forward.

They walked out the door and across an overgrown patch of grass. Maeve could hear the hens inside noisily bawking at each other. Once they were close enough, she stood cautiously at the door, awaiting instruction.

Colin took her by the shoulders and guided her

closer so she could see inside. There were twelve hens, each sitting atop their nests, glaring at the intruders.

"Where are the eggs?" Maeve asked, scanning the ground for loose eggs to collect.

Colin laughed loudly, and a hen started flapping its wings in protest at the outburst. "Under the hens. Where did you think they were?" He was having trouble hiding the smirk on his face, he was enjoying this.

"I don't know, somewhere where I wouldn't get attacked for collecting them," Maeve said, scowling. She was well past her comfort zone this morning and still hadn't finished her coffee. She thought about it sitting in the den, where she'd sat down to read and wished she'd stayed put.

"Go on now, you can do it," Colin encouraged her.

Maeve glared at him in return, not taking the bait.

"Oh, come on, I'll show you how." Colin took her hand in his and guided it toward a hen. He navigated their hands together beneath the hen's body into the nest, and the hen sat there unbothered. "Grab the egg now," he said taking his hand away and allowing Maeve to feel around for it.

Maeve slowly moved her hand around until she

felt the smooth egg against her fingertips. It was deep in the nest, quite warm from being protected by the hen. Maeve pulled her hand out slowly and presented the egg to Colin with a smile.

"I did it!" she squealed.

Colin laughed heartily. "Amazing! Now let's get the rest of them."

The two of them worked around each other in the tiny henhouse, collecting eggs as their elbows bumped clumsily. Colin squeezed behind Maeve as he reached for the eggs in the rafters above where she could reach. She froze when she felt his body press up against her and just stood awkwardly, wondering if he knows what he was doing or if he was just going about his jobs for the day, unaware of the effect he was having on her.

"That's all of them," Colin said ducking out of the henhouse. The moment was gone, and Maeve felt a wash of disappointment come over her, with only a slight twinge of relief. It was much too dangerous to be playing with her emotions like that right now.

"Now it's time to milk the cows!" Colin said cheerfully, walking away from the henhouse, farther into the yard.

Maeve looked at Colin, horrified. "Milking cows

isn't something I want to add to my resume today."

Colin smiled a Cheshire cat grin; he was toying with her. "I'm just joking. I just wanted to see your face and it was well worth it."

Maeve shook her head as they walked back toward the kitchen.

"I have to get some breakfast cooking now for the other guests but let me know if you need to go anywhere today. I'm happy to drive you."

"Thank you, Colin," she said, and she shed her boots by the door. Maeve took her cue to exit, and she padded down the hall to the sitting room to get back to her coffee.

It was cold now, so she refreshed her cup and turned her attention back to the shelves to pick up where she left off reading. But before she could go back to her original choice, Maeve turned her attention to a book that read *Coming Home* by Fiona O'Toole along the spine. She gently plucked it off the shelf, flipping to the back flap, eager to see her mother's face once more. In this photo Fiona looked younger, and the biography identified it as her debut novel. Maeve flipped it over to read the back cover. A quick scan revealed that this was a semi-autobiographical novel about a young girl forced to give up her baby and go home to continue her life, keeping her baby a secret. Maeve's stomach almost dropped through the floor when she read the acknowledgments. There was a line that read, "and a special thank-you to John Horner for all his support over the years." Was it the same Dr. John Horner that had been helping her? She felt like she was the butt of some cruel joke that was running the length of her life, where everyone around her knew what was going on except her.

Maeve couldn't bear to be inside anymore. The damp chill of the house was now suffocating her and making it hard to catch a deep breath. She practically ran out the front door, desperate for fresh air. Maeve looked for a path to follow or a landmark she could use as her North Star. See could see the fence line of the Roundwood House property far in the distance, so she walked as far as she could without losing sight of the house. The walking felt good for her soul while standing still did not, so once she got to one corner of the property, she turned and walked some more in another direction. She wanted to scream—at who, she wasn't sure—but someone needed to answer for all of these strange coincidences that were starting to feel planned and intentional.

Maeve stopped for a break, sat in the grass and leaned up against the fence. She was tired now, and the anger had turned into sadness. She wasn't sure how long she had been out there wandering around, but the sun had now risen high in the sky and warmed up the cold, damp morning air.

"Maaaevvve," she heard faintly in the distance. "Maaaevvve."

Maeve looked around for the source of the voice. Colin was standing in the middle of the field, waving at her to come back to the house. She turned and started walking slowly back toward him. Frustrated by her pace, Colin signaled with his hand the phone sign and waved her in. Her heart thumped in her chest. Maeve's anxiety surged to an all-time high as every worst-case scenario for why someone would be calling her on vacation raced through her mind. She took off toward the house in a full sprint, unsure whose voice she was going to meet at the other end of the line.

20

Maeve was sweating by the time she reached the house. She had wandered out farther than she'd realized, and the run back reminded her how out of shape she was. She was a naturally lean woman, so she never had to work that hard at the gym, but after a morning of collecting eggs, walking and a hard sprint back to the farm, she was out of breath and a bit dizzy. Maeve walked back in through the front door and looked around for Colin.

"Colin?" she called out as she searched for him. He had disappeared back inside when he saw her heading back toward the house.

"In the kitchen," he called back.

Maeve hopped, trying to pull off her shoes as she rushed toward the kitchen. She rounded the corner and found Colin holding the receiver of an old dial phone that was fire engine red secured to the wall.

"Who is it?" she whispered as she approached him.

Colin covered the mouthpiece with his palm and whispered back, "I don't know who, but it's a man." He handed her the phone with his palm still cupped over the receiver.

Maeve took the phone tentatively from him. "Maeve speaking," she said, keeping her eyes locked on Colin. She now had sweat dripping down her face, which she tried wiping away with the sleeve of her shirt.

Colin started busying himself in the kitchen and handed Maeve a glass of cool water, which she gulped at eagerly as she waited for the voice on the other end to respond.

"Maeve, hi," said a quiet male voice on the other end of the line. While she could hardly make out the words, the voice was distinctly Ethan's. Maeve's heart sank; she wasn't ready to talk to him yet. "I was hoping I might get a hold of you here."

"Hi," Maeve said, her heart thumping and hands shaking. She couldn't decipher if it was guilt or anger flooding through her. "How did you know where I was?"

Colin was hovering near her shoulder and Maeve shooed him away with a wave of her arm.

"Your credit card statement, and you share your location on your phone," he said in a more confident voice now.

Maeve ran a hand over her face. While she had "left," their lives were still completely entwined in every way. The guilt rose in her stomach and into her face, where her ears burned hotly against the receiver.

"Now isn't a good time, Ethan. Can I call you later?" she asked, glancing over her shoulder.

"No!" he shouted form the other end of the line. "You cannot call me later. We need to talk now."

Maeve turned her back toward Colin, trying to create a physical barrier of privacy she desperately needed for this conversation. While Ethan deserved an explanation and a conversation, this was not the way to do it. Maeve took a deep breath and tried to remain as calm as possible. "I am currently standing in the kitchen of the bed-and-breakfast using a landline attached to the wall, and there are other people in this room. It is not appropriate for me to have this conversation right now." Maeve took a breath and held it, waiting for his lash back.

"I don't care," he hissed.

Maeve winced. "Just let me call you back from upstairs, okay? My phone is in my room. I've had it off, so I don't get slammed with roaming charges," she lied. She had it off specifically because she was avoiding him.

"Everything all right?" Colin asked, his dark brow furrowed in concern. He took a step toward her from the other side of the kitchen.

Maeve held her hand over the mouthpiece. "All good, just a little misunderstanding," she said, feigning a smile.

Colin's frown stayed put, but he nodded and backed away.

"Just give me five minutes to get back to my room and turn my phone on, okay?" Maeve said, trying desperately to not sound like she was in a hostage situation.

"Fine," Ethan hissed, and then the line went dead.

Maeve replaced the receiver on the wall and turned around to find Colin standing and facing her with his hands on his hips. She offered a fake smile and walked toward him, trying to pass him to get out of the kitchen and up the stairs to her room. The sweat on her body had cooled, and she was starting to feel damp and chilled and uncomfortable. All she wanted was to just deal with Ethan and have a shower at this point. Colin didn't budge as she approached.

"Excuse me," she said, but he just stood there, silently staring her down with his blue eyes. She thought about trying to bodycheck him or squeeze through on one of his sides, but his large muscular frame took up most of the doorway.

"What's going on?" he asked, his normally sparkling friendly eyes now cold and steely.

"It's nothing." Maeve was starting to feel sick to her stomach. Now she had two men angry at her and no way of solving either problem at the moment, but this angry man was stopping her from resolving the other one, and she needed to get upstairs.

"That," he said, pointing at the phone, "wasn't nothing." Colin recrossed her arms, holding his ground in the doorway.

"It's personal," Maeve said, getting defensive now.

"Don't worry about it."

"Well, I am worried about it when some angry man is calling my place of business demanding to speak with a guest. How am I supposed to know if I or you are safe?" he asked.

"We are safe," Maeve said, understanding Colin's investment in this now, "but I have to go make a phone call."

"I can't have angry people calling here. This is my place of business and there are other guests here to consider," Colin said sternly. The softness he'd shown toward Maeve was waning, and she understood she was putting him in a difficult spot.

"I understand, I'm sorry. It won't happen again," Maeve said earnestly.

Colin nodded and turned to the side, freeing up a pathway for Maeve to slip through the doorway. She turned and sidled past him, walking quickly away as she bound up the stairs to go hide in her room. Today had taken a very strange turn, and aside from the fact she needed to calm Ethan down, she needed to figure out a way to assure Colin that she was a completely sane person and not a threat to his business. She would take care of Ethan first and then find a way to make it up to the kind man who had made her feel so welcome here already.

Maeve got to her room and fumbled with the old key and lock with shaky hands. They key was one of those long skeleton-looking keys that took a very specific proper jiggle to open to door, and right as she was ready to throw the key down the hall, she felt the door click and the lock release, granting her entry into her room. She rushed in and barely managed to get the bedside table drawer open before she had her phone in her hands, and she powered it on.

There were twenty-seven missed calls from Ethan. If she hadn't just spoken with him on the phone, she would have been concerned that someone had died, but even knowing he was safe, she was anxious to call him back. Never once in their relationship had he acted this way, controlling and angry and obsessive. They had always lived a relatively boring existence together, but Maeve was now seeing that that was because she fit into his life and what he wanted and just rolled with it. This was the first time she had stood up for what she wanted, ever, and he didn't like it.

She took a deep breath and tapped his name on her phone and hit Dial. The phone rang in echoey long-distance tones, twice, then three times before he picked up.

"Hello?" he said cooly. It sounded like he had calmed down in the five minutes since he last spoke, and Maeve was relieved.

"Hi, Ethan," Maeve said lying down on the bed with the phone to her ear. "Are you all right?"

The line was quiet for a moment before he answered. "No, I'm not," he said flatly.

"Okay," Maeve said, nodding along like he was right in front of her. She pressed her fingertips against her eyes; a headache was now pulsing behind her eyeballs. "I'm sorry," she offered in a whisper.

"Why couldn't you just let me come with you?" Ethan asked, his voice breaking.

Maeve teared up hearing him sound so sad and desperate. "I'm sorry," she whispered.

Ethan sighed. "I just wanted to go with you."

"No, you didn't. You didn't want me to go," Maeve said, gaining some courage back. He was whining and she was starting to see this for what it was, a manipulation.

"Well, of course not!" he snapped back at her. Maeve's brows shot up her forehead in silent response. "We are supposed to be getting married. You don't just run away from your future husband for a solo international adventure to find yourself weeks before your wedding. That's ridiculous!" Ethan was yelling now, and Maeve had the urge to hurl her phone against the wall.

"I understand you're upset—" she started.

"You understand I am upset?" he raged. "You are the most entitled, selfish person—"

"Are you fucking kidding me?" Maeve cut him off. Now she was yelling too. "I haven't done anything for myself beyond surviving and doing whatever you want for the last thirteen years."

"You have gotten to do lots of nice things and have a very nice life. What are you talking about?" Ethan laughed.

"I didn't ask for any of that! That's what you wanted! I can't say no, or I'm ungrateful, but I can't ask for what I want, because it's your family and your money, and I'm just supposed to go along with everything and be grateful and have zero opinion on anything. I didn't even pick out my own wedding dress, for god's sake. Your mother chose it!"

"You're being unreasonable. Of course you get an opinion on things. You chose the bathroom tile, the faucets, every single finish on our house," Ethan said, sounding exasperated.

"Oh, did I?" Maeve yelled. "And who gave me two options to choose from for each? Was I able to go and find options on my own, or was I given two carefully chosen options that you approved before asking me what I wanted?" Maeve's tone turned bitter as she recalled the tenuous process of renovating their house and how infuriating it had been being treated like a child.

"You had no experience," Ethan said. "We knew the distributors and how it works. You wouldn't have known where to start."

"You never gave me the opportunity to even try, you treat me like a child," Maeve said, trying hard not to cry now. Everything she had ever felt and didn't say was flooding to the surface, and he wasn't even listening to her.

"Well, rightfully so, because you're acting like one." Ethan was well past the point of taking any responsibility for the breakdown of their relationship.

"Ethan," Maeve said, sitting up on her elbows in the bed now. She was done taking this kind of attitude from him if he was unwilling to have a conversation about it.

"What?" he snarled back.

"I have to go. This conversation isn't going anywhere. If you want to talk, we can try again in a few days." She got the words out and then held her breath, waiting for his lash back.

"Are you kidding me?" he roared into the phone.

"I'll call you when I'm ready," she said, and hung up the phone before he could sputter any more harsh words her way.

21

Maeve turned off her location sharing before shutting down her phone and hiding in her room for the rest of the day, choosing to focus her energy back into her work to keep her mind from wandering back to Ethan. She was livid at his overstep and embarrassed that he had called the main line and caused a scene in front of Colin. She wasn't sure how she could just walk back downstairs like nothing had happened, so she stayed in her room and poured all of her nervous energy into her work.

While Maeve's foster experience had been in Canada, she was learning that the adoption scandals were international. It had been a centuries-long injustice that involved governments, churches and other backward institutions. The further she dug, the more stories she saw of abandonment and torture of the young unwed mothers who were stripped of their basic human rights as well as their babies.

What Maeve failed to understand, even before this, was how great a health risk pregnancy and childbirth were to a woman. Of course, when she watched movies set in the medieval times, there were many women who died in childbirth, but she thought that centuries later that had all been sorted out. It had not. There were still many women who experienced severe and sometimes even fatal complications of childbirth, and that risk went up exponentially when women went without proper medical care.

Maeve had now read dozens of stories about young girls who died in childbirth after being forced into a maternity home to work manual labor for free during their pregnancy. Because these institutions had to maintain a high level of discretion, these women were woefully under-cared for, left malnourished, and many died in childbirth due to lack of medical resources. There were children out there who would never get the chance to know their mother, because she was never given a chance to do everything, she could to protect the baby and herself from harm.

After hours of typing, Maeve pushed back in her chair and ran her fingers through her hair. She pulled out a piece of hay, which must have been there since she'd collected eggs this morning, lost in her own wild nest of curls. Her stomach was growling now, and she checked the time, it was already four o'clock in the afternoon. She'd missed breakfast and lunch. Maeve stood and stretched her body, her knees cracking from the cross-legged position she'd taken in her chair. She never could just sit at a desk chair and write, her feet didn't reach the ground to sit flat, so she'd adopted a different posture, sitting in some sort of pretzeled position in the chair. It was comfortable most of the time, but after hours like that, her knees ached.

Maeve walked into the bathroom and ran the tub, filling it with hot water. She picked up a little jar of bath salts that was sitting on the counter and sniffed, lavender and eucalyptus. She shook the jar gently, sprinkled some salts into the tub and inhaled the steam in the air around her. She grabbed a towel and padded back out to the bedroom to find a book, and then headed back into the steamy, spa-like bathroom before undressing. Maeve slipped gingerly into the claw-foot tub that overlooked the great expanse of farmland outside the house, letting the water come all the way up to her chin.

Maeve woke up with a start with an intense rapping at her door. After her bath, she had wrapped herself up in the white terry cloth robe that hung on the back of the bathroom door and laid down on the bed. She had intended to keep reading her mother's book she'd picked up earlier, but as soon as she laid down all bundled in her room, warm and relaxed from the tub, her eyes grew heavy. Maeve jumped up off the bed as the rapping continued and opened the door to find Colin on the other side of it.

"Are you all right?" he asked, his face concerned.

"Yes," Maeve said, rubbing her eyes, "is everything okay?"

"After you disappeared earlier and never came back down, I got worried," Colin said, scratching at the back of his head. The look of deep concern that was on his face a moment ago was shifting to embarrassment. "I heard the water running and then you never came down for dinner, and I just—"

"Oh god," Maeve said, understanding what he was trying to say, "I'm fine, really." She reached out to touch his arm. "I think that jet lag finally caught up to me."

Colin nodded. "Of course."

"Sorry about that," she said as he turned to leave.

Maeve grabbed his arm instinctively as he turned, and he looked down at her hand. Embarrassed, she let go. "Did you say I missed dinner?" she asked, sheepishly. She was starving now that she'd missed an entire day's worth of meals.

"You did, but I saved you some if you'd like to come eat," Colin replied with a smile.

"I would love to," Maeve said. "I'll just get changed and come right down." She pointed at her robe.

Colin nodded and gave her a little salute before turning on his heel and walking away. Despite the horrendous timing of all of this, Maeve felt a little flutter in her stomach at the thought of spending some more time with him. She shut the door and riffled through her suitcase, looking for something to slip on.

Colin was sitting at the head of the grand dining room table with a place setting and a plate of foot to the left of him. Maeve walked across the room, sat down in front of the meal and looked over at her host. She had smoothed her hair into a low bun that was pulled back tight from her face, highlighting her green eyes and cheekbones, and wore a comfortable but well-fitting cashmere sweater. She felt pretty, and the way Colin's gaze traveled over her body when she entered the room, she thought he did too.

"Thank you very much," she said graciously before inspecting her plate. While Maeve was not a picky eater, she didn't recognize some of the things on her plate and hoped for an explanation before digging in. "What's on the menu this evening?"

Colin grinned broadly. "This here is a Dublin coddle and soda bread, a classic Irish meal."

Maeve smiled politely, using her fork to poke at the mush and meat on her plate.

"Go on, try it," he urged expectantly.

"What's in it?" she asked, trying to stall.

"Mostly bacon, carrots, sausage, onion and potato. And a good hearty dash of Guinness for good measure," he said, that wicked grin spreading on his face. "Are you scared I'm trying to poison you?" he asked, feigning hurt.

"No, of course not." Maeve laughed. "I just wanted to know what I'm eating, is all." She used her fork to take a real bite this time, chewing slowly and deliberately. "Mm, this is pretty good," Maeve said, going for her second bite.

"That's because the carrots, onions and potatoes are from the garden," Colin said.

"I'm impressed," Maeve said, taking another bite. It was good, and now that she'd started eating, she realized just how hungry she'd been.

"Do you want to talk about what happened earlier?" Colin asked, leaning back in his chair.

"Not really, no," Maeve said, scooping another bite into her mouth so it was too full to speak.

Colin nodded and chewed on his lip, staying quiet for a moment before speaking again. "Are you in danger?" This time his grin was gone, and he looked her deep in the eyes, searching for an answer there if she wasn't going to tell him.

Maeve sighed and put her fork down, trying to decide how much to tell him. He'd been very kind, generous and forthcoming with her, and part of her felt like she should give him something, but after everything she was dealing with Ethan, she didn't want to feel like she owed him anything. Bringing him into the drama would just create the same dynamic she was trying to get herself out of. So, she had two choices: keep him in the dark completely or give him part of the truth and hope that was enough to keep him from prying further. She decided she would give him some of the facts for now, because she liked spending time with him.

"That was my ex. He's upset that I left. But he is harmless," Maeve said, paraphrasing the events of the last week or so quite succinctly.

"Ah, I'd assumed as much," Colin said, raising a brow. "Fresh breakup, then?"

"Fairly recent, yes," Maeve admitted, taking another bite.

"Judging by the last-minute booking, you just took off on him without letting him try to win you back?"

"Something like that, yes," Maeve nodded.

"Why here?" Colin asked.

"You were the only place that had availability," Maeve said as she wiped her mouth with her napkin.

"No, why Kildare?" said Colin.

Maeve squirmed in her seat; she wasn't comfortable with this line of questioning. She sighed and tried to turn the conversation back to him.

"Where did you grow up?"

Colin sat back in his seat and crossed his arms over his chest before answering. "About twenty minutes from here, this was my grandparents' house, as I mentioned, but we lived in a bigger city. Then I moved to Dublin for school and work."

"You said your wife taught at the school here. Did you move back here before she—" Maeve stopped herself before she said too much

"Before she died? Yeah. We met at uni, and she wanted to come back home, so I stayed in Dublin for a few years, and then I moved back here when we got married. Then I commuted into Dublin for work. After she died, I started working on the bed-and-breakfast and quit my day job." Colin stood and walked toward the large cabinet along the far wall of the room, then opened a glass cupboard and removing a bottle of whiskey. "Want one?"

"Sure," Maeve said with a shrug.

Colin poured them each a glass of Irish whiskey and handed one to her, setting the bottle on the table between them.

Maeve took a sip, and the liquor spread like a warmth through her body. A slow smile spread across her lips as she relaxed, and she allowed herself to take a good hard look at the man sitting beside her. He was very handsome. His broad and strong build filled the chair he sat back in, and that cheeky grin on his face was entirely disarming.

"What are you smiling about?" Colin asked, assessing Maeve right back.

"I think it's the whiskey," Maeve said with a giggle.

Colin laughed. "That will do it for sure," he said. "I found a car boot sale for us to go to tomorrow if you're still interested." He took a sip of his whiskey, watching her over the top of the glass.

Maeve's eyes lit up, "Yeah! Let's do it!" she said excitedly.

"Yeah?"

"Yeah, that will be fun," Maeve said, and took another sip.

"All right then, it's decided," Colin said with a smile. He finished his glass of whiskey, stood up from the table and collected the plates and glasses, "I have to get ready for tomorrow then. We'll leave after breakfast. Nine a.m."

Maeve stood as well, tucked the chairs in and followed Colin out of the dining room to the kitchen with her own plate and glass. She followed his lead and loaded her things into the dishwasher. When she stood up, she was looking right at his chest. She could smell the whiskey on his breath and see the pores on his skin. He was a good head taller than her, and he just smiled down at her as she stared back up at him. He placed two warm hands on her shoulders, looked down into her eyes and said, "You don't have to clean up. That's my job." He gently moved her out of the way so he could continue his practiced dance around the kitchen.

Embarrassed, Maeve stepped back toward the kitchen door. "Sorry, I'll just see you in the morning then."

Colin was squatting down at a low cabinet taking some large pan out from the bottom shelf. He looked up at her, surprised. "You can stay."

Maeve considered this for a moment. Every part of her body that was buzzing with whiskey wanted to remain in that kitchen close to him, but she didn't trust herself. "I need to get a bit more work done before I tuck in for the night," she said. "Thank you for dinner. It was delicious."

Colin stood up and wiped his hands on his jeans. "All right then. Nine a.m. tomorrow, be ready to go."

"I will." Maeve slipped out the swinging kitchen door and headed back up the stairs with a flutter of excitement growing inside of her.

22

Maeve woke early the next morning, settling into the time change. She had time to do a little work before heading down for breakfast, so she powered on her laptop to check her emails. As expected, there was an influx of messages waiting in her inbox, but there were only two that she was interested in. She was waiting to hear back from Natalie on her draft, and last night she had sent one more email off when she was restless and couldn't sleep.

After the incident with Ethan and then her private dinner with Colin, she'd almost forgotten why she was upset in the first place. But after she'd come up to go to bed last night, she laid restless in bed thinking about what she read in the back cover of her mother's debut novel: "A special thank-you to John Horner for all of his support over the years."

Surely it must a coincidence, she thought, but something was nagging at her to pursue it further. After she had learned that Orla, her foster mother, had really been her great-aunt and in contact with her mother for most of her life, she didn't quite trust that this could be a pure coincidence. Serendipity, maybe, but coincidence, no. She scanned her inbox and found the reply from Natalie first.

Maeve,

This is good. I don't want to get ahead of us here, but this could be big. I've made some notes and edits in my attached copy below.

Keep going, this is some good stuff.

Natalie

Maeve beamed with pride at the accolades from

her boss. Natalie was not generous with her praise, so this meant a lot. Her brief high was dulled, however, when she opened the file and saw that the entire document was marred with red lines. She sighed and filed the email away for later. She continued to skim the folder, searching for the familiar email address of Dr. John Horner. Maeve chewed on her lip as she scanned and scrolled, anxiously awaking his reply. There was nothing. She sat back in her chair and leaned it back all the way, so she was resting on the two hind legs before going into her Sent folder to reread the email she wrote last night.

Tipsy from the whiskey and little food all day, Maeve had worked up enough courage to ask this man flat-out over email if he knew her mother. While it seemed like the right thing to do last night, this morning her stomach sank as she reread the email.

Dear John,

I know this may be out of the blue, but I was wondering if you knew Fiona O'Toole, (née Grisham)?

Hope you're having a nice week. Let's set up a call for next week!

Maeve

Maeve groaned painfully at her brazenness. She gave the man no context and had just asked him, in the middle of the night, no less. If he was not, in fact, the same John Horner, he might see this for what it was: a drunk message. In that case, she would lose all credibility and his help for her story. However, if it was him, she hoped it would act as a catalyst for answers. She toyed with the idea of a follow-up message, an apology of sorts for the previous email, but decided against it. Instead, she shook off the embarrassment with a cold shower and got dressed for breakfast.

"Good morning, Maeve," Colin said with a grin as she walked into the dining room. He placed a large plate of bacon and sausage in the center of the dining table, which was set for eight, and there were three couples already enjoying their coffee and the beginnings of their breakfast.

"Good morning," Maeve replied, looking around for the coffee urn.

As if Colin could read her mind, he said, "The carafe's just in the den. I'll go fetch it for you."

"Oh, no, I'll get it," Maeve said, slipping back out the door toward the sitting room. She poured herself a mug and walked carefully back toward the dining room. Colin was standing and waiting for her when she returned.

"I'll introduce you to everyone before you can take your seat over there." Colin pointed to a seat at the head of the table, where he had sat last night. She noticed the only other seat unoccupied was at the foot of the table, traditionally where the two hosts sat. She found herself blushing for no reason, so she just nodded and looked around at the other guests of the house.

"Here we have George and Lisa Granger, they are here from Arkansas."

The couple nodded at Maeve and smiled politely. They looked to be in their mid-fifties and well dressed. Maeve was sure it was Lisa's perfume she could smell; she was polished top to bottom, with a full face of makeup on and a hair-sprayed chignon topping off her look. Maeve looked down at her own appearance, regretting not trying harder with her outfit today.

"Nice to meet you," Maeve said at the couple, before turning her attention to the next two in line.

"This is Gregory and Andreas, visiting us from Mykonos on their honeymoon," Colin said, and the two beautiful Greek men smiled at her with their perfectly white teeth. They were both tanned and muscular and really did look like gods.

"Nice to meet you," Maeve said, smiling back at the two beautiful men.

"And last but not least, we have Ling and Steve, visiting from San Francisco," Colin said. A petite Chinese American girl smiled and gave Maeve a finger wave, while her husband, Steve, who very much looked like Ling, worked in the tech sector gave Maeve a half smile, barely looking up from his plate.

"Hello," Maeve said, mostly at Ling.

"And everyone, this here is Maeve Grisham, visiting us from Canada."

Everyone muttered their welcomes and finally she sat down in her chair as they went back to their own private conversations. Maeve sipped her coffee and stole a quick glance at Colin, who was sitting at the opposite end of the table now, checking on a breakfast sausage with that grin plastered on his face. He was in his element here now, with everyone around.

Maeve wasn't sure if it was the air here or the jet lag, but she was starving. The spread Colin had put out for them was full of eggs and sausages, bacon and soda bread, and hand-churned butter. He said proudly that he had carefully grown the herbs and vegetables and selected local meats from farms nearby to give his guests a true farm-to-table experience. The man easily worked sixteen-hour days, and it was paying off. He had happy guests and did what he could to give them a full and authentic Irish experience.

After Maeve gorged herself on breakfast and the other guests retreated off to whatever they had on their agendas for the day, she helped Colin bring the dishes into the kitchen. Today he didn't tell her to stop, and they worked together to wash and dry everything and put it away. While she didn't particularly enjoy cooking or doing the dishes, she was just happy to be spending time with Colin. He had so many stories to share from guests who had stayed with him in the past, and the work went quickly as he told Maeve some of his favorite encounters.

"All right, we're all done here," Colin said, pulling out a picnic basket from the refrigerator. "I packed up some snacks for the road," he said, giving it a pat.

"You think of everything, don't you?" Maeve said.

"I try," he said. "All right, let's go, little lass."

Maeve followed Colin out the side door of the kitchen and back into that old rusty truck. They bumped along the dirt roads on their way to the mythical car boot sale.

"Oh my god," Maeve said as they pulled around a corner and the field full of cars came into view. This was no garage sale. It wasn't like anything she had ever seen before. It looked more to her like a fairground or music festival. There were rows of vehicles lined up ten across and twenty deep. Maeve could see why it was called a car boot sale, because every car had its trunk open, filled with goods for sale. It was like each one was a kiosk, selling anything from books to toy cars to cheese. People roamed up and down the rows smiling and haggling with each other to lower prices, then walked away with their arms full of goods.

Colin laughed beside her. "Not really a garage sale, as you call it."

"Not at all," Maeve said taking it all in, "I've never seen anything like it.

They wandered in silence for a while and stopped at the end of a row to get a cup of coffee from the back of a van. The man had two large carafes, and a jug of milk sat in the trunk of his car. He was charging one euro for a cup, and despite her hesitation, it was the best cup of coffee she'd ever had.

"Are you enjoying your stay so far?" Colin asked between sips.

"Very much so." Maeve's eyes couldn't quite meet his. They were too distracted by everything going on around them. "How do you have time for everything?" she mused out loud, still looking at the vendors. "You're renovating the place and running everything on your own every day and still sitting down for meals with the guests. I don't know how you do it."

Colin chuckled. "I love it. It gives me a sense of purpose, a reason to get up in the morning, you know?"

Maeve nodded.

"At first, I just needed something to focus on, to distract me. And then the more I got into it, I started to love the process, and it became all-consuming. Growing the vegetables, the chickens, making everything from scratch. It's all part of me now."

Maeve turned and looked at him.

He was staring wistfully off into the distance, as if he were finding the words to decide how he felt for the very first time.

"It was your rebirth after your wife died," Maeve said, understanding.

"Exactly," he said with a sad smile. "At first, I needed my space, and I had that when I was renovating. But then when the guests started to come, they filled the house again, and I had families and couples around from all over the world. I get to know all of these people who I never would have come across otherwise and hear their stories and learn about their lives. It's been therapeutic."

"I imagine that takes some getting used to." Maeve made a mental note to talk to the other guests at the next meal. She had been daydreaming this morning and had not made much of an effort.

"Having people around all the time?" Colin asked. Maeve nodded.

"Yeah, it can be overwhelming, but then when you all sit down for a meal together, gathered around the table, everything just shifts. People are laughing and eating and drinking and having a good time. It's hard not to enjoy it."

"It brings a different kind of energy to your day. I could feel that this morning," Maeve said.

"Exactly!" Colin said enthusiastically. "And people who choose to stay at a bed-and-breakfast are looking for that: the community element and the togetherness of the experience. So, most of the time, everyone is in good spirits."

Maeve reddened. She had never stayed at a bed-and-breakfast before, nor knew the etiquette when she booked her stay. She had naively booked the first available lodging she could find that included meals. "I'll admit, I didn't know about the group meals when I booked," Maeve said guiltily.

Colin feigned shock. "You're kidding!"

"You could tell?" She laughed.

That caused Colin to bark out a loud laugh. "Maeve, you have missed almost every meal since you arrived."

"Sorry," she said, wincing.

"Don't be, just try it. You'd be surprised."

"I'll make sure to be there for dinner tonight and get to know them," she said earnestly.

Colin nodded. "Good. Now, the more important question is, why are you here if you didn't come for an authentic bed-and-breakfast experience? We aren't really known for much else around these parts." He gave her a sideways glance.

Maeve sighed heavily, squinting off in the distance as they walked. "I came to find my mother," she said finally, and turned to meet his eyes.

23

Dinner was served at 6:00 p.m. sharp, with cocktails at 5:30 p.m. Tonight Maeve made an effort to dress up for the other guests. When she came downstairs, she took her place at the head of the table and said her hellos to George and Lisa, Gregory and Andreas, Ling and Steve. She felt awkward at first, anticipating the evening to go in the same manner as the writers networking events she'd attending while looking for a job years ago. A hundred introverts in a room desperately trying not to talk to anyone. But this, this was much different. Roundwood House came alive in the evening, and cocktails were served outside. The guests gathered at the back of the house near the herb garden. They stood on a little pea gravel path that had sparse garden furniture, and the breeze that blew by smelled amazing, offering wisps of sage, dill and thyme. Maeve had spent most of her time outside the house around the front where the chicken coop was and the large green expanse of grass, but she hadn't been back here, where the house appeared to be set higher up a hill than she'd noticed before, and they overlooked a pasture with cows and sheep and a little creek on a neighboring property.

Maeve sipped on her cocktail, listening to the other guests for a while. When the liquor worked its way through her system, she built up the courage to speak when there was a lull in the conversation. "So, what did everyone get up to today?"

Everyone turned to look at her, surprised. She flushed and almost ran away before Lisa spoke up. Just as this morning, her hair was perfectly coiffed, and tonight she wore a long flowing caftan that would have looked ridiculous on Maeve, but on Lisa it looked elegant.

"We went to see the Irish National Stud Farm and Japanese Gardens," she said with her thick Southern drawl.

"Ooooh, how was it?" Gregory asked. "We wanted to go."

"It was amazing," John piped in. "You can go see how they raise these racing horses. Very interesting," he said, nodding enthusiastically.

"Oh, yes, the horses are just gorgeous creatures," Lisa said, "and the Japanese Gardens were spectacular. A little oasis back there. You should definitely go before you leave." She gave Gregory and Andreas each their own little wink before she took another sip from her cup.

Maeve smiled and hung back, listening to the banter. She was starting to see why Colin liked having these people around.

Colin came back out at six o'clock sharp and guided them all back to the dining room for their meal. They took their places in the same seats as this morning, and after a quick speech from the host outlining tonight's meal, they all dug in. Maeve watched Colin as he seamlessly transitioned from one conversation to the next, at home here with these strangers he'd known for just a week. This cohort was leaving in the next few days, and Maeve wondered if the next group would get on with the same ease.

When dinner was finished, Maeve said her good-nights and slipped away upstairs to her room. After last night with Colin and their day trip earlier, she was practically a live nerve of emotions, and she needed some time to be alone with her feelings. Once she was tucked away in her room, Maeve pulled out her phone, guiltily checking to see if there were any messages from Ethan. Surprisingly, she had no missed calls or messages. Perhaps she had gotten through to him after all. With that taken care of, she turned her attention to her laptop next. While it was the middle of the night back home, she was still technically working and had a responsibility to her editor. The nice thing about being a journalist was you could work whenever and wherever you were. You weren't confined to the usual nine-to-five structure, but she'd admit she was pushing the boundaries right now.

Maeve worked away on her exposé, using all her feelings to guide her writing. The hurt, betrayal, guilt and lust she felt all came together to form powerful words on the page. The daunting edits Natalie had made earlier just added fuel to her process, and she worked until 3:00 a.m., writing from every fiber in her body. She was just about to give the piece a read-through when she heard the ding of an email in her inbox. She did the math and realized it would be 8:00 a.m. back home—working hours. She debated checking the email or leaving it, knowing once people realized she was available during working hours, she may never sleep. Ultimately, her curiosity got the best of her, and she clicked the little envelope icon and went to her inbox, scanning anxiously.

There it was a reply from Dr. John Horner. Maeve's heart thumped wildly in her chest. Her head shook as she tried to navigate her touch pad to click on the email, and she heard the blood swooshing in her ears as it rose to her face.

Maeve,

Nice to hear from you. I hope you are having a lovely time in Ireland. I think this conversation warrants a phone call. I have some time this morning if you would like to chat.

Let me know what works best for you.

John

Maeve ran to the bathroom and heaved herself over the toilet, vomiting up last night's cocktails and supper. She had been right. He did know her mother. She laid down on the cool tile, trying to regulate herself before working up the courage to message him back and set up a time to talk. She had questions, but there was so much unknown, she was just going to have to let him talk and hope he was forthcoming. Eventually, she peeled herself off the bathroom floor, brushed her teeth, splashed some cold water on her face and sat back down in her chair to face the email.

John,

I'm free now. I'll give you a call.

Maeve

She hit Send and reached for her phone, dialing the out-of-country extension. The phone rang its long droning ring. She almost hung up after the fourth one, realizing he might not have even seen the email yet, but just as she was about to put the phone down, the line clicked, and she heard his familiar voice on the other end of the line.

"Hello, Maeve," he said.

Maeve imagined him sitting in his office with his

kind smile and his round glasses perched on his nose. She took a deep breath before answering him. "Good morning, John."

"How is Ireland?" he asked, like this was just any old conversation between friends.

"It's been really nice, actually. I've been saying at a bed-and-breakfast." Maeve could feel the tension through the phone line, the silence creating even more space than the continent between them.

"Ah, lovely. Always a charming experience," he said.

Maeve was annoyed he wasn't saying anything, so she just jumped right in. "So, about my email ..."

John chuckled on the other end of the line. "Yes, let's get to it."

"Do you know Fiona O'Toole?" Maeve asked, holding her breath as she waited for his response.

"I do, yes," John said.

"How you know her?" Maeve asked. "I saw your name in the back of her book and wondered if you were the same John Horner she mentioned."

"That would be me," John said. "I met her when she was only seventeen, just a young girl visiting her aunt for the summer. She showed me her writing, and it was good! We have stayed in touch over the years, and I've helped her with her writing, and she'd given me feedback on mine."

"I see," Maeve said, waiting for more,

"You know now," he said assuredly.

Maeve frowned. "That she's my my mother? Yes." All the air rushed out of her like a balloon deflating. He had known who she was all along.

"I thought you knew that first time I met you," he said, and she imagined him sitting back in his seat, scratching his head. "You're the spitting image of her. But you never said anything and then I realized that you didn't know," he said.

"Why didn't you say anything?" Maeve asked, her voice cracking.

"It wasn't my story to tell, Maeve. I figured if you didn't know, there was a reason for it."

"Is that why you were helping me?" Maeve asked.

"Because you're Fiona's daughter? No. Well, yes … and no. I think it's an important thing that you're doing, and I wanted to support it. And I also felt connected to you because of Fiona … You really are so much alike."

"I've seen some pictures, it is a little spooky," Maeve laughed nervously.

"Is that why you're in Ireland?" he asked. "To try

and find Fiona?"

"Yes," Maeve said in a whisper.

"Ahhh," John said, and the line went quiet between them again. "Does she know you're there?"

"No," Maeve said. "I haven't gotten that far yet. I'm not sure how to approach it really."

"I see," John said.

Maeve was tired now and just wanted to get off the phone and go to sleep. She was exhausted from her all-nighter and the adrenaline from the last hour had worn off.

"Would you like me to put you in touch with her?" John asked.

"You'd do that?" Maeve said nervously.

"Of course. Why don't you let me reach out to her and let her know that you're there, and see if she's open to meeting you," John said, remaining neutral.

Maeve's heart sank at the realization that Fiona might not want to meet her after all this. "Okay, that sounds good," she said, trying to keep her voice sounding upbeat. "Thank you, John."

"Of course. Leave it with me," he said.

"All right, have a good day then," she said.

"You too," John said, and then hung up.

Maeve crawled into bed and turned off the light,

then sank into a deep sleep.

24

It had been a week since Maeve arrived in County
Kildare, and she was starting to settle in at the bed-
and-breakfast. The incessant calls and texts from
Ethan had ceased, and the last cohort of house guests
had just departed, leaving the main areas of the house
open for her to use as her own. She'd felt a great
weight of relief when she'd padded down the stairs
this morning and found the house quiet and empty.
It appeared that she had woken earlier than Colin this

morning when she went to grab a cup of coffee, and the urn was empty. She took it to the kitchen and washed it out, opening and closing cupboards to locate the ground beans. It was the only time she'd been in the kitchen alone, and she took her time, looking in the fridge and the shelves, getting to know where everything had its place. While she was enjoying her holiday, she did hope Colin might let her help out a bit if it was just the two of them now.

Maeve made herself at home in the den, pulling over a little side table to use as a makeshift desk and sat in the den alone with her laptop, working away with the warmth of the fire burning behind her, cutting the damp of the cool morning. She sipped her coffee as she toiled away at her exposé, deep in the editing process when Colin appeared in the doorway.

"You made coffee," he said, amused.

"I did," Maeve said, looking up from her screen to meet his grin with her own. "Come sit?" she asked hopefully.

"I'd love to, but I have to get to work, we have a new group coming in tomorrow morning."

"Oh," Maeve said, disappointed. Her fantasy of the two of them working together around the house vanished in an instant.

"The next group is only here for a couple of days," Colin said, sensing her shift in demeanor.

"It's great you're getting so much business." Maeve forced a smile.

"I agree," Colin replied enthusiastically, "I have to run to the shops, but I'll put some food out for you in the dining room before I go. Do you need a ride into town at all today?"

Maeve thought about that for a minute before accepting his offer. "Yeah, why don't I just come with you? I can grab breakfast in town." Maeve stood up.

"All right then," Colin said with a nod. "Be ready in ten. We have to get going before all the good meat's gone."

"Yes, sir," Maeve called to him as she ran up the stairs, taking them two at a time.

Maeve and Colin drove to town in silence. At first, she was worried that she'd down something wrong, because the normally chatty Colin didn't have much to say, but she soon understood that he had found a level of comfort with her that allowed him to be quiet around her. She kept stealing glances at him, trying to figure out what he was thinking about. His face was set in a look of concentration with his mouth in a hard line and his forehead creased, it was as if he was a different person than the easygoing man that ran Roundwood House. Now she saw another side of him, the thoughtful, pensive side that made decisions with care. She had already known he was all those things; she just hadn't seen them in action.

As they made the final turn into town and drove once again down Main Street with cobblestone sidewalks lined with beautiful old buildings.

Maeve's phone started buzzing in her purse. She lifted it out to check the caller ID and saw a number and an area code she didn't recognize. She hit Ignore and put it back in her bag. Within seconds the phone started to buzz again, that same number flashing across the screen.

"You can answer that," Colin said, looking over at her.

"I don't know who it is. I don't recognize the number," Maeve said," handing the phone to Colin so he could see.

"That's a local number."

"Oh," Maeve said, racking her brain for who might be calling her. She had called to make a reservation at the Japanese Gardens after George and Lisa recommended it, so she picked up, thinking it could be them confirming.

"Hello?"

"Hi," a female voice on the other line responded, distinctly Irish, as she'd suspected. "Is this Maeve Grisham?"

"It is," Maeve replied, pausing for the woman to continue. When silence hung in the air between them, she said, "May I ask who's calling?"

"Yes, sorry," the woman said, and she cleared her throat. "My name is Fiona O'Toole … John Horner gave me your number."

Maeve froze, unable to verbalize a response.

Colin looked over at her, concerned. "Are you okay?"

Maeve shook her head no, and she could feel the blood draining from her face.

"Who is it?" he asked, already on edge from the past phone call she'd received in his presence.

"It's my mother," Maeve whispered, holding her hand over the microphone.

Colin's eyebrows almost escaped his forehead they shot up so high. Maeve had explained to him why she came here in the first place and that she was here to try and find her mother. But she hadn't indulged with the details of who she was. She felt it would complicate things if she learned about her mother secondhand from an acquaintance versus experiencing it for herself and forming her own opinions.

"Are you going to say anything?" Colin whispered pointing at the phone.

"Right," Maeve said, holding the phone back up to her ear. "Sorry."

"That's all right. Is now a good time?" Fiona asked. Maeve could hear the initial confidence in her voice faltering.

"As good as any, I suppose," Maeve said cautiously.

"This is quite awkward, isn't it?" Fiona said.

Maeve let out a nervous laugh. "It is."

"I hope you don't mind me reaching out like this. When John contacted me and said you were here, I just didn't want to miss the opportunity to meet you."

"No, no. I'm glad you did," Maeve said. "In all honestly, I wasn't even sure when I came here that I was going to reach out to you. I just flew here on a day's notice I don't know what I thought I was going to do."

"Oh." Fiona said, sounding surprised.

"Yeah," Maeve said. That silence hung between them again. Colin had pulled over and parked the car and Maeve was grateful. The motion was making it hard for her to concentrate.

"Were you at the library the other day?" Fiona asked.

"I was," Maeve replied.

"Finn and Garret mentioned they saw someone who looked just like me, but I never expected it to be you," Fiona said. "The boys look so much like your dad."

"My dad?" Maeve sputtered, confused.

"Garret," Fiona said. "Yes, he's your father too."

"Oh," Maeve said, swallowing back a lump in her throat as she tried to work everything out in her mind. "I saw their picture online when I was looking for you. But it was quite a shock to run into them on my first day here."

"I can only imagine," Fiona said. "Would you like come round to our house for dinner this evening?" Fiona cleared her throat awkwardly. "Garret and I would love to properly meet you and get to know each other."

Maeve shot a look at Colin, who was very much eavesdropping but keeping his eyes on the road.

Maeve covered the mouthpiece with her hand. "They want me to come for dinner tonight," she whispered.

"Go!" Colin said in an enthusiastic whisper. "Go. That's why you're here. If it's a disaster, at least you can say you tried."

"Come with me?" she whispered with her hand still over the phone.

"Ehm." He paused and scratched his head. "Okay. Yeah, sure. The Dougals don't arrive until the morning anyways." He nodded as if trying to convince himself that was a good idea and waved her away back to her conversation.

"Dinner tonight sounds great," Maeve said cheerfully. "Do you mind if I bring a friend?"

"Not at all," Fiona said on the other end, almost sounding relieved.

They exchanged addressees and said a polite goodbye, planning to meet at 6:00 p.m.

Maeve put the phone in her lap and Colin looked at her expectantly. "All right, lass, we have some catching up to do here if I'm coming with you to meet your birth parents."

Maeve sighed and nodded her head. She owed Colin some answers. She explained to him the legislation changes in Canada and the connection she made with her foster mother just a few short weeks ago, and how she called off her wedding with only weeks left to come and search for her mother.

"So, that explains the crazy lad on the phone then," Colin said.

Maeve nodded, embarrassed. She told him how she spent days searching the internet trying to find them and located the family here, in Kildare. Colin didn't flinch when she explained that her mother was the famous author, Fiona O'Toole, and that's why she was so interested in the O'Toole boys that day at the library. And finally, she explained the strange connection she had made with John Horner, who was helping her on her exposé, and how he was ultimately the one to connect her with Fiona. Colin listened silently, nodding along, taking it all in as Maeve talked. Finally, when Maeve finished, he reached over and squeezed her leg.

"I had a feeling it was her," he said, completely unfazed.

"Really?" she asked, surprised.

"Yeah, after we ran into the O'Toole's and you were asking about them, I thought that was strange, and then when you told me at the car boot sale you came to find your mother, I realized why you looked so familiar."

"Because I look like her," Maeve said.

"Oh, yes, quite a lot actually," Colin said.

"If you don't want to come, I understand. Sorry for putting you on the spot like that," Maeve said, picking at the skin around her nails. She was already regretting not giving herself more time.

"No, I'm happy to come," Colin said reassuringly. "I just need to run my errands here, and then we can head back to the house."

Maeve nodded, and the two of them got out of the truck. "I think I'm going to head back to the library," she said.

"No problem. I'll come find you when I'm done," he said.

"Thanks, Colin," Maeve said with a sad smile, and she turned to walk up the hill toward the library in search of some answers.

Maeve was a wreck all day. She was anxiously pacing around Colin's old estate, unsure how to handle the impending meeting with her family. She started making lists of questions to ask them in her notebook to prepare, as she would for any other interview she was conducting.

Colin continued to toil away, making preparations for the Dougal family arrival and was setting up their rooms while Maeve was pacing around upstairs. She walked back and forth across the hallway, poking her head in and out of rooms, inspecting their progress, trying to distract herself.

"You all right?" Colin asked, appearing behind her with a concerned look on his face. "You seem fairly unsettled."

Maeve turned around, surprised, and blushed, embarrassed she'd been caught snooping. "Yes, sorry, I can't seem to sit still."

Colin put down the heap of sheets he held in his arms and grabbed Maeve's hand. Maeve froze at the gesture and heat shot into her chest. It was no doubt a platonic gesture, but she still felt the desire to hug him tightly.

"Follow me," he said, pulling her along the upstairs hallway and then around the corner to the other side of the construction zone. Maeve followed in step behind him with a curious excitement. They finally stopped when they were tucked into a far corner of the second floor that had a hidden set of steps.

"Where are we going?" Maeve asked with wide

eyes as she looked around. The steps wound up around a bend and out of sight. This old house offered never-ending surprises.

"Just wait and see," Colin said, and he raced up the steps two at a time, dragging her along with him. They ascended to a small landing with two closed doors off to one side and another narrow spiral staircase off to the right.

"This way," he said, holding on to the rails that lined either side of the staircase as he continued up. Maeve followed behind him, looking up to find they were going up a round tower. After a few corkscrew twists, they came to another landing with windows that offered a 360-degree view of the estate.

"Wow. This is incredible." Maeve walked slowly around the perimeter of the landing to take in the view from all angles.

"This is where I come when I feel overwhelmed," Colin said, leading Maeve to a windowsill. They were a foot deep, and he sat perched inside one, pointing out at the land surrounding them. "It helps to remind me that I am just a very small piece of this intricate work we call life."

Maeve looked out the arched tower window and could see rolling hills and neighboring estates for miles.

"This used to be the lookout tower. You can see all the way to town." Colin pointed out the Newbridge library on the hill, standing tall in the distance.

"Thank you for showing me this, Colin," Maeve said, turning to face him.

"I wanted to show you something else," he said, taking her shoulders gently in his hands and guiding her toward one of the windows. "See over there?" Colin pointed east.

Maeve looked but couldn't tell what he was trying to show her. She shook her head. "What am I looking for?"

He stood behind her, put his right arm under hers and led her arm in the right direction as a sight line for her eye to follow. At the end of her fingertips, she saw another estate similar in size and structure to Roundwood House. She could see that it had a pond and horse barn on its property.

"I see it now," she said, nodding. "What is it?"

"That," Colin said quietly, "is your grandparents' house."

Maeve turned around to look at Colin, overcome by emotion as tears welled in her eyes, and one escaped down her cheek.

Colin used his thumb to wipe away her falling tear. "You can do this, and I'll be right here with you along the way. You came to Ireland for answers, right?"

"I did," Maeve said, wiping her nose with her sleeve like a child.

"Well, in my experience, that means that you're going to find them, good or bad. But that's all part of the adventure," Colin said.

"Thanks, Colin. This is all really very kind of you." Maeve sniffed. "I don't know why you're being so nice to me," she said with a forced laugh.

"I like you, Maeve," Colin said frankly. He searched her eyes with his and cupped her cheek with his hand. She leaned into his hand with her face, relaxing into his touch.

"I like you too," she whispered guiltily.

25

It was time to meet her parents. Maeve had spent the better part of two hours deciding on an outfit and doing her hair to get ready to attend the most important meeting of her life. She showered and washed her hair, then blow-dried her curly mane into a polished straight style. She put on one of the only two dresses she'd packed and spent twenty minutes carefully applying makeup. She checked herself over carefully in the mirror, hardly recognizing the polished woman she saw infant of her. Maeve got dressed up only a handful of times a year, and this version of herself was saved for special occasions and today was just that. The sleek hair and painted-on face also gave her an extra ounce of confidence, which she desperately needed.

At 5:30 p.m. sharp, Maeve and Colin got in his old pickup truck and headed one town over to Kildare. Before getting in, Colin laid a towel down on Maeve's seat to protect her outfit from the dust and debris his truck had collected from being a hardworking vehicle.

"You look lovely," Colin said while helping Maeve into the truck.

"Thank you." She blushed. "Admittedly, I'm nervous," she said, giving him a sheepish look.

"Rightfully so, but it's them who should be nervous," Colin said with a very serious look. "They're the ones who have to face the one they lost and see how wonderful she turned out."

Maeve swallowed a lump in her throat, unsure what to do with his kind words. Naturally, she diverted back to him again. "I noticed another car in the back barn. What's that one for?" When she was out walking the other day, she'd spied a high-end sedan with leather seats that looked a lot cleaner than this truck.

Colin slid her a sideways glance. "That's Delly. She was my car before I moved out here. While technically she still works, I just feel like this truck suits me better now."

Colin looked to be somewhere faraway, and Maeve suspected there was more to the story, but it wasn't the right time to push him. Silence bloomed like a cloud between them, and finally Colin put some music on to soften the awkwardness.

They drove down country roads for a while, like the one that Roundwood House and her grandparents' estates sat on. The roads were narrow and paved and lined with rolling green pastures before entering a quiet suburban area. The homes sat on large lots that reminded her more of neighborhoods from back home than she'd imaged she would see here. While there were no sidewalks, there were sprawling yards with manicured lawns and parks for children to play in. Colin turned left and then took a right, driving slowly down the quiet streets, taking his time as he approached the O'Toole's' home.

"Ready?" he asked Maeve as he pulled in the

driveway and turned off the ignition.

She looked over at him, almost surprised to hear his voice. She had been far away in a daydream, trying to prepare herself for the evening. "I'm ready," Maeve said, nodding toward Colin as she got out of the car.

Before they had a chance to make it up the steps of the house, the front door swung open. Garret and Fiona stood in the doorframe with their arms wrapped around each other, smiling. "Come in!" they said cheerfully.

Maeve stood still for a moment too long. Her eyes were fixed on the woman she'd longed to meet her entire life. Their faces were so similar, but she could spot the differences, and not just those that came with age. They had the same hair, the same softness to their features that made them approachable, but bright and sparkling eyes. Fiona was trim and fit with an athletic body, but Maeve suspected she was a few inches taller than her mother, likely due to her father's size. Garret stood flanking Fiona, towering over her. Maeve shifted her gaze up to his face for a moment, seeing things she'd missed the first time she saw him. She hadn't known he was her father, but now that she knew, she searched his face for a likeness to her own. Maeve's eyes were the same almond shape, and they shared a singular dimple on the right cheek. And while she shared most features with her mother, she could see herself in him now too. Fiona wore a silk blouse that hung perfectly on her figure with a pair of designer jeans. While she looked casual, she did so in a way a celebrity might in a home magazine shoot.

Colin gave Maeve a little nudge, and she took a step forward making her way to her parents. As they moved closer Maeve could smell her Chanel No. 5, a statement scent for a classic beauty.

There was a collective pause as the four of them stood face-to-face on the porch. Normally this would be the time to hug the person you'd come to see, but an embrace didn't feel right for any of them.

"Shall we?" Colin finally said, breaking the tension as he nodded to the door.

"Please come in," Garret said, relieved, stepping aside to let them into the house.

Colin and Maeve followed her parents inside. Maeve was struck by the opposition in the modern architecture and design in the O'Toole house to the traditional and historic buildings she had become accustomed to as part of her stay here in Ireland. It felt almost out of place to the ideation of the Irish life she'd experienced thus far at Roundwood House.

"Has Mr. Walsh been taking good care of you while you've been here?" Garret asked with a kind smile.

"He has," Maeve said, returning a smile. She couldn't help noticing how similar their mouths were. "Roundwood House is lovely. Colin's already put me to work in the henhouse though. I wasn't aware I'd have to work for my meals," Maeve teased, and they all laughed.

"Good, that will give you a taste of the country life we had growing up around here," Garret said, smiling at Fiona.

"Why don't we all go around to the sitting room and have a drink?" Fiona suggested with a gentle smile.

"That sounds like a great idea," Maeve said.

Maeve could feel Fiona keeping herself at a distance while trying to remain a polite hostess. While it bothered Maeve that she hadn't hugged her when she'd arrived, she made a mental note to try and be compassionate with these people, as hard as that may be. She didn't know their story yet. Her journalist's brain was working overtime reading body language and taking in everything around her, while her emotional brain was firing off feelings as a response to it all.

As they walked through the kitchen into the sitting room, a freshly baked loaf of bread on the counter caused more envy than she'd expected. Here they were her parents. They were kind, caring and compassionate people who had a love that stood the test of time. They were both independently successful, but she could tell they spent a lot of time at home and with their children. Maeve was angry that she had been robbed of such an idyllic childhood.

They all took their respective seats around the coffee table, and Maeve waited expectantly for her parents to lead the conversation.

"This must be hard for you," Fiona said, watching Maeve with deep guilt in her eyes. "We always wanted you, Maeve. The timing was just never right for us to bring you home."

"What do you mean?" Maeve asked, desperate for someone to just lay it all out on the table for her. All this cloak-and-dagger information mixed with Orla's untrustworthy account of the matter had Maeve all turned around.

"Oh dear, I don't know where to start. There's

twenty-five years to cover, isn't there?" Fiona said with a distant look in her eyes. "We would love to learn about you, Maeve, what your life has been like, who you are as a person. If you're open to sharing of course." Her gentleness and warmth released a wave of gut-wrenching hurt from Maeve, who had been holding it together for so long now. She started crying big fat tears that rolled down her face, allowing the tension to leave her body.

"I don't know if I'm ready for that yet," Maeve said, wiping at her face with her hand.

Garret passed her a tissue box from across the coffee table.

"That's all right. We understand," Fiona said, nodding politely, like they were working through a negotiation of sorts. "I'm sure you haven't come all this way without a list of questions prepared. Why don't we skip the small talk then, and you can get to asking." Fiona righted herself in her seat, leaning back in her chair with a straight spine, hands folded in her lap. Maeve watched her, fixating on her movements. She not only saw herself in this particular body language, but it reminded her more than anything of Orla.

Maeve caught Colin glancing between the two

women, waiting for the dam to break. Everyone was being so polite; it was bound to get messy soon. The Irish were not known for being fair-tempered, and Maeve was no exception to the rule.

"Yeah, sure," Maeve said with an exhale. She thought she might feel more comfortable in her element anyways. Now that the ball was in her court, she was able to put on her journalist's hat and try and shut out her emotional brain. She decided to play this like she would any other interview and offer an easy question first to get Fiona and Garret comfortable with opening up. "So, how did you two meet?" she asked, looking between Fiona and Garret.

"Oh," Fiona said, smiling over at Garret. "Well, when I was in fifth year, Garret and his family moved to Newbridge from Dublin, and he transferred to my school, Newbridge Secondary. You might have seen it when you were in town yesterday. The boys go there now."

"I did," Maeve said, forcing a smile. She prayed her demeanor put them at ease to continue organically.

"I grew up here, but the towns in County Kildare are small, and the coed secondary school my siblings and I attended was in Newbridge, so I took the bus in each day. When Garret came to our school, I was fourteen, and he was … seventeen?" Fiona looked over at Garret to confirm. He nodded and she continued. "We just kept eyeing each other in the halls for weeks, until he got the nerve to say hello one day. I was already pretty smitten with him at that point, so I offered to show him around."

Garret jumped in next. "That library I saw you at the other day?"

Maeve nodded.

"That was the first place your mother took me, and it became our weekly meeting spot. So, you can imagine my surprise when I saw you standing on the steps. I felt like I'd been transported back in time."

"That must have given you quite a start." Maeve laughed. She found herself relaxing enough to enjoy the story at face value.

"Aye, it did." Garret laughed. "Finn too. He was already a bit shook up after seeing you inside. The boys knew they had a sister in Canada who they had never met, so when he saw you, he suspected who you might be. He's a shy lad though, never would have said anything."

Fiona nodded in agreement and Maeve felt a pang seeing her parents speak with such knowing about their son.

"The boys are excited to properly meet you as well. We just thought we'd wait until we spent some time with you first," Fiona said.

"I understand," Maeve said, brushing that off. She tried to switch gears by asking another question. "I'm guessing it wasn't a planned pregnancy?"

They both laughed nervously again. "Ah, no, that was quite a shock to us both. You have to understand, the Irish Catholic community wasn't well informed about birth control back then. I come from a family of eight kids myself," Fiona said. "You were not meant to be intimate with anyone but your husband, and I knew that, but we were in love and made some decisions when we were much too young. And those decisions led us to you."

"What happened when you told your parents?" Maeve asked, trying to look past this perfect woman sitting in front of her and see her as a scared young teenager who made a bad decision and now was left with a lifetime of consequences.

"Well, that didn't go very well, as you can imagine," Garret said. He and Fiona shared a look. "In the long run, everything was okay, but at the time there was a lot of tension between our families. I was older than your mother, so a lot of blame was put on me by her parents, who didn't want me anywhere near your mother. And my parents, as their only child, wanted to see me follow my plan and be successful, not be a teenage father."

"There were a lot of tense conversations for many months about what we were going to do," Fiona said. "Luckily I was able to conceal the pregnancy for a long while and stay in school for the majority of the year." Fiona paused and glanced at Maeve's torso. "I'm sure if you have children one day, you'll be the same."

Maeve offered an awkward smile in return, and Fiona continued. "But my parents did not want anyone finding out about my pregnancy and offered me no choice to keep the baby." Fiona picked at the skin around her nails nervously, the same habit Maeve shared.

"Ah, yes, a child is considered a minor for medical and legal purposes in Ireland until they are eighteen. Fiona had no choice in the matter—what was happening to her or the baby," Garret said before catching himself. "What was happening to you."

Maeve's stomach twisted, remembering she was a part of this story too.

"That was very hard on us both. We started to

envision our life together as a family," he said. It was Garret now who had tears in his eyes.

"Then one day I woke up, and my belly was too big to hide. I couldn't go to school," Fiona said, touching her stomach absentmindedly. "I came downstairs, and my mother told me she had made arrangements for me to go and live with her older sister, Orla, in Canada and I was leaving almost immediately. Within a few days I was shipped off to go hide out for the remainder of my pregnancy while my parents told all our family and friends that I was doing a 'summer abroad.'" Fiona used her fingers to make air quotes.

"That must have been very painful," Maeve said sadly. She felt some of the resentment she'd been carrying around slip away as these people sat in front of her, clearly still hurting from what they experienced twenty-five years before, even with the happy ending they'd created for themselves.

"It was. And then when you came, Maeve, and you were so beautiful …" Fiona was crying now, and Garret reached over to hold his hand in hers. "I couldn't leave you," she said, her voice catching on a tiny sob.

"It's true," Garret said, looking at Maeve. "I flew

over when you were born, because your mother wouldn't give you up, and she wouldn't come home. She brought you to Orla's and wouldn't leave. The entire pregnancy, she wouldn't talk to any adoption agencies or even have a conversation about it. She wanted to keep you even though she knew we couldn't. I had been saving up all summer so I could bring Fiona home, but she wouldn't come back with me. She wouldn't leave you." Garret squeezed Fiona's hand and added, "I had to go back for university. I had a scholarship, and they wouldn't defer it."

"You had tufts of bright copper hair that stuck up all over your head. It was so cute," Fiona said, wiping at her eyes, "and the milkiest skin. You were a dream come true." Fiona smiled at her daughter with this tender confession. Despite the vulnerability, she stayed seated across the room with a table between them to make sure no lines were crossed today. "I stayed for six months after you were born, wonderfully immersed in the newborn bubble with Orla by my side. And then one day the bubble popped, and my parents insisted I come home and finish secondary school in Ireland." Fiona looked off in the distance and chewed nervously at her lips, still upset with the decision that was made on her behalf.

"And I stayed with Orla," Maeve said, filling in the pieces.

Fiona nodded. "She was ready to retire. Orla had never married or had kids of her own, and she fell in love with you too. She said she would keep you until I was ready to come back and get you after I'd finished my schooling."

"And then what happened?" Maeve was on the edge of her seat now, losing the professional composure that had kept her steady this whole time.

"And then you lived with Orla, who loved you dearly and gave you a beautiful life. You were thriving. You excelled at sports, academics, you had friends. She would send us pictures and letters almost weekly, filling us in on your progress and achievements. By the time I had finished university, you were eight years old. I didn't think it was fair to come pluck you from your life and move you to another country."

"Your mother and I also took a relationship break for a few years after everything we had gone through," Garret said. "We needed time and space to heal from all of it separately. Eventually we found our way back to each other." Garret squeezed Fiona's hand, and she nodded.

"When we heard what was happening with Orla a few years later, Garret and I had just gotten married. We knew the right thing to do was bring you home then, and we started to make plans for you to come and live with us."

Maeve was teary as she heard her parents recount the story that Orla had been unable to continue. "Why didn't I come?" she asked impatiently. She was reliving the pain of being taken out of her home and placed in state care over and over again for two years until she settled in the Clarkes' home.

Fiona inhaled sharply. "Because I left the country when you were an infant, I technically surrendered you to the government. Orla had taken the role as your foster mother with the intention of us one day being reunited." Fiona paused, trying to find the right words, clearly still riddled with guilt. "Once she lost the ability to be her own medical and legal proxy, she could no longer be yours, so we lost any chance of getting you back as a minor."

"Fiona felt sick about it," Garret said reassuringly. "We should have gone back for you sooner, but there was nothing we could do."

"We tried for years, and then we found out you had

moved in with a lovely family and we stopped trying. We didn't want to take you out of a safe place and move you again after being moved all over," Fiona said sadly.

"So, you knew where I was this whole time?" Maeve said, standing. She was fuming and could feel physical heat rising off her chest, unable to sit calmly with this news anymore. "You knew exactly where I was and how I was doing, and you did ... nothing?"

"Not nothing, Maeve," Garret said sternly, trying to protect his wife. "We tried very hard, but there were forces we could not fight against that were in the way. We thought you'd been through enough, and when you were old enough and ready, you could find us, if that's what you wanted to do."

"We tried to give you the best chance of a good life with the information and tools we had at the time," Fiona said sadly, knowing this wasn't what Maeve wanted to hear.

"I think need to leave now," Maeve said, looking over at Colin, who had sat there silently this entire time.

"I'll go start the truck," Colin said, standing up and slipping away out through the kitchen.

"We'd love to see you again when you're ready,"

Fiona said, standing to face Maeve. She was calm and looked sad, like Maeve had disappointed her in some way. "Garret, can you go get the trunk for Maeve?"

Garret nodded and disappeared down the stairs to the basement, returning a few minutes later with a large trunk.

"We saved all your baby stuff, and letters from Orla if you'd like to look through them," Fiona said, gesturing at it.

"Oh," Maeve said, looking at her mother, embarrassed now by her outburst. "Yes, I'd like that. Thank you," Maeve put her shoes on. She stood awkwardly on the front mat, waiting for this to be over. "I'm sorry. This is all just so much at once," Maeve said, rubbing at her temples.

Fiona put a hand on Maeve's shoulder. "It is for us too. But we are here and so happy to finally meet you. We would love to try this again if you're up for it." Fiona searched Maeve's eyes for a flicker of hope.

"Okay," Maeve said.

Garret came up the stairs with the trunk and signaled to Colin, who came back from the truck to retrieve it for her. Colin loaded the trunk into the bed of the truck as Maeve said her goodbyes, feeling her parents hug for the first time … and possibly the last.

26

Colin carried the trunk up the stairs to Maeve's room and placed it at the foot of her bed. "Do you want to talk about it?" he asked, searching her face for answers.

"I don't know if I do. I haven't made sense of what I think, to be honest," Maeve replied.

Colin nodded. "Shall I leave you to go through your trunk then?" She picked up a hint of disappointment in his tone.

"I don't think I'm ready for that either." Maeve sighed, raking her fingers through her hair.

"A drink then," Colin said, deciding for her. "Come on now," he said as he grabbed her hand and led her downstairs.

"All right, twist my arm," Maeve said, laughing, glad for someone else to take the lead. She couldn't be left with her own feelings right now. They were too fresh. Too raw.

"Go sit in the den, I'll be back with drinks and food," he said.

Maeve's stomach grumbled, announcing that she was starving. She hadn't eaten all day due to nerves, and then they had left her parents' house before the promised meal.

Colin came back a few moments later with two plates full of chicken, potatoes and green beans and a gravy boat hanging off his pinky. Tucked under his right arm was a bottle of red wine, and under his left, a bottle of whiskey.

"What's all this?" Maeve laughed at the sight of him.

"Well, I had an inkling we wouldn't make it to dinner, and you didn't eat all day, so I prepared this before we left just in case," Colin said, and it almost looked like he was blushing.

"Well, that was very thoughtful of you, and you read me like a book." Maeve rested her hand on his knee. "Thank you."

"Of course. You're my guest after all. It's my job to feed you," he said, brushing it off. "Wine or whiskey?" Colin asked, holding up a bottle in each of his hands.

"Both?" Maeve asked, grinning, and Colin laughed, rolling his eyes at her.

"I didn't realize Canadians were as drunk as the Irish," he joked.

"It's in my blood, remember?" she said with a shrug.

"Oh, hold on. I'll be right back!" Colin said, then placed everything neatly on the coffee table and disappeared back into the kitchen.

Moments later he reemerged with cutlery, napkins and glasses for both wine and whiskey. He set the places neatly beside one another and poured them each two drinks. A tumbler of whiskey and a glass of wine.

When he was set, Colin raised his wineglass toward Maeve. "Sláinte," he said with a nod.

Maeve and Colin sat around for hours drinking and eating. She felt warm from the buzz of the mixed alcohols combining in her bloodstream, causing a smile to slip across her lips. She felt at ease here with Colin despite the turbulence of the day. As they talked, Maeve learned that Colin was thirty-three, eight years older than Maeve. In those extra years lived, he had quite a few stories to tell that made Maeve laugh and cry and want to curl up onto his lap and listen all night. He told her stories about his early years in the accounting firm, his post-university backpacking travel, and his nieces and nephews, who he loved very much. The later it got, the more Maeve wanted the night to stretch on forever.

"How long are the Dougals staying?" Maeve asked, wondering when they would get to be here alone in this big house again.

"They're just here for two nights, then it's just you and me for a while," Colin said locking eyes with her.

He leaned across the table to grab the bottle of whiskey, and his hand brushed the sensitive part of her inner thigh just above her knee. Maeve felt a spark shoot up through her groin that sent her heart into a flutter. She looked around for a clock, trying to get out of here before she did something she would later regret. It was half past midnight, a reasonable time to slip back to her room alone.

"Oh my, it's late," Maeve said awkwardly, feigning a yawn.

Colin looked up from his glass, surprised. "Ah, it is," he said after turning to glance at the clock behind him. "The night slipped away from us."

"I should probably be getting to bed," Maeve said, standing up with a slight wobble.

Colin stood with her. "Let me make sure you get up the stairs all right," he said, slipping an arm around her waist to steady her. He held her firmly all the way up the stairs until they reached her bedroom door.

Maeve turned to face him, and he was standing so close that her body pressed against his. "Thank you for everything you did today, it was more kindness than I deserve from … I mean I'm just a guest. You have hundreds of us …" Maeve's voice trailed off.

"It was my pleasure," he said, tilting his head down so their foreheads touched, "and after today I wouldn't consider you just another guest," he said, slipping his arms around the lower part of her back.

Maeve tilted her chin up and pressed her lips against his. She let out a small unfamiliar noise as she did. Her whole body reacted as they stood entwined, and she kissed him deeper. Colin's hands slipped from around her waist up to her face, cupping it between them. Maeve slipped her hands around his back and under his shirt in response, feeling his skin hot against her hands. They kissed with a hunger she had not felt before, like every neuron in her body was firing and heat rushed through her, edging her on further.

"Let's go inside," Maeve said in between kisses as her back pressed up against her bedroom door. The handle was digging into her spine, but she didn't want this to stop.

"Are you sure?" Colin asked, moving from her mouth down her neck.

She let out another little moan. "I'm sure," she said.

In one swift motion, Colin hoisted her up with one arm as he opened the door with the other. Maeve wrapped her legs around his waist as he carried her into the room and threw her onto her bed. Colin climbed on top of her, kissing her from her head all the way to her toes, finding every bit of bare skin as he removed her clothes.

Maeve awoke to that familiar buzzing of her phone

beside her head and reached for it with one eye open. Ethan again. Maeve rubbed her eyes and sat up to see Colin sleeping soundly beside her. Her heart flipped over in her chest as she replayed last night. Maeve pulled back the covers and tiptoed out of the room, shutting the door quietly behind her.

"Ethan, you have to stop calling," Maeve said when she answered the phone. It rang twice in a row, and had it not been 2 o'clock in the morning back home, she would have been worried, but she knew this was most likely a drunk dial.

"Maeve you have to talk to me," Ethan said tearfully.

"I don't and you're drunk. Go to bed," Maeve said, and hung up. She opened her bedroom door back up, trying to sneak in quietly. Colin was awake, propped up on a heap of pillows with his hands behind his head.

"Who were you arguing with?" Colin asked, head cocked in concern.

"Oh, uh, no, no one," Maeve lied, trying to brush off the call.

Colin shot her a look that said, *Bullshit*, and she knew she needed to be honest with him now or lose his trust.

Maeve walked over and sat on the edge of the bed. "I haven't been totally honest with you, Colin," she said, biting the skin around her nails.

"What do you mean?" Colin said, sitting more upright so that the covers fell to his waist, revealing his bare chest. His brows knit together with concern.

"I wasn't honest with you about how recently I broke off my engagement." Her words hung in the air between them as Colin nodded slowly, seeming to understand.

"I figured as much when he called the other day."

Maeve reddened with embarrassment.

"When did you split?" he asked, his tone remaining calm.

"The day before I left for Ireland," Maeve said, keeping her eyes fixed on her hands. She tossed the phone back and forth between her palms nervously.

"When were you supposed to get married?" Colin asked, his tone cooling.

"In a few weeks," Maeve whispered, ashamed.

Colin blew out a long exhale and rubbed his eyes. "For fucks sake, Maeve."

"I know." Maeve was sweating now, the alcohol from last night seeping out of her pores fragrantly.

"Do you love him?" Colin asked, trying to make

sense of all this.

"I did, but I don't anymore," Maeve said, surprising herself with her honesty.

Colin stood up to get dressed, finding his clothes strewn around the room. "I'm going to go take a shower," he said, then walked out the door past Maeve without so much as a touch on the shoulder.

"Okay," she whispered after him, the intoxication of last night's tryst turning into a red-hot anxiety.

27

Maeve came downstairs for coffee an hour later, last night a mix of emotions wreaking havoc on her stomach. She could smell the coffee and bacon as she reached the bottom of the stairs, and she followed the scent into the dining room. Coffee was brewed, breakfast was made, and Colin was nowhere to be found. As Maeve poured her coffee, she saw a corner of a note sticking out from under the breadbasket. She pulled at it to reveal a note Colin had left for her.

Maeve,

Had to run out and do some errands.

Colin

Maeve's heart sank in her chest. She really wanted to talk to Colin about this more. Although she'd only known him for a short time, there was a strong sense of connection, and a deep pull toward him that she felt even when he was across the room. She was truly comfortable with Colin, something that didn't come easily to her. She had only felt that way when she was alone and let her guard down after a long day of protecting herself. While Ethan and the Clarke family offered a sense of security, there was no peace when they were around. When Colin was there, she felt it. Like he was just meant to be with her. Maeve feared that she'd just ruined any chance of something more between them now.

The day dragged on while Colin was out doing errands in preparation for the next family to arrive. Maeve wandered through most of the estate, taking everything in in detail, as she hadn't been able to do with others around. When her stomach started to rumble, she checked the clock. It was 2:00 p.m. and Colin was still gone. Maeve found her way to the kitchen and poked through the drawers and cupboards for snacks, tucking a box of crackers under her arm. In the fridge she found a block of cheese and some chicken salad. She carried her findings back to the large dining room table, meant for all guests to share a meal family style, and spread out her provisions. Meticulously creating uniform bites with a bit of cheese and chicken salad towered on each cracker, Maeve sat there so focused she didn't hear when someone came in the room behind her.

Maeve jumped in her seat when she felt hand on her shoulder. Expecting to see Colin, Maeve's face drained of color when she turned around to see Ethan standing in front of her.

"What are you doing here?" Maeve asked, her tone flecked with annoyance and concern.

"I just wanted to talk. I've been trying to call you," Ethan said, trying to reach for her hand.

Maeve pulled it away, standing to face him. "Ethan, this is not okay." She took a step back from him, feeling slightly frightened by his unexpected appearance.

"Please, Maeve. I understand why you came, but you have to realize how hard this is for me. You left and called off our wedding. Do you have any idea what these past few days have been like for me trying to explain this to my family and friends?" Ethan said, pleading with her. He looked like a wreck. He had black crescent moons under his eyes, like he hadn't slept and had been drinking heavily since she left. He was making every effort to show her that he cared and wanted to work this all out, but all Maeve could think about was getting Ethan out of here before Colin came back.

"How did you even find me?" Maeve asked, and the hair on the back of her neck stood up.

"I told you, the credit card statements," Ethan said defensively.

"But how did you know I'd be here right now?" she asked accusingly, looking him in the eyes now.

Ethan went red and rubbed his neck, fidgeting. "Uh, the tracker on your phone. It shows your location."

"I turned off my location sharing," Maeve said, crossing her arms over her chest.

"I know. Since that's my old phone, I turned on Find My Phone from my laptop," he confessed, looking at his feet. "I was worried about you. You just left."

"You know that's insane, right?" Maeve yelled at

him. She was angry now. "You need to leave!"

"I just came all this way to talk to you, Maeve! I'm not leaving," Ethan said. He crossed his arms over his chest and widened his stance, punctuating his seriousness.

"Yes, you are," Maeve said, grabbing his elbow and giving it a tug, trying to guide him back to the entryway. "You don't just get to show up, barge in here and tell me what to do. That's over, Ethan. We are over, and this conversation did not need to take place on another continent. Go home."

"Maeve, please!" Ethan yelled, grabbing her arms tight in his fists.

"Get your hands off her" came a voice from behind them.

Maeve turned her head, her arms still stuck in Ethan's grasp.

"Who the fuck are you?" Ethan asked with a scowl. "This is my fiancé."

"No, I'm not," Maeve said, shrugging out of his grasp and moving toward Colin.

"You heard the lady. I'd suggest you get off my property before I call the Garda," Colin said, standing in front of Maeve.

"I'm not leaving without her," Ethan said,

practically spitting his words.

"Ethan, leave. Now. You never should have come," Maeve said from behind Colin, afraid of what was going to happen next.

Ethan took a step forward to grab her again, and Colin put his arm out in front of Ethan's chest to stop him. "That's enough now. Carry on and get out of here."

Ethan pushed Colin with two hands, and Colin took a swing in defense, hitting Ethan in the jaw. Ethan staggered backward from the blow as rage flashed in his eyes. When he regained balance, he lunged toward Colin again in retaliation.

Colin cocked his head, amused. "I wouldn't do that, bud. Leave now, and I won't call the Garda. Come at me again and you'll be in an Irish cell for the weekend."

That shut Ethan down pretty fast as he grumbled obscenities as he backed away, opening the door. "You're going to regret this, Maeve," he said, attempting to get the last word in.

"Is that a threat?" Maeve retorted and Colin put his hand out to quiet her.

They watched as he walked away and got into his rental car, then drove off down the long gravel road.

When he was out of sight, Colin asked, "Should I call the police? Has he hurt you before?" Colin's brows were twisted in concern, searching Maeve's face for hints at what life was like back home with that man.

"No, never," Maeve said, looking down at her hands, which were now shaking. "This is honestly so out of character for him, he's not really one to go the extra mile. I think he's really upset," she said as a surge of guilt shot through her stomach.

"Yeah, I'd be too if I lost you right before our wedding," Colin said, giving Maeve a look that made her feel even worse for what she'd done to Ethan, and for not being honest with Colin. "I expect he'll be back tomorrow, so you might want to figure out how you want to handle … that." Colin gestured flippantly at the door and walked toward the kitchen.

Maeve followed him, shaken and more concerned about Colin's feelings than her partner of ten long years. "Are you mad?" she asked, too impatient to let any more time pass between them without talking about last night or this morning.

"Wouldn't you be?" Colin said, looking Maeve in the eyes.

"I'm sorry," Maeve said, casting her eyes to her

feet. "It didn't feel right to unload more on you after you'd been so kind already, and then everything happened so fast last night …"

"Clearly this is still fresh and resolving itself," Colin said dismissively. He started toward the door, trying to create space between them.

"I know. I'm sorry," Maeve said, following behind him.

Colin turned around and put his hand out, motioning her to stop. "Look, I like you, Maeve, but I think it's best we keep things professional for now. This is my place of business after all, and I need to treat it as such," he said firmly. He crossed his arms over his chest. It was decided. He slipped away into the kitchen, leaving her standing alone in the hallway, not sure what to do next.

Colin was right. Ethan did show up the next day and the next day and the next. Every morning, he would show up on the front steps like a stray dog leaving gifts at the door. First it was flowers, then the next day it was a case of Guinness, and the next an Irish Claddagh ring to remind her they were partners for life. Day after day Maeve sent him away, but he was relentless. He said it was penance for his behavior, clearly still not seeing the irony in his actions. His behavior was starting to concern her; she had never seen him this distraught with such lack of composure before. But she still held her ground, worried if she gave in even the slightest bit that it would fuel his efforts, and he'd become hopeful that she would return with him.

Ethan had always lived a delightfully charmed life. He had "champagne problems," he'd often joked, only the kind of small grievances that came with having all the comfort, money and love he needed. In all the time they had been together, Maeve had never seen him have to endure something truly difficult. He had a loving family, was set to inherit a family business, all of his grandparents were still alive and well, and he'd maintained a small group of friends from childhood. Everything in Ethan's life was lovely and perfect, and Maeve leaving had just sent shock waves through all of it, fracturing every little bit out of his control. He was grasping for anything that would pull everything back into place, but Maeve couldn't do that for him. Things were never going to be as they were, no matter how hard he tried, because Maeve wanted more than the life she had with Ethan. She felt a level of guilt, but now that she had left and truly been on her own and was okay, she didn't need him to protect her anymore.

The Dougal's had come and gone, and Colin was avoiding her beyond any duties he had to fulfill as the host of Roundwood House. When it was just the two of them for a few days, he left out meals for her but wouldn't sit and eat with her. There were two more families now staying at Roundwood House, and Colin was becoming increasingly more irritated by Ethan dropping by in front of the other guests. It was one thing for him to make a scene privately, but now there was an audience, and it was reflecting poorly on his business. Colin and Maeve hardly spoke, as it was now so awkward between them the tension was palpable. It was getting to the point where she wanted to leave and go elsewhere but was afraid of what would happen if she didn't have him looking out for her while Ethan was still here. She hated that she was reliant on a man yet again, but she didn't see a way out without going home to Ethan.

Finally, after the fifth night of showing up and interrupting their family-style dinner, Maeve's phone vibrated on her bedside table with a text from Ethan that read, I'm going home.

"Thank you," Maeve replied, saying the words out

loud as a release as she typed them into her phone. She exhaled a week's worth of pent-up stress, anger and fear, feeling a steady calm settle over her body in waves. She placed the phone down on the side table beside her in the den, and it started buzzing loudly against the marble tabletop

Maeve picked it back up to read the incoming message.

> I'm sorry. I just love you and thought this was the only way to get you to come home with me.

Maeve exhaled through her nostrils, annoyed that this still wasn't over before typing back.

> I understand. I just need you to listen to me when I tell you what I mean. If I say I need space, following me and showing up repeatedly is going to push me further away.

Maeve hit Send, and within seconds another income message appeared on her screen.

> I'm just so afraid of losing you forever.

Maeve's feelings were so close to the surface she

started to tear up, knowing the feeling of being alone very well. But for the first time in her life, she wasn't afraid of being alone, and she needed to do this for herself.

We can talk when I get home.

Maeve paused before hitting Send and deleted the message. She typed instead, have a safe flight, before turning her phone off and tucking it away.

28

Maeve waited until the sun set that evening and she knew Colin would be in the kitchen prepping for the next morning's breakfast. She hadn't quite worked out what she was going to say to him yet, but she knew she owed him an apology.

"Hey," Maeve leaned in through kitchen door, testing the water before she got closer.

Colin stood at the sink washing fruit and vegetables and looked over his shoulder. When he spotted Maeve, tensely perched in the doorway, chewing on the side of her cheek with anxiety, he inhaled sharply before he turned back to his food prepping.

"Hi, Maeve," Colin said to the sink.

"Do you think we could talk?" Maeve asked, staying put at her post in the doorway.

Colin cracked his neck with a roll of his head and let out a sigh. "I don't know what you want to talk about. I'm busy and I really don't have time for more of your drama. It's cost me enough already."

Maeve felt her heart hit her stomach, that heavy twisting knot of emotions leaving her without the right words to fix anything. "Okay," she said, turning to walk away. "I just wanted to apologize and let you know I'll be leaving. This is awkward and I feel so bad about the last few days with the other guests." She shook her head and gazed down at her palms.

"Okay," Colin said, still not looking at her.

"If you have any recommendations on where to stay, please let me know," Maeve added before she started toward the staircase.

"What? You're not going home?" Colin asked, surprised. He finally turned around, and his face was twisted in confusion.

"I need to stay and finish what I've started here with my birth parents." Maeve's heart was fluttering inside her chest, making her dizzy. There were so many people she had disappointed in the last week.

"I thought surely you'd be headed back home to go get married after all of"—he waved his hand in the air like a tornado— "whatever that was." Colin wiped his wet hands on a tea towel and threw it over his shoulder, then leaned back against the sink as he crossed his arms over his chest and looked Maeve up and down.

She took a step toward the doorway of the kitchen again, closing the space between them. "That was honestly very out of character for him, and stressful. But, no, that part of my life is over," Maeve said with a sad smile. "That was why I didn't want to tell you to begin with. I knew the moment I stepped foot off the plane I wouldn't be going back to him."

"Oh," Colin said softly, some of the ice around him melting away.

"Yeah, I could have never guessed all of that would have happened. I'm very embarrassed and I'd like to get out of your hair so you can focus on your guests."

Colin took a step forward, stopping at the butcher's block island to brace himself against it before speaking again. "You don't have to leave," he said quietly. "Everyone checks out tomorrow. Why don't you wait until they go, and we can chat properly when it's just the two of us."

Maeve stalled, feeling a little bit of hope rise up in her, "I don't want to put you out, I've been such a burden already."

"Just stay until the other guests leave," Colin said in that authoritative and decisive tone of his. "Then, if you still want to leave, I'll give you some recommendations." And then the strangest thing happened. He smiled at Maeve for the first time in a week.

Maeve almost cried she was so relieved. "That sounds like a good plan." She smiled back at him and took a step forward. "Can I hug you?"

Colin softened with a smile and stepped around the island toward her. "I'm Irish, of course. Come here," he said, holding out his arms.

Maeve stepped forward into his embrace. It felt so good to be wrapped up in his arms and to smell him again, she almost lingered too long and caught herself, then pulled back. "Okay, well thank you for the chat. Again, I'm really sorry for all of that." She gave his arm a squeeze and said, "Goodnight, Colin."

"G'night, Maeve." Colin waved and watched her walk away through the corridor and up the winding staircase back to the bedroom suites.

Caught up in the moment of her reconciliation with Colin and daydreams of what tomorrow might bring, Maeve nearly tripped over the trunk in her room. It had been sitting on her bedroom floor inconspicuously, hidden under a heap of clothes for over a week now. With the stress of the last week, Maeve hadn't touched the keepsakes her parents had thoughtfully collected over the years. She heaved the pile of clothes off the trunk and onto a chair to deal with at a later time. The leather was a dark mahogany with iron buckles that snapped over the top of the lid. It resembled what she imagined a pirates' chest might look like: rustic with a flat top and leather straps punctuated by metal studs. Maeve wondered if her parents chose this specifically for her, or if it just became the receptacle for her things over the years. Maeve unbuckled the latches and lifted the lid to peer inside.

The trunk was packed to the brim with albums, baby clothes and file folders. She carefully took each item out of the trunk, one by one, and laid them on the floor around her, encasing herself with bits of her past that were unknown to her. She took her time with each item, sorting them into piles once a pattern started to emerge.

Orla had kept some of her art and school projects when she was growing up and left her a memory box that she took with her when she moved out. It was sparse and felt haphazard. Maeve had remembered being angry with her for giving her a box of meaningless things to take with her. It felt worse to see all of those items scattered in a box that had no significance to her or any connection to Orla.

This trunk, on the other hand, was a comprehensive box of memories woven through clothing, paper and photos. It had been thoughtfully arranged and cared for over the last twenty-five years, each item representing an important moment or milestone in Maeve's life. Fiona had carefully labeled folders and envelopes with dates and brief descriptions of the contents inside. She teared up at the care that had been taken to preserve these moments for Maeve. She had been so hurt when she learned of all the time that had passed since her mother left her broken and alone and didn't come save her. Seeing this was proof that she cared and was more than Maeve could handle right now. She stood up and stepped over the circle of memories that surrounded her, freeing herself from someone else's version of her life, and walked toward the four-poster bed. She tripped over a folder, and the contents scattered in every direction. She started to pick up a series of letters and some photographs. After a brief inspection, she saw that these were letters from Orla, sent along with photos of Maeve at various points in her life. Orla sent a letter with every one of Maeve's achievements, big or small, and detailed what going on in Maeve's life at that moment. A flash of memory sent Maeve back to when Orla would ask her to stand and pose with her artwork or school essay that she got an A on. Maeve had never seen any of those pictures, and now she knew why.

Her anger deflated as she read through the letters, looking back on the small accomplishments that marked the various phases of her childhood. They weren't just hers anymore, she realized. They never were. They were shared memories, shared accomplishments, which were cherished across an ocean by her parents in secret. Maeve stacked the letters neatly on the desk and crouched back down by a small pile of clothes. She picked up pair of pajamas small enough for a doll. Maeve inspected the clothing delicately. There was a onesie, pink with bows, and a tiny, knitted hat that fit in the palm of her hand. Maeve's eyes stung as tears prickled at them from the thought that someone had so much love for her as an infant, when her entire life she thought she was truly unwanted.

She put the small clothes back down and picked up an album-like book with a cloth cover that had her name embroidered on the front. She traced her fingers along the precious letters before cracking the spine to peer inside. It was her baby book. Every detail of her mother's pregnancy, Maeve's birth and the first six months of her life were recorded in detail. Every first, every special moment cherished by her mother and preserved in this book forever. Maeve wasn't ready for this just yet. She put it down and turned to the next group of items in the small piles around her.

She picked up an accordion folder next. It felt full but light, like it was stuffed with papers. She reached her hand inside and pulled out card-sized envelopes, twenty-five of them, each labeled by year with her birthdate on them. Twenty-five years of missed birthdays with her parents reduced to these envelopes. She set them down and stood up to get some water. Had she not been so tired, she might have taken out her laptop to write away her feelings, but Maeve was utterly exhausted. She lay on the bed and closed her eyes, not waking again until morning.

29

"Was that the last of them, then?" Maeve asked.

Colin shut the front door of Roundwood House behind the most recent family who had been visiting. They were a kind family, and Maeve enjoyed the reprieve from all the drama, but she was happy to be alone with Colin again, even if it would be short-lived.

"That was all of them." Colin smiled at Maeve; his face relaxing.

"Do you like having all these strangers pass through your home all the time?" Maeve asked. "Don't you ever just want to be alone?"

"I've spent enough time feeling alone to last me a lifetime," Colin said, his eyes looking sad. "I like the commotion and distraction. Not as much commotion as you threw at me this week, but the regular kind." He laughed, and Maeve shook her head, embarrassed.

"Again, I'm very sorry about that. I, too, have yet to recover from the commotion that Ethan brought. That completely distracted me from my birth parents, which was another thing entirely," Maeve said, exhaling a loud sigh. She still wasn't sure how she was going to approach that situation.

"And the sleeping together thing," Colin added with a wink.

Maeve flushed a hot red. "Are you ready to talk about all of that?" she asked nervously.

Colin nodded. "Why don't you go get settled in the study, and I'll grab some refreshments." Then he disappeared again.

Maeve did as she was told for once and went and sat down in front of the fire and waited for Colin, who reappeared shortly with a bottle of chardonnay and two glasses.

"I figured this time we could take it a bit easier on the drink," he said, setting the glasses down between them. He popped the cork and poured them each a small amount.

"Good call." Maeve laughed, accepting the wine from Colin and clinking it lightly against his own. They tilted their glasses back, testing the wine, maintaining eye contact for good luck.

Colin put down his glass and settled on the sofa beside Maeve, then turned to face her.

"Well, now that I know that you're staying, you're staying here with me," Colin said definitively. "And not just because I want to get you back in bed, but everywhere else is booked up for the month."

Maeve laughed. Colin was letting his guard back down now, and Maeve was happy to feel like something was going right for once.

"I'd like that very much," Maeve said earnestly and put her hand on Colin's knee. "Thank you for understanding. I don't know if I would have been so kind if the circumstances were reversed."

Colin roared with laughter at this. "Maeve, you were on the other end of it, and I watched you hold a pretty firm ground. You were scary. But I liked it."

Colin grinned and grabbed her hand. "I haven't had this much excitement in a long time. I think you shocked me back to life."

"Well, I'm glad, because it looks good on you," she said taking a mother sip of her wine.

"So, how long are you planning on staying?" Colin asked cautiously.

"Do you need me out by a certain date?" Maeve knew she was taking up a room in his place of business.

"I have a large family coming in a few week's time and your room is booked, but we can figure that out if and when the time comes." He leaned back into the couch and got comfortable.

Maeve nodded. "I really don't know if there is a life for me that I care to return to, if I'm honest. Being here has started to feel like home."

Colin looked down at his lap, and when he looked back up, his eyes were wet with tears.

"What is it?" she asked.

"Having you here feels like I just came home too." He swiped at his eyes with the back of his hand quickly, embarrassed for the display of emotion. "Sorry, I know that's ridiculous, it's just been a hard few years. And then you came along, and for the first

time in a long time, things seemed like they might...
be okay."

Maeve put her wineglass down, reached across the
love seat and took his hands in hers. She squeezed
them tight and looked into his eyes, which were
searching hers for reassurance.

"Things are going to be more than okay, Colin,"
she said to him, sure of it.

He nodded and took a deep inhale, righting
himself. "And what will you do for work then?" He
was trying to focus on more practical matters than
those of the heart.

"I'm an excellent egg collector," she joked, and that
made him smile. "I have some leeway at work right
now. I completed month worth of articles before I left,
anticipating I might be gone for a while. And I've
started writing a new investigative journalism series
about internationally adopted children. So, if that if
all goes well, maybe it will get picked up by a bigger
outlet than the local one I work for."

"Would you leave your job?" he asked.

"I don't have a return flight," Maeve admitted.

Colin raised his eyebrows in amusement. "Are you
planning to stay then?"

"I don't know, but I can't imagine going back

now," she said.

Colin nodded.

"I've always had greater ambitions than working for a small local paper," Maeve said, "but I've never had a story big enough to even let me fantasize about it."

"And you think this is the one?" Colin asked.

"I think it might be," she said.

Over the last few days, she and Natalie had been going back and forth about the first installment of her exposé series. Maeve didn't typically enjoy the editing process, but with this piece being so close to her heart, she wanted to make sure it was perfect before sharing it with the world. She felt this one was something special, and she appreciated the feedback and keen eye for detail that Natalie had provided. Maeve had just sent the most recent version to John as well, along with a thank-you note for connecting her with her mother. She wasn't ready to go back there yet. She had a few more pressing matters to attend to first and figured if her parents could wait twenty-five years, they could wait a few more weeks for Maeve to get acclimated to Ireland and her new life without the Clarkes.

"I bet your mother could connect you to some

people around here in her line of work as well." Colin said, thinking out loud.

"Maybe one day. Right now, I think I'll stick to just taking things slow with them." Maeve picked at her nails again.

"Have you popped the trunk open yet?" Colin asked.

"I did last night actually. It was … overwhelming. I've left everything in piles on the floor," Maeve said sheepishly. "Care to see?" She secretly hoped he would. Having him there might make it easier to look through.

"Sure, let's go," Colin said, setting his wineglass down. He took her hand in his as she led him back upstairs to her chaos.

Maeve opened the door to her room to reveal the disaster she left earlier. She tiptoed around the mess and sat down on the bed, which she had made earlier in an effort to be somewhat civilized.

"What's your plan for all this?" Colin asked, scratching his head as he took in the papers and piles strewn across the floor.

"Well, I'll have to read all the letters first," she said, pointing at the stack, "but I think I'll probably organize and log it all on my computer to use as part of my research."

Colin nodded while taking it all in. "I'll be right back." He disappeared out the door and returned moments later. Maeve could barely see him behind a massive corkboard that was six feet tall by six feet wide.

"I thought this might help you get organized," he said, wiping his brow as he set the board along the far wall, and he handed her a package of thumbtacks.

"This is perfect!" Maeve jumped up from the bed and ran over to hug him. He squeezed her back tightly, and Maeve could have sworn he was sniffing her hair.

Once he let her go, she grabbed a pile of papers from the floor and got to work. She had a pad of sticky notes and started arranging a timeline on the board, not just from her life but from before, as part of her mother's journey. They worked together to sort the pieces, their shoulders bumping and hands brushing as they worked together to untangle Maeve's lost history.

Maeve hoped to write the second installment of her exposé on the social constructs that allowed for the adoptions to happen in the first place and then prevented children from being reunited with their families. The further she dug, the more she learned about the church and government involvement that pulled children so far away from their families that they became broken children and didn't have the chance to thrive, like Maeve did. Maeve and Fiona, all things considered, had been on the lucky end of circumstances. They were both healthy, successful women who had had a support system and lived a nice life. Many pregnant teens and unwed mothers had died or spent their lives carrying so much shame, they went down a very bad path. Maeve wanted to shine a light on these untold stories and expose the systems that allowed it and profited from it.

Colin helped her assemble the research and findings from her trunk up on the board until it was completed fully, organized by time and place. Maeve had only seen the side of Colin so far that was the social bed-and-breakfast owner who worked with his hands and liked to create things from scratch. What she got to see today was how his mind worked. An accountant by trade, she watched as he skillfully arranged a timeline in a careful pattern, picking out details she'd overlooked. Maeve liked to work alone, but she had to admit she was having fun. Hours passed in an instant, and they stepped back to admire their work.

"See, there's a method to my chaos," Maeve said with a grin, holding her arms out like Vanna White.

Colin stepped forward and wrapped Maeve in his arms. "What am I going to do with you, Miss Grisham?"

"Well, for starters, you can kiss me," Maeve said, leaning into Colin's embrace and feeling that rush of heat shoot through her body once more.

30

Maeve and Colin were inseparable in the following weeks. He helped her take trips to the library to do research, and she helped him with chores around the house. They painted the guest rooms, installed a new toilet and cooked together each evening, then collected fresh eggs in the morning and gathered herbs from the garden. With the impending arrival of a group of new guests, they had moved Maeve into Colin's master suite for the time being, even though she had been sleeping there every night since they made up. Her guest room had effectively become her office, where she wrote and used the corkboard to map out her articles. They had to move it all into Colin's room and find a more suitable place once the next cohort of guests left.

Maeve had completed her first piece about finding the truth about her family and meeting them for the first time. Before they published it in *The Guelph Tribune*, however, she wanted to take it to her parents to read and get their permission. It was very intimate and used quotes and pieces of information from their story, which was theirs to tell, and she would not move forward without their go-ahead. If they agreed, she also was hoping they would be up for a second interview, but it was an awkward line to toe with their relationship being so new and fragile. In no way did she want them to think she was using them or her mother's fame to benefit from that.

Maeve printed her piece and stapled it together, the top page reading "'Coming Home to County Kildare' by Maeve Grisham." She was meeting with her parents tonight, taking Colin's car that was sitting unused to see them. While she was gone, he would welcome and feed the incoming guests. Colin had taken her out the last few days to acclimate her to driving on the other side of the road, and while she wasn't overly confident, she figured she would be able to make it there in one piece since she would be on back roads most of the way.

Maeve kissed Colin goodbye in the kitchen before stepping out, waving at the guests in sitting room. They were a real couple now. She wasn't sure how it was going to translate into the real world since they had been holed up in their homesteading bubble, but time would tell. A slow start was what she needed after a decade in another relationship entirely. This new set of guests coming in were breaking up the honeymoon stage of their relationship, and it would be the first test to see how they would fair in this bed-and-breakfast life. The next test would be when Maeve needed to go home to get all of her belongings. But that was too much to think about right now.

The drive was nerve-racking as she bumped along the farm roads having to correct herself every time she started to naturally veer across the median to the familiar side of the road. Thankfully, her only companions on this drive were the cows and sheep that grazed in the meadows she passed by. It was a far cry from the world she knew, but she was enjoying every new challenge she faced as she gained new skills.

Maeve made it to her parents' home and stood once again on the doorstep with her article in her messenger bag slung across her body. She knocked firmly, a double rap, and Fiona appeared with a smile.

"Maeve, come on in, dear," she said, standing back so Maeve could pass through the threshold.

Maeve stepped inside and smelled a hearty, savory aroma coming from the kitchen. "It smells wonderful in here." She smiled at Fiona.

An ease had settled between the two women in the time that had passed since their last meeting. The wonderful thing about working away from home in another country was that Maeve had had enough time to read all of Fiona's letters and journals, along with her semiautobiographical novel, gaining an understanding of why it wasn't until now that they could meet. While her heart still ached for her lost childhood, she felt renewed in starting over and leaving that behind. For both their sakes, Maeve was glad she was able to leave her resentment at the door today.

"Oh, thank you, that's your grandmother's famous

Guinness stew cooking. One of my favorites," Fiona said with a wink as she ushered Maeve into the kitchen. "I'm so glad you called, although we were surprised. We thought you might've gone home by now." Fiona offered Maeve a kitchen stool to perch at as she flitted around the kitchen, making the final preparations to the meal.

"Hello, Maeve, dear," Garret said warmly, entering the kitchen from the garage. "Lovely to see you." He shed his coat on a chair and leaned in to kiss her on the cheek. Maeve blushed, she'd never had a father before, and this warm kindness she felt was overwhelming. "What have you been up to the last few weeks? Are you enjoying our little part of Ireland?"

"I am!" Maeve said enthusiastically. "I'm getting a taste for the country life, that's for sure. Due to my extended stay, Colin's put me to work at Roundwood House," Maeve said with a faraway smile, and Fiona and Garret exchanged a knowing glance.

"Ahhh, Mr. Walsh is taking good care of you then?" Garret asked, and once again, Maeve blushed.

"He is." She nodded, not comfortable indulging more than that at the moment.

"From what I've heard around town, you two are

hot and heavy," Fiona said, surprising Maeve with her forwardness.

"Uh, well, I—" Maeve blew a fast breath out, caught off guard. "I guess the cat's out of the bag then."

"It's good, Maeve. That's how it's supposed to be! From what I heard, Colin's not been himself the last few years since everything with his wife, and you seem to have sparked a light back in him."

"He's done the same for me," Maeve said earnestly.

"I'm so glad to hear that, love," Fiona said, coming up behind Maeve to give her shoulders a light rub. "You yourself seem different than the woman I meet a few weeks ago. It seems like you and Ireland agree with one another."

"Did you expect anything less?" Garret asked. "This is her home after all."

"I suppose it is," Fiona said with a smile. "How long are you planning on staying?"

"Indefinitely," Maeve said, and again, her parents exchanged a glance Maeve couldn't quite read. Perhaps they wanted her gone, the novelty of her arrival having worn off. "Of course I won't bother you. I know this is...a lot," she added, trying to preemptively temper any negative reaction.

"You're always welcome here. We lost the last twenty-five years with you. We'd like to make sure we don't miss any more of your life. But have you sorted out the logistics of how it is you'll stay and live here?" Fiona asked, a frown creasing her face. Even though they didn't raise her, they were still acting like her parents, and it was a strange yet comforting dynamic. "I'm sure you know you can't just move countries without quite a bit of red tape."

"Yes, I'm still working that part out," Maeve said, her tone sounding more annoyed to her ears than she intended. "I actually was hoping to show you something I've been working on." She pulled her article out of her bag and placed it on the island. "I'm working on an investigative series about international adoption rights and started the series with my story—well, our story." Maeve was getting nervous. "Of course, I wouldn't want to publish it without your permission, due to the personal nature of it." Maeve stopped talking then and waited for her parents to speak next.

Fiona picked up the article first, flipping through it with care. Having her mother's professional eye scanning her work unearthed a new level of anxiety that hid beneath her more rational anxieties. After a few minutes, Fiona put the piece down and looked at Maeve.

"This is very well written. I'd read some of your work before." It was Fiona who now blushed at the confession. "But this has heart. Well done," she said and handed it to Garret, who read it next.

"This is a very brave thing to do. Most people in your position wouldn't be able to separate their feelings and turn it into something productive. I'm impressed." Garret smiled at her. "You have my approval."

"Mine too," Fiona said, smiling back at her daughter, one who may not have shared a home with her but shared many of her same qualities—physically and intellectually. It was almost alarming how similar the women were.

Maeve relaxed, having gotten the hard part of the evening out of the way. Now she was able to sit and enjoy her time getting to know her parents. The three of them sat around the dinner table, eating Fiona's favorite meal while they laughed, cried and shared stories of their lives. The awkwardness dwindled the more honest they became with one another, and while Maeve knew she'd never get a chance to relive her childhood, she had the chance to build a relationship with her parents as an adult.

There was, however, one factor they had yet to discuss, which was introducing Maeve to the rest of the family. She'd met Finn, sort of, but integrating her into everyone's life was going to be an adjustment for them too. While Fiona's brothers and sisters were aware she had a baby in high school, it was never discussed among the family. No one had once said a word about it. They all just moved on and allowed Fiona to live her life, afraid any mention of it would send her spiraling.

"Maeve, we'd like to host a little party here for you, if you're going to stay a while," Fiona said as she was tidying up their meal.

"Oh, for what?" she asked, surprised at such a concept.

"Well, since your arrival, news has been spreading like wildfire across the county about you. We'd like to properly introduce you to the whole family."

"That sounds lovely." Maeve smiled with her whole face.

"I'm not sure 'lovely' is the word you'll use after you meet them," Garret said with a wink, and they laughed.

"I have to get back to Roundwood House before

dark," Maeve said, looking outside as the sun lowered in the sky. "I don't trust myself out on these roads."

Her parents stood on the porch and waved as she drove home into the sunset, on the wrong side of the road, filled with an unfamiliar warm buzz of parental love.

31

Months passed and winter approached, and Maeve
knew it was time to pack up her things and go home.
Colin and Maeve had settled into a new life together,
a balance of calm and adventure with the stillness of
living in the countryside bringing her great peace, but
the excitement of new guests staying with them
weekly kept it fresh. She could see her life here for

decades to come in a way she'd never been able to look forward to before.

Maeve had been doing research for further installments in her series, which was set to debut next week, and she was so anxious for it to hit the press. She had been corresponding with John over email frequently since he put her and her mother in touch and had been a keen eye in preparing her first piece to go to live. Today, the immediate feedback you received from the internet was explosive and all-consuming, and she knew with a publication this size, good or bad, her name would be out there, and it would change the course of her future as a journalist. She couldn't sleep or eat in anticipation and because, quite frankly, she was proud of herself.

Colin and Maeve's most recent guests has just packed up and left, giving them a few days on their own before the next group was set to arrive. These little mid-week breaks had become precious to them, a time when they could play house in their home, rather than see it as their place of work. Maeve had learned a lot during the renovations she did on her house in Guelph and had proved to be quite a useful companion for Colin. The pair of them worked well together and Maeve couldn't imagine another life for herself better than this.

"Well, they're off," Colin said, coming up behind Maeve and giving her a little squeeze and a kiss on the cheek.

"Well, thank god, I missed you," she said, turning around to wrap her arms around his neck.

"I missed you too," Colin said with a grin. "Although I did have fun watching that hen get you this morning."

"She wasn't happy with me today," Maeve said, showing off the nip where the hen got her, and Colin took her hand in his.

"Ouch." Colin winced at the mark and gave it a kiss.

"We need to talk about something," Maeve said, changing her tone from jest to a more serious one.

Colin pulled back, noting her voice, and searched her eyes for a clue.

"It's getting cold here, and I need to go back to Canada to collect my things." Maeve hadn't been prepared for the damp cold that Ireland would bring in winter, and she still only had her summer wardrobe with her. While she'd visited the local shops for a thick sweater and wool socks, she needed her things. "As you know, that brings up a few challenging conversations." Maeve braced for Colin's reaction. She shifted her weight nervously from one foot to another as she absentmindedly picked at her nails.

"Ahhh." Colin sighed with no particular affection to his voice. "When are you going to go?"

Maeve knew the real question he wanted to ask was *Where are you going to stay?* and *Are you going to talk to Ethan?* And she wanted to ask him, *Are you willing to let me move all my stuff in here?*

Until now, she was the easiest house guest one could imagine: she did chores, helped out and only had a bag full of clothes. Collecting her things from Canada meant a lot more than just a temporary stay and brought up conversations about their future that she wasn't sure they were ready for.

"Well, I wanted to talk to you about that," Maeve said, continuing her nervous sway. "I was wondering if you'd like to come with me?"

Colin looked at her with surprise and Maeve continued. "As much as I'm glad to leave that world behind, it has been my home for the last twenty-five years, and it is a part of me. I know we don't have much time between guests, but if you wanted to come along, I'd love to have you." Maeve thought him coming with her might help ease some of the awkwardness surrounding her departure.

"I don't know if it's the right time for that kind of a trip," Colin said after a quiet moment of consideration.

That sent a shot of disappointment through Maeve's chest. "Right, of course," she said, nodding.

Colin grabbed her hands to steady her nerves. "I think you need to go and have a proper chat with Ethan and say your goodbyes to your old life, if this is what you really want. And I think you need to do that on your own. I will be here waiting for you when you come back, ready to put you to work," he said, offering her his kind smile, which always put her at ease.

"That's a relief," Maeve said. "I thought you're going to send me packing."

"Never," Colin said, squeezing her hands again, "I want you here with me. I know it's only been a few months, but they've been some of the best of my life." He pulled her in close, wrapping his arms around her waist. "I love you, Maeve Grisham," he whispered barely loud enough for her to hear it.

"I love you too, Colin Walsh."

Maeve found herself once again on an international flight across the Atlantic. The flight on the way to Ireland was a red-eye and she'd been able to rest her eyes and drift off into a semi-sleep for most of it. This time, however, the seven-hour flight took up most of her day and brought along with it a distracted anxiety about how she would be received on the other end. She tried to work, read and watch an in-flight movie, but she kept getting pulled back to thoughts of Ethan and the Clarke family. She had given Ethan a heads-up that she was coming to collect her things, and he'd been polite through text, but she couldn't be certain how the visit would go. It was a strange thing returning to a home that wasn't her home anymore. Maeve had booked a hotel, and while the location was rather inconvenient, her only other choice was to stay with Ethan. He, of course, had offered to let her stay at their house, as it was hers too after all, but she couldn't very well do that to Colin.

Aside from packing up her things in boxes to send back to Ireland, Maeve and Ethan also needed to talk about what to do with the house. While his parents had given him the down payment and the money for renovations, Maeve had paid half the mortgage and bought her fair share of the furniture. She didn't want to be petty and take his home away from him, but it was all she really had to her name, and she wasn't ready to part with it all just yet. Maeve wasn't worried about that part of the conversation though. Ethan would be fair; she knew that. What she was nervous about was the conversation she owed him about how things ended. Now that she had enough space from it, she understood how hard that must have been for him, and she did feel guilty. There wasn't ever going to be any way to make that up to him. But, despite her guilt, she was confident that it was the right decision for both of them. She would have never been able to give Ethan all of herself, knowing her family was on the other side of the world waiting for her.

Maeve decided she would go straight to her old home first and get the tough part out of the way. The taxi pulled to a stop in front of Ethan's house, and Maeve stepped out to the snow-covered sidewalk, shivering as her foot sunk into the snow and it snuck up her pant leg. She gave the cab a wave and hefted her carry-on over the sidewalk and up the front porch steps to knock on her own front door.

Within seconds, Ethan answered, looking as nervous as she felt.

"Come on in," he said with a forced smile, opening the door and stepping aside to let her pass through.

She stepped into the warm home, a stark contrast to the icy chill of the wet pant leg stuck to her ankle. She looked around, inspecting the place as if it hadn't been her home for the last few years. Upon brief inspection, nothing had changed in the four months she'd been gone, but it felt different. She did notice that their engagement pictures hanging on the wall when she left had been replaced by some generic art from Home Sense. It wasn't her home anymore.

"It smells good in here," Maeve said with a smile, trying to break the ice.

"Oh, yeah. I, uh, made your favorite meatballs," Ethan said sheepishly as he rubbed his neck, and Maeve's heart sank.

This was going to be harder than she thought. She stood awkwardly with her hands by her side, wanting to hug Ethan and make him feel better, but she was afraid that would just send him the wrong message.

"Thank you, Ethan," she said instead. "That was so thoughtful."

"Of course. Come on in. Let's eat. I'm sure you're starving after such a long day." And he was right. It was 6:00 p.m. and she'd been traveling for twelve hours already. While she hadn't planned on sharing a meal at their kitchen table, she was grateful for the kindness and was, quite frankly, ravenous.

They at mostly in silence before Maeve finally spoke. "I'm sorry things ended the way they did," Maeve said wiping marinara sauce from her mouth. "I think I knew for a long time that this wasn't going to work out, but we had just been together for long, I didn't see a way out."

Ethan teared up across the table and nodded slowly. "I could feel you pulling away for a while. That's why I followed you out there. I knew it was my only chance left at keeping you. You'd already felt so far away for so long."

"I'm sorry. I know this hasn't been easy for you. And I'm sorry for your family. They must be so angry with me." Maeve stared into her pasta bowl.

"Well, yes. But—" He stood to go and grab something from the living room and returned with a copy of her article. "This certainly has helped everyone to understand. I'm really proud of you, Maeve. We all are."

"Thank you," she said. "I was pretty mad when you came all the way over to Ireland to get me back and didn't once ask about finding my parents." A crease grew between her eyes. Until she'd said it out loud, she hadn't allowed that hurt to surface.

Ethan groaned. "I know. That was stupid of me. Would it have changed anything though?"

Maeve thought for a moment and replied, "No, probably not." And that broke the tension between them both, and they laughed the kind of ridiculous deep belly laugh that stirs up tears.

"I miss you, Maeve. It's been strange living in this house we built all by myself," Ethan said wistfully.

Maeve flinched as if she'd been struck. It hurt her to know that he was suffering when she felt happy, like she was living for the first time in her life, not just surviving.

"We need to talk about that too. I'm planning to stay in Ireland, which is why I came back to collect my belongings. I was able to apply for my Irish citizenship since I am a direct descendant, and I'm freelancing now. There's been a lot of interest since my exposé got so much attention." Maeve tried to swallow down the lump in her throat. Since her exposé had gone live it was picked up by a larger national news outlet, and then an international one once word got out who her mother was. Maeve had been fielding offers from different companies to publish the rest of the series.

"Ah," Ethan said nodding, then looking around the house, making a mental note of everything they'd bought or built together.

"I owe everything we had here to you and your parents," Maeve said, "and I have no way of transporting furniture to Ireland or anywhere to put it."

Ethan nodded along trying to follow where she was going. "You want me to keep everything? That hardly seems fair." He frowned. The house was the only thing tethering the two of them together.

"Well, would you keep it for now?" she asked. "And if I ever need anything, I'll come knocking."

"Sure" he said after a long pause. "The door will always be open for you."

Maeve spent the next hour packing up all of her clothes into three suitcases. Ethan had stayed downstairs while she packed, and she was thankful he couldn't see her crying on the floor of the custom closet from Ikea that they had spent a weekend building. Her life here was over.

Later, she sat in her hotel room in the city she used to call her own, looking at her old life neatly packed and ready for transport. She was eager for her new life to begin.

32

Maeve tossed and turned all night, unable to get comfortable. Her belly had swollen to the size of a watermelon, and the baby girl inside was insistent on swimming around all night. She checked the clock, 5:30 a.m. With a sigh, she figured she might as well get up now rather than lie there uncomfortable.

Rolling herself over and upright was harder than it looked at thirty-six weeks pregnant, any remnants of an abdominal muscle long gone by this point. She was purely reliant on flexibility and strategy to get things done these days. Maeve waddled down the stairs and started a pot of coffee, opening the blinds to let in the first glimpse of a rising sun.

Now that she was up and moving, the baby had stopping kicking, lulled back to sleep by her motion, and Maeve could get to work. Between managing Roundwood House, getting the nursery ready and writing her newest exposé about Irish immigration, Maeve felt like she was running out of time to get everything done before the baby came. Not to mention, she had the *Vogue* Ireland team coming this week to do a tandem interview with her and her mother here at Roundwood House. After her international adoption series took off five years ago, Maeve gained some fame in the writer's world, and then the internet came barreling in and sleuthed its way into finding out who her mother really was. Maeve and Fiona became an overnight sensation, their story touching hearts of mothers and daughters worldwide.

The success from their sensational story brought

them closer together as mother and daughter, and they got to know each other as they did talk shows and interviews, giving their sides of the story and both building up an audience for their work. While the hype died down after a few years, Maeve's pregnancy rekindled the public's interest and *Vogue* Ireland now wanted to do a follow-up interview as they prepared to welcome the new baby as a family. It was going to be a multimedia piece, a video interview for their website and socials and a written four-page spread for the magazine.

Thankfully, Colin and Maeve had finished the major renovations and restorations to Roundwood House last year after she was paid a large advance for her memoir by a Random House imprint and Colin was happily taking over more and more of the bed-and-breakfast as she got closer to her due date. With their own daughter arriving soon, they had blocked all bookings for three months after she was due, giving them time to adjust and spend time together as a family.

Fiona and Maeve had grown exceptionally close, and Fiona was so excited to be a grandmother to a baby girl. She never had the chance to raise her own little girl and had made it abundantly clear to Maeve that she was on call night or day for the rest of her life for Maeve and the baby. Maeve joked they would have to lock the doors at night so they wouldn't wake up to Fiona in the house once the baby came. Maeve was unable to sleep most nights these days, but she thanked God for the turnaround her life had made. While there were still ups and downs, it seemed that having this strong family and community around her, living in this beautiful home with her beautiful husband, Maeve could say she had truly loved and been loved, cared deeply, worked hard and achieved success in her life. The next greatest thing was about to come, and then that would be her focus, and she could say she accomplished everything she had ever wanted in her life.

Maeve sat and made endless lists while she sipped her coffee and rubbed her belly, preparing for the shift ahead and navigating motherhood. She and Colin had been overjoyed when they found out Maeve was pregnant, they had dreamt of adding a family to this great estate and talked about it endlessly at night wrapped up in bed together. When they found out she was with child, a sudden fear overtook Maeve, unsure how to be a mother when she had not had one of her own. She tried to prepare by choosing character traits from Fiona; Ethan's mother, Rose; and Orla that she loved to try and emulate, but she wasn't sure how that would translate when the time came to care for an infant. Anxiety-ridden, she often turned to internet forums late at night when she couldn't sleep to search for answers. Most women would talk to their friends or their own mothers for advice, but as strong as her relationship had become with Fiona, it was a still new, and she feared she would fracture it if she unloaded on her that she didn't feel fit to be a mother because she'd been abandoned. And so, Maeve worried alone, quietly doing everything in her power to set up the perfect start to life for her daughter.

It was *Vogue* Day. The camera operators, lighting technicians, assistants and reporters showed up in hordes with their arms filled with equipment, props and wardrobe and filed toward the front entrance of Roundwood House. Maeve opened the door with her best warm smile, usually reserved for their bed-and-breakfast guests.

"Welcome to Roundwood House." Maeve was the glowing cliché of impending motherhood as she stood in a maxi dress, her bump peeking through the pleats in the cotton. "Please come in." She stood aside to allow the large crew to flood into her home. Everyone filed in and stood waiting for direction as Lynn O'Keefe, the reporter here today surveyed the entryway and peeked her head around corners.

"Nice to see you again, Maeve." Lynn reached out her hand and gave it a firm shake. "Where is your lovely mother?" Her eyes traveled around the main floor as if she were surprised she, too, wasn't here to greet them.

"She is with my husband upstairs checking out the nursery," Maeve said smiling. "We just finished it." She rubbed her belly absentmindedly, then heard footsteps above her head as Colin and Fiona descended the spiral staircase. "Here they come now." Maeve nodded toward the two most important people in her life, who were soon to be eclipsed by the little one inside of her.

Lynn waved, and they introduced themselves. Colin took the camera crew to get some B-roll footage of the nursery and the estate while hair, makeup and wardrobe set up in the dining room. Some of the assistants shuffled the furniture around in the sitting room to get the best lighting for the interview, taking out nearly half of the furniture and putting it in the foyer, while another assistant rearranged the books on the shelves to create a more *Vogue*-approved aesthetic.

Colin came back in with the camera crew and gave Maeve a thumbs-up from across the room. She and Fiona were getting the final touches of hair and makeup done by the famed *Vogue* glam squad. Fiona squeezed her hand under the table, and they somehow managed to share a knowing glance without turning their heads. Each woman had someone tending to their lipstick, which required them to be painfully still. Colin was grinning ear to ear. He was proud of Maeve for what she'd accomplished, but he was equally excited for Roundwood House to get some publicity. Finally, all his hard work paying off. This interview would not only be great for Maeve's career, but it would put their beautiful home on the map of must-visit destinations when visiting Ireland.

After an hour of hair and makeup, Maeve and Fiona emerged from the dining room. They were clad in outfits that complemented the decor, perfectly styled hair and a no-makeup makeup look that was appropriate for a day out at a country estate. Maeve looked in the mirror to admire the transformation.

Her usually air-dried mass of curls had been blown out into soft waves, with a bit of rouge on her cheeks to accent her high cheekbones. The brown eyeliner they used set off her green eyes, and she wore a flowing white empire waist dress with a brown tweed blazer with elbow patches. A pair of tasteful cowboy boots completed her look. While not the most practical of outfits for a day managing the bed-and-breakfast, she had to admit she looked *Vogue* ready.

Lynn took the two women in and slapped her hands together with a smile.

"Gorgeous," she said looking at Maeve and Fiona standing side by side, the mother-daughter writing powerhouse as regal as ever. "All right, ladies, let do this." Lynn signaled to the camera crew as the three women took their places. With a nod he held up three fingers and said, "Ready to roll in, three, two, one ... go."

A Family Affair, Five Years Later

An Intimate Conversation with Fiona O'Toole and Maeve Walsh

by Lynn O'Keefe

Driving through the rolling hills of County Kildare,

Ireland, our crew rolls up to a stunning estate
perched on ten acres of land just outside the city of
Newbridge. The estate, called Roundwood House,
had been owned by Declan Walsh for seventy years
before passing it down to his grandson, Colin, when
he passed. Colin Walsh, a successful tax accountant
born and raised in Ireland, decided to take a chance
and leave his job to turn Roundwood House from a
rundown home into a thriving business. Now touted
as a top place in Ireland to stay, Colin attributes its
success to his wife, Maeve Grisham, renowned
investigative journalist and long-lost daughter of
local writer, Fiona O'Toole.

Five years after we interviewed the mother-
daughter duo upon their initial reunion, we are back
today at Maeve's home, Roundwood House, with
Maeve and Fiona as the family prepares to
welcome the next generation of women into the
family.

Lynn: Maeve you have a beautiful home

Maeve: It's a funny story actually. When I
came over to Ireland in search of my
mother, I stayed here at the bed-and-
breakfast. This is where Colin and I met
and fell in love, and I never left.

Lynn: I can't imagine why anyone would ever
want to leave; this is a gorgeous home.
You're welcoming a baby soon. Have you

completed the nursery yet?

Maeve: We have! Due to my current condition, I couldn't put as much elbow grease in as I normally do, so Colin was the muscle behind it and brought my vision to life. We are so excited to welcome our daughter to this special place.

Lynn: Fiona, this must be special for you too, becoming a grandmother after not being present for Maeve's childhood.

Fiona: (with tears in her eyes) While I was able to experience motherhood with my boys, it's very special to be able to be a part of Maeve and her daughter's life. I think we are both excited for what the chapter will bring to our family.

Sitting here with Maeve and Fiona feels like a warm hug. The two women, while having spent most of their lives apart, are in sync. In tough moments, they share a glance, or a squeeze of the hand, showing unwavering support for one another. Maeve, due just weeks from now is glowing with excitement, her bump perfectly round, like she's hiding a basketball under her dress.

We go to the nursery that has recently been renovated in a separate wing of the house than the guests stay. Up a second secret set of stairs off the kitchen lies a staircase behind a closed door. We end up on a landing that has three doors. To the right is the master suite where Maeve and Colin stay and then a bathroom and then next to that a door to the nursery.

Upon entering, the first thing you notice is the large lookout window that wraps around half of the curved wall from where you can see over almost the entirety of the estate. The other half of the wall is a mural that continues the scenery with a princess and horses added in for flare. Finn O'Toole, soon to be uncle to Baby Walsh, painted the mural as a gift to his niece. There is no shortage of skilled artistry in this family, as the mural is absolutely breathtaking fairy-tale realism at its finest.

Under the window lies a daybed adorned with pillows for Mom and Dad to lay down and cuddle with their newborn.

"That was my mom's suggestion." Maeve laughs and points at the bed. "Apparently they don't like to sleep alone for the first few years," she says, rubbing her belly.

The stylish crib is adorned with a patterned fitted sheet matching the fairy-tale theme. Fiona shakes her head knowingly in the corner and I think back to when my son was born, all the sleepless nights that felt like they dragged on forever, only to get up the next morning as if nothing had happened, met with a toothless smile and a gummy kiss to start your day.

We tour the rest of Roundwood House, admiring the new guest suites and sunroom addition off the back. Colin has done almost everything himself, an impressive feat with an old house like this. After our interview, Colin served a delicious lunch in the dining room, proving he has multiple talents and is a gracious host.

You'd never know by watching these women that until five years ago, they didn't know each other. They have every making of a traditional mother-daughter dynamic, with the added advantage of understanding each other as adults, as most children find hard to do with their parents.

> Lynn: Fiona, what is your favorite thing about your daughter after imagining who she might be after all these years, now that you really have gotten to know her?

> Fiona: That's a great question. Her resilience is admirable, but I knew the moment she was born she would be tough. I think her perseverance to never give up in pursuit of getting what she deserves is my favorite thing about her. I know that no matter what, Maeve won't just let things be wrong. She will work hard to create a better life for herself and for her daughter.

> Lynn: And, Maeve, what about you? What is

the thing about your mother that you cherish most, now that you finally have her in your life?

Maeve: That is a tough one, Lynn. You know, I spent twenty-five years imagining who my mother might be, wishing I had been able to meet her, wondering if I'd be different if I had. Now I'm expecting my own daughter and questioning how I can make sure that she feels loved and secure and doesn't have those questions. And the one thing that is extra special for her, and that I will cherish forever, is that my mother will get to be a part of my daughter's life, and give her a grandmother, something else I never had. I just cherish her being here in my life and stepping right into her role as my mother as soon as I showed up. She opened up her heart, her home, her family—everything for me when I decided to just show up out of the blue. Despite some initial awkwardness there were no boundaries placed. She was ready and willing to take me for all that I was and all that I'll be, and I'd say that's pretty amazing.

Only days after the interview, Maeve gave birth to a beautiful baby girl, Aisling Orla

Walsh. Maeve turned to the last page of the article to see the three generations of Grisham women together in the nursery, smiling blissfully into the camera. Aisling, who was wearing a white embroidered dress, her tufts of copper hair and sparkling green that match her mother and grandmothers. Maeve closed the magazine and tucked it beside her on the linen rocking chair in the corner of Aislings nursery. She buried her nose in Aisling's hair and smelled her for as long as her inhale would allow. She'd never tire of that soft powdery baby smell she had. Maeve held her close, unwilling to put her down even as she slept peacefully in her arms. This feeling of closeness and maternal bond was still otherworldly to her. She often surprised herself with the ferocity she protected her child. She was exhausted, elated, stripped down and felt herself blossoming into something new. Maeve craned her neck to look out that turret window that overlooked the Roundwood House property and saw Colin emerging from the hen house with a basket full of eggs. A laugh escaped her as she

remembered her first time inside that coop
with Colin, they'd come so far from that day.
Aisling startled and started to fuss on her chest
from the sudden jolt of Maeve's laughter.
"Shhh, shhh, shhh," Maeve said rocking back
and forth, comforting her daughter in the way
she'd always longed for.

AUTHORS NOTE

Thank you for reading County Kildare. If you enjoyed it, please consider leaving a review on Amazon or Goodreads to help grow awareness of my debut novel!

County Kildare is a work of fiction, although certain elements of the story are inspired by real life people and places. Below is a list of some standout places referenced in the novel that have real family history and significance woven throughout the story.

County Kildare

First and foremost, the title of the book, County
Kildare, is the county in Ireland where my mother's
birth mother was born and raised, and I found it
vital to root the story there. Many of my mother's 11
aunts and uncles, nieces and nephews still reside
there, and my parents had the pleasure of meeting
them a few years back on their own journey to
County Kildare. I was able to collect little bits of
research and memories through photographs of my
parent's time in Ireland and construct my story
based on what I knew and what I learned during my
research. While the county and city names are real,
the school and library that are mentioned in Fiona's
narrative are fictional.

Our Lady Immaculate

In the book there is a scene where some characters
take a tour of the Guelph churches, making their
final stop at The Church of Our Lady Immaculate in
Guelph. This Church really does sit at the top of the
high street in Guelph and the city bylaws are set in
place so that from no point in the city can a building
be built higher than the church so you can always
see it. While the church itself is stunning, its known
to be one of the most impressive works of Irish

architect Joseph Connelly, it also holds personal significance for me. This church was where my grandparents got married in the 1940's and its where my husband proposed to me! It is a very special place, and I was excited to be able to include it in my novel.

Roundwood House

Roundwood House is name of the Bed and Breakfast in my novel, and it is based on the most beautiful Bed and Breakfast in Ireland located in County Laois of the same name. In Fact, that building you see on my book cover is an oil painting of the real Roundwood House by Mike Rafter, who graciously let me use the pointing for my cover! If you want to check out any more of his work, he is local to County Laois and has some pretty stunning work. Roundwood House is owned by Hannah and Paddy Flynn, and while I haven't had the pleasure of staying there yet (it's on my list for our Ireland trip next year), but my parents raved about their experience. I grew up down the street from Paddy's parents in Canada and can say that the Flynn's (globally) are the loveliest family. I got lost in the photographs of this gorgeous establishment while I

was writing County Kildare and encourage you to
check it out if you are planning on heading to
Ireland anytime soon.

AKNOWLEDGEMENTS

I wrote County Kildare as an ode to my mother who never go the chance to meet her own. This story was inspired by her journey to County Kildare in search of answers about where she came from. I owe a big thank you to her and my dad who both gave me encouragement and were relentless in their feedback, pushing me to work harder every step along the way.

When I was about 8 years old, my dad gifted me a box set of books called "Girls to the Rescue," which were historical retellings of folklore written to offset the stories of the helpless heroine. It was those books that shaped how I viewed myself, and they were in the back of my mind while I wrote this novel and wrote the main character, Maeve Grisham.

Thank you to Will Tyler, my editor who taught me so much during the editing process and provided guidance and support along the way. Thank you to Rachel Mulhall, who created the perfect cover to represent this novel, and to Mike Rafter, who graciously let me use his beautiful oil painting on my cover.

I also owe a huge thank you to my original beta readers Carly Manderson and Kelsie Smith who read the first version of County Kildare, in its very raw form and gave great feedback along with the confidence to keep going.

Thank you to my book club, Mia Huber, Emma Sandrock, Hannah Sandrock and Arden Grischow and who read the first version of the first novel I ever wrote and were kind in their feedback.

And finally, a big thank you to my husband who has been endlessly patient with me during the writing process and given me the time and space to write this beautiful book.

ABOUT THE AUTHOR

This is B. E. Kennedy's debut novel. She lives in Southwestern Ontario with her husband, Matt, and their daughter, Violet. Her children's book work includes a series called Violet and George's Adventures. You can follow along on Instagram @b.e.kennedy or at baileykennedybooks.ca

www.ingramcontent.com/pod-product-compliance
Lightning Source LLC
Chambersburg PA
CBHW021843010726
47493CB00005B/1525